THE WRONG STRANGER

HE'S BEEN WATCHING AND WAITING.

K. LUCAS

Copyright © 2021 by K. Lucas

All rights reserved.

No part of this book may be reproduced in any form or by any electronic or mechanical means, including information storage and retrieval systems, without written permission from the author, except for the use of brief quotations in a book review.

This is a work of fiction. Unless otherwise indicated, all the names, characters, businesses, places, events and incidents in this book are either the product of the author's imagination or used in a fictitious manner. Any resemblance to actual persons, living or dead, or actual events is purely coincidental.

Cover Design by Taylor Dawn of Sweet 15 Designs

Editor: Whitney Morsillo of Whitney's Book Works

For my son

PROLOGUE

Twenty-three Years Ago

A little girl sat on the kitchen floor underneath the table, holding her doll and its brush—both covered in dirt. She hummed to herself quietly as she brushed the doll's hair. The kitchen chairs were pulled in close, so she was blocked in from all sides. Sitting there alone for most of the afternoon, she felt hidden.

But now she was feeling hot, and her tummy was starting to feel hungry. It was July and there was no air conditioning in the house. Her diaper, the only thing she was wearing, was getting full.

At just four years old, being alone was something the little girl was already used to. Her mommy was always in bed, and her daddy was never at home. So, the little girl spent her days with her doll and her only book. She was used to waiting until she could no longer bear the hunger before she tried asking her mommy for something to eat.

Normally, her mommy would come get her some chips

down from the top cupboard, if the little girl could wait long enough before going to get her. The little girl knew her mommy was usually grouchy if someone bothered her too early in the day. It would only result in a spanking and no food.

Her daddy said one time, "Mommy only cooks on special occasions." The little girl wasn't sure what a special occasion was, but it didn't happen very often. She only ate chips or cereal, or really anything that came in a package and didn't have to be put together. The girl had tried pushing a chair over to climb up to the cupboard before, but she still wasn't able to reach anything by herself; she was too short.

She hated to get her mommy when she was in her bedroom. Her mommy would get so mad and yell at her, and it usually made her cry. "This is my fucking space, goddammit," she would scream. Her mommy would spank or hit her, too, if it was a bad day. The room always smelled funny, and the girl didn't like that stinky smell. There were a lot of empty bottles on the floor, piled on top of clothes and trash, so it was always hard for her to walk in her mommy's bedroom. She decided she would rather spend her time playing with her dolly or pretending to read while she waited.

Her daddy drove a big truck and was usually gone for a long time before he came home again. When he came home, he always made sure to play with her for a while and gave her what she thought of as, *special daddy time*. It was always while mommy was sleeping. She enjoyed having someone to play with when her daddy came home and missed him while he was away. But special daddy time scared her sometimes.

She got headaches during a lot of those times and would fall asleep in the middle of their playtime. When she woke up, she hurt, and she had a hard time remembering what

The Wrong Stranger

they did together. She was too afraid to tell him about her owies or not remembering their fun time, thinking he would stop playing with her if she told him. She didn't want him to leave her alone the way that her mommy did. But he continued playing with her, even though she always fell asleep. The little girl was so lonely that she craved attention of any kind. She was thankful her daddy made time for her, even after all the time he spent working.

When her daddy was home, he and her mommy would yell at each other a lot, too. Sometimes her mommy threw things at him, or he would accidentally break something with his hand. This never failed to scare the little girl, and she would run and hide under the kitchen table.

She didn't have a bedroom of her own, and no brothers or sisters to turn to for comfort, so she felt like under the table was her safest place. Anytime something scary happened, or if her parents were yelling at each other, this was the spot she would run to. She would always tuck the chairs back underneath the table as far as they would go, and hide right in the middle, holding her doll or book as tightly as she could.

The family lived in rural, northeastern Washington. They had a big yard and some chickens, too, but her mommy forbade her from going outside alone. She wanted more than anything to go outside to play but knew she wasn't allowed to. One time, when her mommy hadn't been up all day and it was nearly nighttime, the little girl tried going outside by herself to play with the chickens. After only a few minutes, her mommy walked outside and caught her. Her mommy had slapped her until she bled from her nose and sent her to bed with no dinner. Her hunger pains that day were worse than any of the slaps that her mommy gave.

After that, the little girl was too afraid to try going

outside alone again. She was too afraid to do anything that would get her in trouble. She was too hungry for that. Instead, she waited. She waited and waited and waited. Her mommy would come out of her bedroom eventually. She just had to wait.

The girl had also become so used to being in a wet diaper; she thought it was normal to wear one all day. When it leaked out the top or sides, she would take it off, but her mommy didn't like to see her naked when she came out of her room. The little girl had a diaper rash that hurt and itched, but it had been there so long that she didn't know what it was like to be without it.

At four years old, she still had not learned how to use the potty, and because she was so neglected, isolated, and abused, she had a speech impediment. The fear that she felt almost daily, contributed to her stuttering the few words that she could say. The lack of nutrition in her diet didn't help her learning abilities. It caused her to appear severely underweight, despite the high calorie junk food that was her only source of nutrition. But the little girl did not know there was anything out of the ordinary with her health. The only thing the girl felt was truly wrong, was her loneliness.

That day in July, the little girl was under the kitchen table with her dolly because her parents were fighting again. Her daddy came home, and within minutes, he and her mommy were yelling at each other. "She looks like she's starving to death, goddammit!" The little girl heard her daddy roar.

"Don't tell me how to take care of my own fucking kid!"

"You're not taking care of her at all! I can see her ribs!" Something pounded against the wall, so she covered her ears, trying to drown out the sound. They were both in her mommy's room with the door closed, and she was in her safe place. She heard them yelling some more and heard things breaking. She hummed loudly then, with hands still covering her ears.

Her favorite song was "Twinkle Twinkle Little Star;" she knew almost all the words. Her head started to hurt, so she hummed as loud as she could, thinking that her favorite song would help keep her safe. Sometimes singing helped her head feel better and drowned out the scary sounds that her parents made.

Then, it was quiet. The little girl let out a sigh of relief, but knew they could start back up any second. After a moment, she tentatively took her hands off her ears. She never knew how long the fighting would last, and since she wasn't allowed to go outside, she had no choice but to stay there and listen. The house was so small, and her parents were so loud, that even if she wasn't in her safe spot under the table, she would've still heard their argument.

A few minutes passed. Instead of both of her parents yelling, she started to hear just her mommy yelling. She didn't sound angry anymore, though. She sounded happy because she was yelling over and over, "Yes! Yes!"

The little girl was glad her mommy finally sounded happy, but she was still scared. She hated all the loud noises and all the yelling. She was so lonely and wished someone would come out and play with her. Her head hurt her so badly. This time, singing hasn't helped.

She blacked out, curled underneath the table, with her doll in one hand and the doll's brush on the floor beside her. She woke up later, in the same spot. Someone was making noise in the kitchen. The little girl blinked. She saw her mommy cooking something. She thought, *it must be a special occasion.*

There was music playing and her mommy was at the counter, chopping something, while she was dancing. "H-hi, M-m-mom-m-my," the girl said, hesitating.

"Hi, baby girl." Her mommy's words sounded funny, and she smelled yucky, but the little girl didn't mind. When her mommy was happy, the girl was happy, too. She crawled out from under the table and went to give her mommy a hug. "Watch out for my knife, silly," her mommy said, dodging away from the girl. She held the chopping knife in the air. "Your daddy had to leave again for more work."

"Okay," the little girl said and then pointed to her diaper. "P-p-pee pee."

Her mommy sighed, looking irritated. "You haven't figured out how to use the potty yet?" The little girl shook her head back and forth, looking down in shame. She wanted to learn, but just couldn't. She wanted to ask her mommy to teach her how, but she was afraid of making her mad. Her mommy pulled the diaper off, so the little girl was naked. "Go run, and grab me a new diaper," she said, patting the girl lightly on the butt.

The little girl plodded down the hallway toward the bathroom where they kept the extra diapers. She rubbed her eyes, still groggy. Her head didn't hurt anymore, and she was relieved that her mommy was happy now. She smiled to herself, excited for the food and thinking that maybe Mommy would even play with her for a while.

She might even read my book, she thought. She made it to the bathroom, then heard a breaking sound, followed by a loud thud. The girl frowned at the loud noises. Her hopes of playing with her mommy were quickly fading. The little girl was used to things breaking, but it normally meant that her mommy was *not* happy, and if she wasn't happy, she didn't play.

The girl heard the noises clearly. She was worried that she was the cause for making her mommy's good mood go away. Was Mommy mad because she went potty in her diaper? Mommy hated how she talked. Could that have upset her, too? She was afraid of going back to the kitchen.

The bathroom door was already open, so the little girl continued walking in and turned toward the cupboard under the sink. Pulling it open, she reached in to grab a diaper. It was a new pack, which meant they were packed in tight, and it took her a second to wiggle one out. Once she had it, she closed the cupboard and reluctantly turned to go back to the kitchen.

When the little girl returned, she gasped in horror. Losing control of her bladder from the overwhelming fear, she began to cry. Urine streamed down the side of her leg, even though she'd just gone in her diaper a short while ago. Broken glass was all over the kitchen floor. Her mommy was sprawled on the ground. The kitchen knife her mommy had been using to cut dinner with was now sticking out of the side of her neck. Her legs were twisted and had glass sticking out of them, and her feet, too. Blood was already pooling around her. She had tripped and fallen, knife in hand. A simple accident in the blink of an eye.

Her mommy made gurgling noises as blood came up through her mouth. She was gasping for air, trying to say something, but nothing came out. Her mommy was hurt, but the little girl didn't realize that she was dying. She sat on the floor next to her fading mommy and said, "M-m-m-mom-mmy?" The girl was still naked, sitting on pieces of glass without knowing or realizing that they were cutting her bottom. More gurgling and choking came from her mommy, but no words. Her eyes were wide open, gazing at the ceiling. The girl was crying even harder now, not knowing what to do or how to help.

Moments later, her mommy was dead. The girl believed her mommy had fallen asleep. She didn't know what to do, other than try to wake her mommy up. She had been taught her whole tiny existence that she should never wake up Mommy. The little girl was shaking with fear. She didn't know if she should risk getting into trouble or just wait for her to wake up on her own.

She thought it was weird that her mommy's eyes were open while she was sleeping. Her mommy normally closed her eyes to sleep, so this scared the little girl even more. She ran to the table and crawled underneath, thinking maybe her safe place would protect her and make her feel better. But this time, it didn't work. Her head was pounding again. She could see her mommy laying on the floor from where she's sitting. Gasping, she put her hands over her face, turning the other way. Minutes passed while she tried to think as logically as a four-year-old was able.

The little girl was afraid to get in trouble. She remembered what happened the last time she woke her mommy up. She remembered she had thought her mommy was hurt *then*, too, but it didn't matter. Her tears fell harder as she remembered the beating that her mommy gave and could give again. She hated getting spankings; they hurt so much! She thought as hard as she could and then decided that she didn't care.

The little girl knew she should try to wake her mommy up. She knew what blood was. The girl had blood on her and coming out of her all the time, and blood usually meant that there was an owie. She'd seen it so much that it didn't make her squeamish at all. It just gave her the awareness of pain, and she thought that with the amount of blood coming out of her mommy, she had to be in a lot of pain.

The girl remembered her daddy had just left for work. It meant it could be a long time before he came home. He wouldn't be able to help right now, and she had no one else. The girl gritted her tiny teeth. With all the strength she could muster, she shook her mommy, trying her hardest to wake her up. She shook and shook, but her mommy didn't move. She cried and screamed, relentlessly trying to wake her sleeping mommy.

Her small naked body was covered in her mommy's blood, but she didn't notice. The fear of being spanked faded, and she was more afraid of her mommy not waking up than anything else. There were little bloody handprints all over her mommy's face. When she could not wake her mommy, the little girl laid down on the floor beside her body, listening to the sounds of the radio still playing above on the counter. She wondered how long it would be before her daddy came home from work this time. Even though she woke up a short while ago, the little girl fell back asleep, exhausted from sadness and fear and the pain in her head.

She was left alone with her dead mommy for three days before her daddy came home. The first day, she pushed a chair up to the counter, in search of what her mommy was cooking the night before. She found raw chicken that was partially cut into little chunks. The girl also saw a can of green beans that was open, and two potatoes. She tried to wake her mommy up again, offering some of the food to her. Her mommy still didn't wake up.

The next day, she tried to eat the potatoes and could get a little of the skin off, but they were too hard for her little teeth, so she left them. She wasn't strong enough to get the refrigerator open, to look for anything else to eat. By now, her mommy was starting to reek and looked really scary, so she stopped trying to wake her up.

The little girl was still naked with cuts on her feet, legs, and bottom from lying next to her mommy. She tried to get her diaper on by herself, but it was crooked and when she went potty, some of it leaked out the side, dripping down her leg. She would just wait for her daddy to come home and help her. He would know what to do.

She spent her time playing with her doll, looking at the pictures in her book, and sleeping. She played pretend games, imagining her daddy coming home to rescue them. The little girl made up a pretend friend to talk to and play games with. She called her friend Ashley. The little girl was so hungry and thirsty that she cried again. She cried, even when her body had no more tears to shed.

When Joe Taylor finally came home, he took one step into the house and knew that something was wrong. The smell hit him like a slap to the face, nearly gagging him. Covering his mouth and nose with his shirt, he gave a muffled yell, "What the fuck?" There was soft music playing from the radio that was plugged in in the kitchen. Other than the music, the house was eerily silent. He didn't hear the normal sounds of his daughter playing or his wife watching TV. He rushed in, calling out for either of them, "Willow! Daisy!"

He reached the kitchen, seeing his seventeen-year-old wife's dead body. "Jesus!" He cried. "Willow, fuck! What happened? Oh God, what the fuck?" He went to her, dropping his shirt from his face, for a moment forgetting the smell. Then, he heaved and vomited, over and over. He was panting, trying to catch his breath. "Fuck, fuck, fuck!" He called for his daughter again, "Daisy! Daisy! Goddammit, Daisy, where are you?" But she still didn't answer. Pulling out his phone, he called 911. After hanging up, he searched the house, finally finding Daisy asleep in the bathroom. She was filthy, covered in dried blood, urine, and God only knew what else.

She looked nearly starved to death and had pieces of glass sticking out of her.

The police and the ambulance came. The mess was cleaned up, and their lives were forever changed. Because of the girl's severe malnourishment, CPS was called, and she stayed at the hospital for recovery. After she felt better, she stayed with another nice family for a while. They played with her and never forgot to feed her.

They had other children, a boy and a girl. Her headaches mostly went away, and she had a lot more energy than she ever remembered having. They taught her how to use the potty and brush her teeth, and she was so proud of herself. She even lost her stutter while with them.

She was happy with the new family and never wanted to leave. They filled her days with playtime and so much food that she nearly made herself sick from eating so much. She started kindergarten while she was living with the new family. She loved learning, and every day came home to share every new thing that she could remember. They took her to the library for the first time, and she fell in love with all the books. It became her new favorite place in the entire world, her new haven. Her new family also bought her new clothes and toys, too. She had never been so happy in her whole life.

She overheard some grownups talking about what a tragedy her life was. She heard how sad it was that her mommy died, and hearing this made her head hurt again. When that happened, the little girl cried. She tried to not be sad, but thinking about her mommy always made her sad. If she thought about her mommy dying, or being left alone for a long time like before, her headaches came back.

Her daddy got a new job, one that didn't make him stay away for long periods of time anymore. She went back home with him, even though she'd rather stay with the new family. No one asked her what she wanted to do. Her daddy made sure to play with her every day. He never forgot to give her special daddy time. He told her how much she looked like mommy, and that made her happy. Mommy was so pretty. Her headaches returned, and she was sleepy all the time again. She and her daddy lived alone for thirteen years, until Daisy turned seventeen and ran away forever.

PART I

1

Bill Wright stood in the shade of an oak tree, in front of a two-story Victorian that was listed for sale. He was watching Claire Fette, his real estate agent, arrive. The neighborhood he'd asked her to see was on the outskirts of town, where the lots were larger and had more privacy.

She'd sent a text to her waiting client, "I'm so sorry. Stuck in traffic! Will be there in ten or less." That was twelve minutes ago. Claire, who prided herself on professionalism, was late. Still in her car now, she seemed to be flustered. She was trying to arrange her short chestnut hair into something that would make a good impression.

Bill thought, *If I was a real buyer, I wouldn't be happy right about now.* He wasn't a real buyer, though. He had other intentions with Ms. Fette, and couldn't care less that she was running late. Bill had been watching her for some time now. He knew where she lived. And he knew what she'd been doing until a few minutes before she left the house. He also knew that she was not stuck in traffic when she texted him.

Bill knew these things because, until half an hour ago, he was in her attic, watching her.

Claire hated being late at all, but especially hated it with a new client. As she pulled up to park, she glanced at the clock again. *Shit, shit, shit!* She thought. Grabbing her notes, keys, and phone, she peeked out the window to see where her new buyer was. It only took a moment for her to find him in the shadows of the front yard.

He was leaning against a massive tree with his arms crossed. Because of the lighting, she couldn't make out his features. He seemed tall, taller than she'd expected somehow. Claire checked herself in the mirror. Then, she pasted a smile on and climbed out of the car.

"Mr. Hayworth, I'm terribly sorry! I can't apologize enough for my tardiness," she called, approaching. Bill had given her a false name when contacting her to set up the appointment. As she walked closer to him, Claire realized what a handsome man he was. His jet-black hair had blended in with the shadow of the tree. When Bill smiled at her, reassuring her all was well, his black eyes crinkled in the corners, and Claire felt her stomach do a somersault.

"Things happen, Ms. Fette. I'm sure it's not within your power to control traffic, or if it was, I'd bet you would have a different profession altogether." She seemed to visibly relax. Now she knew he wouldn't bite her head off.

"Let's take a peek inside this beauty, shall we?" As she moved toward the lockbox on the front door, Claire saw Bill reaching for a black duffel bag that had been at the base of the tree. He saw her notice the bag, so he explained how it was his overnight work bag that he kept his iPad and more expensive tools in, and he rarely liked to leave it in the car. As they walked toward the front door, she asked, "Mr. Hayward, I understand you're a truck driver?"

"Yes, ma'am, sure am. That's why it's so important for me

to keep some important tools on hand." Claire thought it was odd that he would want to carry his tools with him in a duffel bag, but also knew little about truck drivers. She supposed that if he had some expensive wrench, more power to him for wanting to keep an eye on it.

"I can imagine having those tools on hand comes in handy."

"You bet," Bill chuckled. "It's true that truck stops offer some tools and supplies for the trucker in need, but they're pretty limited in their selection."

"Oh, I bet." She nodded her understanding.

His black duffel bag was normally kept in his truck at all times, except for when he used it, during times like these. Inside were essential tools that he regularly needed for his truck, but more importantly, there were tools for his hobby. Part of Bill's hobby involved selecting individuals and causing them pain. In the duffel were various tools that he used to detain a target, and temporarily make that person unconscious, including preloaded syringes.

There were also various other tools that he would use later, once a target was obtained. For example, household tools like scissors, screwdrivers, hammers, etc. These items looked innocent enough, and their presence could be relatively easily explained if someone uninvited opened the bag. If Claire would have looked inside, she would not have been concerned.

It was one reason Bill chose and loved his occupation. He had a job that allowed him to explain away everything. He loved to travel, meet new people, and have the convenience of doing what he loved with little-to-no questions asked. His primary goal was to be ready when he wanted to pick up a target or visit a playroom. Today, he had his target right where he wanted her, and she led him straight into their playroom.

Bill was an avid planner and was regularly on the lookout for a good playroom location. He never used the same one twice, unless it was completely safe to do so, and it usually wasn't. Since he traveled the country to find his targets, he liked to find a playroom location first, and then find a target within a convenient distance from that particular playroom.

Playrooms were usually old, abandoned buildings, or a house that he knew the owners wouldn't be in. Sometimes he chose properties that were for sale and vacant. Many times, he chose rural locations. It was convenient for him to find realtors to show him vacant properties, and this was the first time that he'd chosen a realtor as a target. It made things much more convenient, which was a double-edged sword because it also meant there was more room for error, especially if he left a paper trail.

Because he was such a passionate planner, even after spotting a playroom location, Bill often took a lot of time before he committed. He took his time staking out the location to make sure it was safe. He was not ready to be caught yet and was going to make damn sure that laziness would not trip him up.

Not only did he scope out each new playroom, but he also scoped out his targets. Occasionally, targets were unplanned, but most often, he took time before making the commitment. Once he'd found Claire's profile online, he'd put in the footwork to make sure she was what he wanted before he made his move.

Bill liked to choose someone at random and then follow that person to observe. He would even get into their house and watch them up close, which is what he'd chosen to do with Claire. This was his favorite part of planning. Bill was obsessed with the power he felt when he was in a stranger's home, watching from another room, under the house, or in the attic. And they had no clue that he was there.

The Wrong Stranger

He was always smart about the decisions he made, usually starting off by watching from outside the home first, before moving inside. His target of choice was usually a woman he knew would be alone or with small children. These were the targets he liked to watch for long periods of time. This morning had been quite interesting so far, for Ms. Fette.

Claire and Bill stepped inside the vacant home, their voices echoing. She allowed him several minutes to explore the home on his own before making any commentary. Bill played the part of an interested buyer, examining the rooms, walking through the house, and asking questions. While he was alone, he dropped his duffel into the cellar. Claire didn't notice that he was no longer carrying it.

While they were climbing the stairs, he in front of her, Bill stopped without warning. Turning back to her, he said, "By the way, I almost forgot to ask: an affair with your neighbor? Is that really a good idea? And screwing him before meeting a new client? Tsk, tsk, Ms. Fette."

Claire was caught completely off guard. She blinked, thinking she must've misheard. She had no idea what to say. For a moment, she forgot she was standing on a staircase. Out of shock, she took a step back. As soon as she did, her ankle twisted, and she lost her footing. She let out a cry of surprise as she fell backwards down the staircase. Claire was not knocked unconscious from the fall, but she was in pain, which temporarily took her mind off the question that Bill had thrown at her.

Bill loved to punish, to cause pain. There was nothing in the world that was better than making one of his targets scream out in agony. To see someone writhing in misery and hear their cries brought him joy, but also fulfilled an urge that was buried deep within.

Emotional pain could be as terrible as physical pain, which is why he attempted to inflict it whenever possible. He loved to manipulate, surprise, and horrify his targets. Sometimes it was not a scream that he wanted, but the look in their eyes that said he'd reached their soul. He was waiting for the perfect opportunity with Claire, and it had been priceless. To see that look in her eyes was what he lived for.

Bill calmly walked down to the foot of the stairs where she was lying on the ground. She was attempting to get up, but he stopped her. Now that he'd caught her off guard, he was ready to play. Without saying another word, he reached into his pocket to pull out one of his pre-filled syringes. Claire finally realized that something was wrong, but it was too late. She didn't have time to scream or fight. He injected her, and her fate was sealed.

He dragged her limp body to the cellar where his supplies were waiting. Claire wasn't unconscious, but heavily sedated. Bill laid her on her back so she was looking up at him.

"Now, I know you can't move, Claire, but don't worry. You'll still feel everything." Bill pulled her clothes off, so she was completely naked. Then, he tied her up before he began to cut.

It was satisfying for him in every imaginable way. Every stroke of the blade was one push closer to the ultimate release. This was his hobby, but it was so much more than that. It was at the center of his life. He could never give it up and would never want to. This was his reason for needing to appear normal to the rest of the world. He needed to keep suspicion off himself, and the only way to do that was to blend in.

Once Bill finished, he left the house, walking back down the sidewalk to his waiting car. He drove away to a parked black semi. Making sure that there were no witnesses first, Bill opened the back of the semi's trailer, then drove his car up into it. He got into the cab of the truck and drove away.

2

"Mom, when can we go over to Jake's?" An eager six-year-old Chris asked his mom, with shining eyes and a broad smile. He hadn't seen his best friend, Jake Carter, since school got out for summer break. Jake's family went on vacation for two weeks, and it had been nearly three since the boys last saw each other. Ashley gave a smile full of warmth and love to her only son, as she tousled his short blonde hair.

"We'll go over around noon, baby, after we have some lunch." He dodged back, not liking for her to mess with his hair.

He whined, "Why can't we go now?"

"Because that's when Joy asked us to come over. Now, let's get your swim stuff together. It'll be noon before you know it."

Jake's mom, Joy, and Ashley were close friends. Usually when the boys got together to play, the women would enjoy each other's company, too. They liked to gossip and catch up on the latest news about each other's lives. It was sunny and hot, and Joy invited Ashley and Chris over for a swim date.

Joy and her husband, Fred, had a beautiful built-in pool and barbecue area. At one point, they pulled out money from the equity in their home and invested in a total outdoor landscape renovation. Fred hired landscapers to install full grown palm trees, the built-in pool, surround sound system, and barbecue area. They frequently hosted get togethers in their backyard oasis, and since Ashley and her husband, Bill, did not have a pool, most of the hot summers were happily spent at the Carter residence.

Ashley and Chris walked to the Carters' in leu of driving. Chris ran up the driveway, to the front steps, ahead of Ashley. As soon as he knocked, the door flung open to reveal Jake with an enormous grin. Without a word, the boys performed their secret handshake, then high-fived each other. "What's up, man," Jake asked. The boy was so excited, he forgot to step out of the way to let his friend in the house.

Chris gave a mock frown, asking, "You gonna let us in or what?" They both laughed, and Jake stepped back to let Ashley and Chris enter.

At the sound of the boys' laughter, Joy called, "I'm in the kitchen!"

Ashley met her there, giving her a tight hug. "How was the trip?" The women chatted for a while, catching up on the details of the Carter family vacation, while the boys caught up in their own way.

"So, how's Bill's job?"

"Oh, it's the same. Busy, busy, always gone," Ashley said, trying to sound cheerful about it. Bill was a long-haul truck driver, which forced him to be gone from home several nights of the week, under normal conditions. It was hard but better than some drivers who were gone for weeks at a time. Bill would travel the country, dropping off and picking up loads in all contiguous forty-eight states. Being a driver, though, meant that he could only be on the road for so many hours at a time, and eventually, he had to rest for thirty-six hours before taking another shift. When he ran out of driving hours, he often made sure he was far away and, therefore, unable to come home.

"Uh huh. So, he owns the company, but still drives, too?"

"Yeah, well, that's the nature of being a truck driver, I suppose."

"I just don't understand why he can't give himself the local routes and let the other guys go cross-country?"

"You and me both. But there's no telling Bill that. Let's talk about something else." Ashley hated talking about Bill's work and didn't want to sour their reunion. Soon, the group headed outside to the patio, all dawning swim gear and each mom holding a cocktail in her right hand.

Joy and Ashley settled up to the patio table and chairs, Joy turning on the surround sound music. The boys grabbed some water toys and jumped into the pool. The women sat at the table, about ten feet from the pool. They faced each other, Ashley with an unobstructed view of the pool, and Joy with her back toward it.

They were already having a great time, enjoying each other's company. The music was loud, and the boys' splashing and yelling made it even louder, but nobody cared. It was nice to visit with good friends who they were used to seeing on almost a daily basis.

It wasn't long before both women drained their drinks, and Joy got up from her chair to head into the house. When she did, both women spotted the boys being rough with each other, dunking each other's heads under the water. They didn't seem to be fighting, but Ashley didn't like the way they had started to get rough. "Boys, don't be so rough," she called.

She said it with a smile and a wave, as if to reassure them they weren't in trouble, but she still wanted them to pay attention and listen. The boys stopped, swimming away from each other to each grab a pool noodle.

Chris called back, "Sorry, Mom."

"It's okay, baby. Have fun! Just you boys be a little more careful, I don't want either of you to get hurt." Then, the boys went back to playing.

Joy, who was still standing next to the table, smiled at Ashley. "You know, Ash, boys will be boys." She laughed, adding, "You don't have to worry so much. We're right here."

Ashley blushed. "You know I can't help it."

Joy patted Ashley on the shoulder, giving her an understanding smile. "I know, babe," she said, then headed toward the house. She turned her head, calling back to Ashley, "BRB!"

While Joy was gone, Ashley thought about how different her mothering style was from Joy. Joy was always so carefree and seemed to never stress about anything. She hardly ever watched Jake and never seemed worried about him getting hurt. Ashley wished she could be so carefree, but despite all her efforts, she was too high strung. She worried about everything when it came to her son.

She supposed it was because of how hard it was for her to get pregnant. She had wanted a baby more than anything in the world, and after years of trying and heartbreak, she had finally become pregnant with Chris and successfully gave birth to her precious boy. After all the pain and suffering of lost pregnancies, she would rather die than let something happen to him, especially if it was something preventable. She was his mother, after all. Wasn't it her job to protect him?

This was one reason that she never let Joy watch Chris alone. Joy had offered several times to have Chris over for the night, to give Ashley and Bill a night to themselves. Ashley knew Bill would love to take her up on this offer, but she just couldn't trust her best friend enough to watch her son without herself present. She loved Joy to death, but something inside Ashley told her that Joy was just too careless.

It wasn't long before Joy came back, carrying a whole pitcher of margarita mix for refills. Ashley laughed. "Damn, how drunk do you want to get me?"

Smiling, Joy winked. "As drunk as you want, babe."

Ashley snorted. "I'm only having one more." This would make two drinks for Ashley, which she thought was more than enough for a pool date. She held up her empty glass for a refill. Joy shrugged. "Fine, more for me." They had been going slow, talking and sipping, how they always did when drinking adult beverages. For two women who normally saw each other so often, their long period apart was a little hard on the both of them. They were each other's support system. Each of the stay-at-home moms had their own troubles, the deepest of which was loneliness.

Now, the women were simultaneously delighted and relaxed, caught up in one another's company. Sitting in the shade, under the awning, listening to music and the laughter of their little boys, in the company of a dear friend, life was nearly perfect at that moment. There was a light breeze that blew through the palm trees, providing a respite from the heat.

Ashley glanced at her watch, noticing they had been outside for nearly three hours. She thought Chris was probably getting tired from all the swimming and playing. The women had intended to swim, too, but had been so caught up in chatting, that they hadn't moved from their spot on the patio.

Ashley felt a buzz now from the cocktails Joy had shared

with her. Her whole body tingled. She was a little beyond buzzed, if she admitted the truth.

She hadn't stopped at two drinks, as she had said, but had gone for three, at Joy's insistence. Ashley only drank about half of the third, stopping because she felt too guilty to finish it. She had eaten little, and with her slight build, the alcohol was going straight to her head. With Chris in her company, she felt she needed to be more responsible for his sake. Ashley rarely drank three glasses, ever, no matter how slowly, and especially not during the day at a play date.

She stood up. "I've got to pee and then we'd better get going soon."

"Will you guys eat some snacks with us first? The boys are probably starving."

Ashley glanced back at her watch and nodded. She swayed a little. "Sure, we'll eat something, but just a little. I have to make dinner soon; Bill will be home tonight." Joy nodded, as Ashley headed to the house. Ashley walked toward the guest bathroom, going through the kitchen, and setting her glass on the counter.

She took her time in the bathroom, hoping her buzz would be mostly gone before they left. By the time she was done, at least ten minutes had passed since she left the patio. It surprised her to hear noise coming from the kitchen. She thought she was the only one in the house, but when she got back to the kitchen, Joy was fixing a platter of cold snacks. Ashley was a little irritated because she thought Joy would watch the boys.

"Did the boys get out?"

Joy shook her head. "No, I told them it would be time to get out in a few minutes."

"How long have they been out there alone?"

Joy smiled. "I came in the house right after you." Ashley immediately felt one of her headaches coming on. She was heading straight for the pool, but Joy stopped her, asking for help. Joy knew what Ashley was thinking without her saying a word.

Joy laughed at her friend. "Don't worry! They're fine for two minutes, girl!" Ashley gritted her teeth, sighed, and helped Joy with what she needed. Then, she walked as quickly as she could, without running, to the pool.

For the rest of her life, she would never forget walking back into that backyard. Ashley stepped through the French doors, into a ghost-like atmosphere. The music was still playing, but there was no other noise or movement. When she left to use the bathroom, there had been the sounds of the boys playing, and the trees moving. There had been life and happiness. Now, it was too quiet and too still. There were no sounds coming from the pool. There was no splashing or waves rippling the top of the water. Ashley felt apprehension rise in her chest. As she walked toward the pool, she called, "Chris?" There was no answer. She called out again, "Boys?" Now, nearly at the pool, she could hear someone crying.

It made sense to Ashley why they wouldn't answer, and she was somewhat relieved. With neither of the boys answering her when she called, the worst thoughts ran through her head. But now that she could hear the sound of crying, at least she knew they were still in the backyard. Someone had been hurt, and they didn't answer her because they were afraid of getting into trouble.

Ashley took a steadying breath, hoping neither of the boys was hurt badly. She had known they were playing too rough. Ashley felt a small sense of vindication, recognizing she had been right in asking them to take it easy. She wondered what Joy would say, or if she would admit that Ashley had been right to ask them to not play so rough. Ashley knew it was better to be safe, and one day, Joy was going to regret being so lax with her parental supervision. Of course, knowing Joy, she might just play it off as if it was no big deal. "Boys will be boys," she would say.

She saw Jake huddled in the fetal position, sobbing. Ashley bent to rub his back, which made him bawl even louder. She tried to shush him and offer comfort, but when she looked around for Chris, she couldn't see him. "Chris!" When he still didn't answer, she asked Jake, "Baby, where's Chris?" Hearing the question, Jake began to howl as if he was in agony. Ashley was taken aback, worrying all over again. Her sense of relief disappeared. She shook Jake gently, asking, "What is it? What's wrong?"

She was nearly yelling, in order to be heard over his howls. He wouldn't answer her. He said nothing, just kept wailing and howling as if he was dying. Ashley looked him over as best she could. She didn't see any blood, and he didn't seem to be physically hurt, as far as she could tell. Her head was pounding now, and she was having a hard time thinking clearly.

Standing up, Ashley yelled for Joy as loud as she could. She waited a few seconds and yelled her name again. Ashley didn't know if Joy would hear, especially over the music, but didn't want to take the time going back into the house to get her. She needed to find Chris. Ashley turned her head, searching for Chris again. Then, she stopped.

Her universe froze in place, as if time stood still. She couldn't move, couldn't breathe, couldn't think. Across the pool, in the far corner, under the waterfall, she saw him. He was barely visible, but she saw him because of his bright red swim trunks and his legs. His legs were floating out, toes facing down. After what seemed like an eternity, Ashley regained her ability to move. She dove into the water, half swimming, half walking across the pool to get to him.

Chris was floating in the water, face down. He was still.

Lifeless. She flipped him over, crying his name over and over. "Mommy's here, baby. It's okay now, Mommy's here." His eyes were wide open, unblinking. Ashley could barely see through the tears, but she managed to pull Chris to the edge of the pool and push him up and out. She began screaming at the top of her lungs for Joy, who was still not outside. "Call 911!" She yelled over and over. She yelled at Jake, "Goddammit, go get your mom! Call 911!" She was shaking, teeth chattering from the adrenaline.

Her screaming seemed to finally break through to him. Jake got up and ran to the house, still bawling. Ashley tried CPR on Chris, begging and pleading with God to spare her son.

When Joy came out, she looked dazed and confused. "What's going on," she asked.

Ashley snapped, "Did you call 911?"

Joy said, "No. Jake—"

"Go call 911, goddammit! He needs a fucking ambulance!" Ashley cut her off with so much force that all the color drained from Joy's face. Ashley never spoke that way to her or anyone else, as far as Joy knew, and it frightened her. She turned around, sprinting back into the house. "Please, God!" Ashley cried.

She counted the minutes in her head, continuing to try to breathe life into her little boy. Ashley thought she'd been gone from the backyard for less than twenty minutes, but then it had taken her several minutes to find Chris, and now several more to call an ambulance. She wondered how quickly they would get there and prayed again for mercy for her son.

It took four minutes for the ambulance to arrive once they were called. It was too late. They could not resuscitate Chris. He was dead.

Ashley was crying and screaming over his body. She

begged for them to let her stay with her baby, not to take him away from her. It was heart wrenching for them to see a mother broken, but they had their jobs to do. The police were called to file a report, and a counselor would also be called to speak with Ashley and her husband about their loss.

Jake told the police that he and Chris had been dunking each other under the water when things got heated. "We were punching each other. We were just playing but Chris started getting rough," Jake said. "I held him under. I didn't know it was too long. I'm so sorry!"

"What happened next?" An officer asked.

"When he didn't move, just floated there, I didn't know what to do."

"Why didn't you run for help?"

Jake was crying too hard to answer. He had no answer. He didn't know. No one understood why he didn't run for the house to get Ashley or Joy for help. The precious minutes he wasted, laying there crying and not going for help, were what sealed Chris's fate.

Ashley was devastated. She was almost instantly a shell of her former self, and although she heard Jake's story, she couldn't speak. She couldn't ask him anything or say anything to the police because she couldn't stop crying. It was as if her soul had died with Chris.

She wanted to lash out at the boy who'd killed her son, wanted to beat him, scratch his eyes and face, slam his head into the concrete. She wanted to cause him and his mother pain, but she couldn't move. All she could do was cry and wallow in her own agony, imagining causing him the worst physical pain imaginable.

Before leaving the house, Ashley looked Joy straight in the eyes. She didn't say a word. Joy didn't know what to say, didn't think that anything could be said. She realized it was probably the end of their friendship. A tear dropped down

Joy's cheek as Ashley turned her back and walked out. Her throat was raw, eyes red and swollen, and heart shattered. She allowed an officer to give her a ride home despite the short distance because she didn't think her legs would hold her up for even a block. Ashley asked the officer to call her husband and give him the news because she couldn't say the words out loud.

Unlocking the front door and walking inside, Ashley dropped her bag on the kitchen counter and went into her bedroom. She locked the door behind her, laid down on the bed, and cried. She cried until her body had no more tears to shed and screamed until the only sound that came from her was a dry rasp. Bill did not come home that night. He stayed away until the funeral a few days later. Even if he had come home, Ashley wouldn't have heard him or been able to communicate with him. She was lost in her own misery. Ashley stayed in her bedroom for the next three days. She didn't eat and didn't say a word. She just laid on the bed and cried.

3

Jenny Jackson, single mother of three-year-old Tyler and four-year-old Avery, had the day off work. It was a beautiful summer day in north Idaho, and she was spending her day off playing with her boys while doing chores around the house. She wanted to be outside on such a nice day but knew if she didn't get some clothes washed, they'd all be going naked soon. She hoped to get the house cleaned and laundry done so the next day she could spend relaxing, as much as she could with two littles.

She was a server at a local diner, which was why she usually had a couple of weekdays off. Weekends were prime time for the busy crowd, and tips, too, so she didn't mind what her schedule looked like, as long as she got some down time with her boys.

The boys woke her up at six o'clock sharp, no matter what day it was. When their internal alarm clocks went off, they got up, bright eyed and bushy tailed. They were full of eager innocence, excited to seize the day, every day. Jenny was thankful that her boys were so happy and in love with life, but wished they would grasp the concept of sleeping in, or at least allow Mommy to sleep in a little on her days off. They were still too young to understand, but luckily for Jenny, she found the perfect way to get an extra hour or two of shut eye.

Tyler and Avery were both obsessed with their cartoon show, "Zoonies." All their friends from daycare watched the show, too, and it seemed like every kid in the entire world was obsessed with the little animals that drove in cars, finding different adventures all over the globe. They were always searching for different things on their adventures, and one Zoonie, "Todie," was always getting lost. The other Zoonies were constantly calling for him, trying to find him when he wandered off.

The kids seemed to love the mystery of finding him, almost like the game hide and seek. Tyler and Avery were so in love with the show that their shared bedroom was decorated in all things Zoonies. Every day, that's the show they wanted to watch, and Jenny had a hard time getting either of them to watch anything else.

One morning, Jenny was so tired when they woke her up, she turned on their show and went to pass back out. She'd been exhausted from a late shift at the diner the night before, and the boys had woken her up after only four hours of sleep. She'd startled herself awake, remembering that the boys were up and alone, with no adult supervision.

Filled with guilt and concern, she scrambled up, back out to the living room, where she saw them sitting peacefully on the couch, zoned out, still watching their show. She said a silent prayer of thanks, relieved they were both fine.

The more she thought about it, the more she didn't feel so guilty. Jenny asked herself, what was the harm in letting them watch some TV alone while she got some extra rest?

She saw they were so zoned out that they weren't about to move an inch away from their show, and besides, it wasn't like she was leaving them home alone. She would wake up if one of them started screaming for help.

Jenny began making a habit of this routine on her days off. She woke up, turned on Zoonies for the boys, made sure they were settled, then went back to bed for some extra sleep.

This new routine worked nicely for both mother and sons. Everyone was happy with the arrangement. The only side effect that Jenny noticed, other than feeling well rested and having more energy, was the boys' captivation with the show seemed to grow even more intense, which she hadn't realized was possible.

The boys lived and breathed for the show now. Even when they weren't watching it, they played games where they imagined themselves as characters from it. They ran around the house searching for Todie, calling his name over and over until Jenny had to shush them. She was becoming concerned with how obsessed they were growing.

She tried to get them interested in other shows and characters, but nothing peaked their passion the way Zoonies did. Finally, she had to reassure herself that eventually they would get bored with it and move on to the next show. She found it both annoying that they were so into the show, and also endearing. Because both her boys were such fanatics, she became an expert on the show, too, so she could play along with them.

Jenny had just finished loading the dishwasher and was grabbing all the boys' dirty clothes. They were young enough that she still helped them get dressed and undressed, but they had a habit of stripping naked and running around the house that way. They tended to leave their clothes wherever they took them off. When the weather was warmer was the most likely time for the boys to practice this art.

Jenny was moving from room to room, lifting things, trying to straighten as best she could, while searching for abandoned pieces of clothing. While she was doing this, the naked little boys were both searching for Todie.

Avery called, "Todie! Where are you?"

Followed by Tyler crying, "Oh, Toe-deeeeee!" They ran from room to room, calling for the elusive Todie.

Jenny asked, "Where do you think he could be?"

Tyler said, "Yeah!" Jenny chuckled at his one-word response.

Avery said, "He's not answering."

The boys looked crestfallen, so Jenny said, "Well, maybe he's just sleeping and can't hear you." This seemed to brighten them both up. They looked at each other then began to shout, "Todie," even louder than before. Jenny flinched but continued picking up clothes, moving to the laundry room to start a load.

Once she had a full load in the washer, she moved to pick up towels from the bathroom floors. She didn't normally pick up that much on her workdays, which resulted in the house being a mess by her day off. She was continuing to pick up, going back and forth from room to room, when Avery ran up to her. "Oh, he can't hear us!"

She smiled indulgently. "No, babe, remember, he's sleeping."

"Why won't he wake up?"

"I bet he's super tired. Let's let him rest, okay?"

"No! Please wake him up! Pleaaaase!" He was whining but not really looking for her to answer. He ran back into the other room to continue playing with his brother. Jenny sighed, moving to finish with the chores.

She was trying to get things done as quickly as she could, but it meant she wasn't keeping a close eye on the boys. Sometimes she wanted to cry from loneliness, thinking of how nice it would be to have a father figure in the house to play with them while she got a few things done. Or even better, he could do some of the picking up while she got to spend precious time with her sons. She refused to feel sorry for herself, knowing full well that even if she had a partner, it might not make things picture-perfect. Plenty of married women had men that didn't help at all.

Jenny was concentrated on the task at hand for some time when she realized she no longer heard the boys playing. Their silence was more of a concern than anything, so she dropped what she was doing and moved to check on them. Jenny peeked into the doorway of their bedroom. She saw both boys on the floor, staring down into the floor vent.

The home they lived in had a raised foundation with heater vents in the floor instead of in the wall or ceiling. Seeing the boys sitting cross-legged next to each other, staring down the dark slats in silence, sent a bolt of fear through Jenny. She watched them for a second to see what they were doing, but when neither boy moved nor made a sound, she stepped farther into the room. She figured she was probably being irrational to think this was worrisome behavior, but this was definitely not a normal part of their games.

Trying to sound as casual as she was able, Jenny asked, "What are you doing?" Both boys jumped. They looked at each other with guilty eyes, like they'd been caught doing something they weren't supposed to be doing. Jenny saw the look that passed between them, and it made her even more afraid.

Attempting to maintain her calm, she said, "Boys, listen to me, please." She crouched down next to them, putting an arm

The Wrong Stranger

on each. She eyed the vent, which looked completely normal, but she was suddenly afraid to be anywhere near it. "You guys are freakin' Mommy out. Please tell me what you're doing." She didn't want to scare them, but dammit, they were scaring the hell out of her. They had looked like they were trying to perform a séance or some other ritual.

Avery spoke first. "We found Todie."

Tyler nodded, adding, "Not nice to wake someone up."

Jenny breathed a sigh of relief. She thought, *they're still playing that damned game*. "Oh, I'm glad you found him, finally. Mommy is just tired boys, I'm sorry." She gave them each a hug. "Let's leave the vents alone, ok?" Jenny wasn't sure why she was so freaked seeing them like that, but she had learned to trust her gut over the years.

The boys didn't want to, but finally agreed to leave the vents alone. "Do you guys want a snack?" They wanted one, so they all went into the kitchen to eat. The rest of the day, the boys move on to play other games. They seemed to forget all about Todie for the time being, which was an enormous relief for Jenny.

THAT NIGHT, WHEN SHE WAS WINDING DOWN IN HER bathroom, getting ready to take a shower, Shadow, the family cat, was meowing nonstop. Shadow was the type of cat who had an attitude, but also loved to give love. When he wanted something, he meowed to let Jenny know his needs were not being met. If he was hungry or in need of something (like the litter box being changed), he never hesitated to let her know. When the cat was happy, he purred his contentment. Shadow never meowed for no reason, and he never purred for no reason. He was a sassy little thing, which was why Jenny loved him so much. He had a habit of meowing in response to Jenny, like he was having a conversation with her.

Jenny stripped down to her underclothes, about to step into a nice, hot shower before getting into bed and watching some Netflix. Shadow was meowing, rubbing against her bare legs, walking in circles around her. She leaned down to pet him, thinking maybe he just wanted some loving. But Shadow did not purr. Instead, he continued to meow, looking at her like she was an idiot.

She asked, "What?" and then flicked his tail. He stopped circling her, then walked between her legs. He laid on top of the bathroom vent, still meowing. His meowing was different somehow, more urgent. She noticed the difference but didn't understand what he wanted.

Jenny turned from the cat, climbing into the steaming water. While she was washing, she could still see Shadow through the clear glass door. Now he was standing up over the vent, pawing at it. She couldn't hear him meow over the sound of the water but thought he was probably still complaining about something. With the boys looking down the vent and now Shadow, she wondered if they had mice under the house or some other kind of rodent. That had to be it. She thought maybe the boys heard something big under there, shuffling around. It would explain everything. "Great. Now I have to call damned pest control."

As a single-income parent, Jenny could support herself and the boys, but money was not something they had in excess. She couldn't afford much more than rent and groceries. Daycare was taken care of with state help. She wondered if there was some kind of help for pest control, too, or if it was something the landlord was supposed to take care of for her.

Jenny was terrified of pissing off her landlord. He was giving her an amazing deal on rent, which she could still barely afford. She was fully aware he was only giving her a deal because he had the hots for her and had hopes of

The Wrong Stranger

hooking up. Jenny may or may not have flirted with him when she was first interested in the house, despite not being attracted to the man in any way, shape, or form. A woman had to use what she's got, to the best of her advantage, if it meant taking care of her family.

Jenny thought there was a good probability she would have to flirt with Mike again if she wanted him to fix anything for her. She wondered when he was going to figure out she was playing him. Jenny didn't want to play him. She knew leading him on was wrong, of course, but at the same time, she had made no promises.

Thinking about dealing with it all sent anxiety flooding through her. She tried to calm herself by taking deep breaths. Jenny inhaled slowly, counting to three, then slowly exhaled. She let the warm water fall over her as she closed her eyes to block out the rest of the world and her problems.

As Jenny was trying to relax, Shadow was toying with a small wire poking up through the floor vent. It was nearly invisible, only sticking up by a hair. At the end of the wire, was a tiny camera. It was too small for Jenny to see from the shower, but it saw her. It has appeared, disappeared, and reappeared several times. If the boys were awake, they might've said, "Shadow found Todie!"

By the time she was in bed under the covers, Jenny had calmed back down. She looked at Shadow laying on the bedroom vent, still not understanding what his problem was but having too much on her mind to think about it anymore. Before going to sleep, she thought,

There is no pest problem. Damned cat is just taking notes from the boys on how to freak Mom out.

She had the following day off from work, too. The boys went back to their game of calling for Todie. They ran through the house from room to room, crying out for him. They opened doors to closets and cupboards, pretending to search high and low. Jenny decided it was about time for them to all get out of the house, so she piled them into the car, and they headed out.

They lived in a rural area, about ten minutes outside of the nearest town. She drove down their unpaved road until she could turn onto the main highway. As she turned right, to merge into traffic, she passed a black semi parked on the side of the road. It wasn't an uncommon sight, having a semi parked so close.

Living that close to a highway, truckers often pulled over nearby if they needed to. Town was ten minutes in one direction, but if you didn't stop there, the next town was forty minutes in the other direction. Its frequent use had widened this area of shoulder so it was wide enough to support a semi driver to stop for a break or emergency and not worry about blocking traffic. It was not a spot for overnighters, but it also wasn't like the sheriff was monitoring it closely.

Jenny took Tyler and Avery to the town park, letting them get some energy out on the playground. Even there, they searched for Todie, and she admired their dedication. "They still haven't tired of that damned show," she said to herself. She let them burn some energy, then afterward, they stopped to get some ice cream cones before making a quick run to the grocery store.

They were gone from the house for a few hours, and when they pulled off the highway on their way back home, they passed the same semi that was parked earlier. Jenny noticed the truck, but it didn't register in her mind that it was the same one from when they left the house earlier.

Over the next several weeks, Jenny went back to work as normal.

Jenny left the house a little early so she could drop the boys off at daycare before heading to the diner for her shift.

She saw some other cars come and go from the spot on the side of the highway, but hadn't noticed a black semi again. The boys continued to play their game of searching for Todie anytime they had an opportunity, and the cat was still obsessing over the floor vents.

4

On a Sunday morning, one of Jenny's busiest days at work, she got a call from the boys' daycare. Tyler was sick with a fever and threw up all over a little girl after snack time. Jenny had no choice but to leave work to pick them both up. As she drove, all she could think about was losing five hours of pay and tips. She racked her brain, thinking of how she could make up for the lost hours. She's worked at the diner for years, but because it was such a small business, there was no paid time off or sick leave benefits.

When she saw how pale and weak Tyler looked, guilt consumed her. She'd been worried about money instead of how her baby was feeling, which made her feel like the worst kind of mother. She held him close, whispering, "I love you, baby," into his ear.

"I love you too, Mama." She grabbed his hand with her left, and Avery's hand with her right, leading them to the car. On the way home, she stopped to rent a movie so the three of them could enjoy movie night together. Jenny decided if Tyler was too sick for movie night, then she would tuck him in her bed, and they could just watch the movie in her room. Or, if that still didn't work out, then they would all snuggle up and call for Todie until the boys fell asleep.

They made it home, and the boys loved the idea of snuggling in their mom's bed to watch a movie together. Tyler insisted he was feeling a lot better, even though Jenny could clearly see he was as pale as a sheet. Hoping it wasn't the flu or something worse, she put him on the edge of the bed, next to her nightstand. She set the small bathroom trash can on the table next to him in case he needed to throw up again. She gave him some medicine and set some water and apple juice on the table next to the trash can. Avery was on the other edge of the bed, with Jenny planning to snuggle in the middle of her two boys.

She was rummaging in the kitchen for a few more things before she got the movie started when she spilled the bag of fish crackers. She was trying to open it, but the bag was stuck. Jenny yanked and pulled until finally the opening ripped apart, spilling fish crackers all over the kitchen floor.

Jenny bent to pick them up. She saw a single fish piece that was on top of the floor vent, tipping down into one of the slats. She moved to pick it up before it could fall.

As she approached the vent, she stopped and listened. Jenny tilted her head in confusion. She could've sworn she heard heavy breathing. It sounded like something was panting right next to her. She looked down into the vent, staring into the darkness. She started to lean closer when she felt a small tap on her back.

Jenny held back a scream, nearly jumping out of her skin. She turned to see Avery. The light of the kitchen was like a spotlight on him with the contrast of the rest of the dark house behind him.

"Did you find Todie?"

Jenny shook her head. "No, babe. I think we have a rat under the house."

He cried, "Todie isn't a rat!"

"Well, it must not be Todie, then."

"But he said he was!"

At this proclamation, Jenny felt the hair on the back of her neck stand up. She thought, *something isn't right.* She couldn't put her finger on it, but that feeling in her gut wouldn't go away. Jenny put her hand under her chin, as if she was thinking hard about a complicated problem. "If that old rat says he's Todie, then he's being naughty and telling lies. I think we shouldn't play with him anymore. What do you think?"

"But I like playing with him."

"If he's telling lies, Avery, I don't think he's being a good friend to you." Avery looked heartbroken. His little chin wobbled as he fought back the tears. Jenny felt the familiar mom guilt coming back again with a vengeance. She bent to hold Avery close. Jenny believed the boys were pretending to talk to some kind of rodent that was underneath the house. Her primary concern was that the rat would find a way into the house.

The boys kept bending over the floor vents, trying to keep it a secret because they knew they weren't supposed to.

She didn't like it. So, she told Avery, "I'm sorry, love. I know you guys have fun with Todie. Just please be careful around the vents. I don't want any rats to get up into the house and bite you or Ty." Avery wiped his nose into her shoulder. Sniffing and wiping his eyes, he pulled back to look at her. The boy brightened, easily forgiving his mother.

"Yes, Mama!"

Jenny left the rest of the fish crackers on the floor for Shadow to get. She grabbed a few other snacks, moving as fast as she could so she didn't have to be in the kitchen

The Wrong Stranger

longer than necessary. Then, the little family relaxed together on her bed to watch their movie. During the show, Tyler fell asleep. By the time the movie was over, it was dinnertime.

While she was making dinner, Jenny glanced back at the kitchen floor vent. She tried to ignore it but couldn't help glancing back at it over and over. She was going to call the landlord the next day to get the rat problem taken care of, but something in her told her it was no rat that was under the house. What kind of rat *panted* like that? The more she thought about it, the more she wanted to call Mike right away and not wait. She was ashamed she'd let the possible infestation go on for so long, as it was.

Jenny let both boys stay in her bed that night. After she put them to bed, she went back into the living room to call her landlord. He picked up the phone on the second ring. "Jenny!"

"Hi, Mike, how are you?"

"I'm just fine! It's great to hear from you. How's everything?"

"Actually, that's why I'm calling. I think there might be a rat under the house." There was a pause, and she had to ask if he was still there.

"I'm here. Say, how about we talk about it over dinner tomorrow night?" Now it was her turn to pause. She knew this would happen. She knew it, she knew it, she knew it. If she said no, there was no way he was going to get someone to go under the house for her. If she said yes, though, he was probably going to expect sex. There was no way she was about to go down that road, but Mike didn't know that. Jenny clenched her fists, but thought if the boys were around during dinner, she might be saved.

"I'd love to talk about it over dinner. Come over around

five, tomorrow. The boys are looking forward to spaghetti night."

"Oh. I didn't mean for you to have to cook."

"No, no, I'd love to!" Jenny put on her most charming voice.

"Alright, if you insist. I'll see you tomorrow."

"Sounds great!"

The following night at dinner, Mike listened to Jenny's concerns about the supposed rodent under the house.

"The boys have been hearing it through the floor vents, and Shadow has been obsessed, too. It's really been freaking me out." Mike had a strong suspicion it wasn't just a single rat causing all that noise, if there really were any noises at all.

"Are you sure the boys aren't just making it up for a game?"

Jenny tried not to be frustrated. "I thought that at first, too, which is why I didn't call you right away. But now I'm pretty sure there's something down there."

"Pretty sure?"

"Yeah. Well, for not going under the house, myself." She smiled.

Mike had no intention of calling anyone to check it out. It would cost too much. And, if there was an infestation it would cost even more. Nope. He thought if he put her off, she would forget all about it. Mike knew she would never get in bed with him, no matter how much she teased, so he was going to find a new tenant who would pay him some real rent. No more favors.

He smiled back at Jenny. "Look, Jen, I just know how the boys have some intense imaginations. No worries, though! I'll have my guy come to check things out."

Jenny breathed a sigh of relief. "Thanks, Mike, I really appreciate it."

"No problemo! He's been real busy, though, so don't be

surprised if he takes a little while to get out here."

"Oh, yes, of course."

Laying in the dark, below the vent in the kitchen floor, there was someone listening to the conversation going on above. He was the rat under the house, also known as Todie, and he was far more sinister than Jenny suspected. He's been watching and waiting. Observing. This was what he lived for, and he's been relishing every moment. Even now, on the brink of discovery, he was excited. He hadn't been caught yet, and almost wished that Mike really would send someone under the house.

After listening to the conversation between Mike and Jenny, he decided he would make his move soon. He'd just gotten some bad news from home and needed to wrap things up here anyway. He had a strong intuition that Jenny's landlord did not really mean to send anyone under the house, but if she was serious enough to bring up the topic to her landlord, then she would eventually take matters into her own hands. Women like Jenny were like that. He liked to keep an upper hand and the element of surprise, so he'd be the one making the first move in this relationship.

Jenny was lying in bed that night, next to both of her boys. She kept dozing off and waking back up to toss and turn. It was a restless night. She considered getting up to take a sleeping pill but decided against it, thinking she'd never wake up in time for her morning shift if she took one.

She was in the twilight zone when she felt the cat biting her foot. It was not uncommon for him to gnaw on her toes, so she shook her foot gently to encourage his playfulness. She was lying on her stomach, holding the pillow with both arms, eyes closed. Jenny wiggled her toes, then felt him pull back and jump off the bed instead of continuing to play. Only half awake, she mumbled, "Oh, Shadow." To her horror, a man's voice responded.

"Did I wake you?" It was a deep, masculine voice that spoke low and soft. It would've been extremely sexy if she knew who it belonged to, and if it had actually been

invited into her bedroom. She was awake immediately, terror gripping her. Jenny tried to roll over, but he stopped her. "No, no, love. Stay down like that for me." He put a hand on her head to hold her down.

She couldn't see his face from her position. He was leaning over Avery in order to hold her down and was covering her right eye with his hand. She could see Avery still asleep, but wasn't able to look at Tyler. Reaching with her left hand to feel for him, she touched nothing but sheets. Jenny began to panic. She didn't know if Tyler had gotten up to pee and was hiding, or if the man took him, or what the hell was happening. Images ran through Jenny's mind of her baby boy being taken from bed while he was asleep. Finally, her hand brushed against him.

Thank God.

She wanted to wiggle, to fight her way free, but couldn't bring herself to make a scene in front of her boys. She didn't want to scare them more than they already would be. Whatever happened to her, she needed to keep this psycho away from them. The man seemed to know what was going through her mind because he laughed. "Don't worry, I'm not interested in Tyler or Avery." At the use of her sons' names, Jenny's panic grew exponentially. She felt like her throat was closing. Her eyes grew wide. She felt like her heart was about to beat right out of her chest. She wondered, *who is this man?*

"What do you want?"

"Just a little playtime." He injected a syringe into Jenny's neck. She didn't have time to say anything else, or to even think. Her world went dark. The man went to each of the boys, also injecting each of them with a sedative, but with much smaller doses. He didn't want to play with them, but he

The Wrong Stranger

didn't want them to wake up and spoil his fun, either. He wanted to take his time and enjoy every minute of Jenny's company.

The next day, a 911 operator received an emergency call from a little boy. He was crying so hard that the operator could barely make out anything he was saying, other than him crying for his mommy. She had to trace the call, in order to get his address. Police showed up, but the little boy was too afraid to open the door. He and his brother huddled together in their mommy's bed while they heard pounding on the front door. After busting the door in, the officers followed the sounds of the children crying. The police found the boys holding each other, both crying uncontrollably on their mother's bed.

Upon entering the bedroom, the two officers saw a sight that would haunt them for the rest of their lives. "Oh my god!" one officer screamed before gagging and turning from the room. The two little boys were on the bed, next to their dead mother. Her body was mutilated beyond recognition, but her face was untouched. The bed was not bloody, so they suspected she was killed elsewhere before being transported back to the bed.

The boys were holding each other like a lifeline, pushing themselves back up against the headboard. Their mother was lying face up, naked. Her torso was mutilated and missing both of her legs. Three fingers were gone from her right hand. She had deep gashes everywhere, and it looked like someone had bludgeoned her with a hammer. In the middle of it all was a gray cat, who was staring at the officers, as if he was guarding the boys. The cat lay between the little boys and their mother, and as the remaining officer approached, he backed closer to the boys. He gave a warning meow, then began to growl and hiss as the officer reached the bed.

"We're here to help, boys. Close your eyes, now. We're

police officers, we're going to help you." The officer tried to sound as soothing as possible, but he was having a hard time controlling his stomach.

The boys were still crying, unable to speak through their tears and confusion. Social services showed up to take the boys, who insisted that their cat come with them. It wasn't something that was normally done. The cat would go to the SPCA or other rescue organization, but in this extreme case of tragedy, the social worker assigned to Tyler and Avery made the boys a promise. They would be able to keep their cat. She vowed no matter what happened, they would keep him. Even if she had to adopt the cat herself and bring him to them on every visit, she would not let them down.

The story of the violent murder hit the news and flooded social media. The story of the boys' loss was on every news station throughout the country. Everyone was dying to know what happened. The mystery involving the case was unbearable for the public. There was a large portion of spectators who could not believe the boys didn't remember a thing.

There were many who believed Tyler and Avery actually had a hand in their mother's murder, but these accusations were given no merit. The extent of Jenny's injuries had been far too violent and extreme for two little boys to have done it. The officers who found the boys adamantly believed in their innocence, and so did most of the world.

Jenny's landlord was under suspicion by investigators, as he was the last person to see her alive. His fingerprints were fresh, all over the living room and other areas of the house. When investigators got a search warrant to take a look at his home, they found what appeared to be a shrine dedicated to Jenny. At the top of the shrine was a used pair of her underwear. They arrested Mike for the murder of Jenny Jackson, mother of two.

5

Bill planned Chris's funeral. Ashley was surprised he would do it, but relieved to let him. At the funeral, Ashley remained speechless. People greeted her, offering sincere condolences, but it was as if she was a statue. No tears left her eyes, and her lips didn't quiver once. She didn't respond to anyone, despite their efforts to console her. As soon as the service was over, she returned home to her bedroom.

After Chris's death, Ashley's entire world ended. She felt like her still-beating heart had been ripped from her body and crushed. Initially, all she did was cry and sleep, sleep and cry. Over and over again, she would relive the memory of his death. She would torture herself with thoughts of what she could've done differently, replaying that afternoon in her mind until her head throbbed with pain. Every time she thought about it, it brought on one of her headaches, but she couldn't help herself. The guilt consumed her every waking moment, but she refused to see a therapist for help.

Ashley locked herself in her bedroom most days and stopped leaving the house. Slowly, the agony grew, multiplying into anger and a bitter hate. A burning rage started to consume her. Ashley hated Joy and her son with every fiber of her being. She would spend hours imagining torturing them, causing untold amounts of pain, grinding her teeth at the thought of revenge. They'd gotten away with the murder of her son with no punishment whatsoever from the law.

She wanted them both to suffer twice as much as she had, and especially twice as much as Chris. She thought about how scared he must've been, with his head being held under the water, not being able to breathe. Imagining his pain and fear brought on her headaches, too, but she welcomed the pain, feeling she deserved every ounce of it for letting her boy die. Anger would eventually overwhelm her, and she would sleep for entire days at a time before waking and doing it all over again.

It took six months for Ashley to stop isolating herself in her bedroom. One day, she opened the door and came out to sit on the living room couch for a while before returning to bed. Then, the next day she came out to make dinner before breaking down into tears and returning to bed. Once she made that first step to come out, though, it only took her a short while to live life like a human being again. She still stayed in the house and wouldn't even go into the yard, but she was getting out of bed and out of her bedroom.

Once she left her room, it didn't take long for something to trigger her into either tears or a searing fury, but she now seemed to resist going back to bed for entire days at a time. The hardest part for her was walking past Chris's bedroom without him being in there. She felt so alone without him; it was like a part of herself was missing.

Bill was grieving Chris's loss, too, but he handled it in a much different way than she did. Instead of never leaving the house, he hardly came home. He worked as much as he could, and if he wasn't able to work, he still stayed away. Bill had his hobby, which also kept him busy. He threw himself into it, committing all his attention to his targets, which seemed to keep his mind off his loss.

Being at home was hard for him because he couldn't stand to see Ashley how she was. Instead of dealing with Ashley by confronting her grief, he stayed away. She didn't even notice he was gone most of the time, until she started leaving the bedroom regularly. Knowing she wouldn't leave the house, Bill got Ashley groceries and pre-cooked meals because he didn't want her to starve to death. Some of the neighborhood women cooked meals and brought them over once a week, which was a tremendous help. There was no shortage of food, but Ashley refused to eat; she had no appetite.

After six months of self-isolation and starvation, Ashley lost an enormous amount of weight and was beginning to look sick. She had been a small size before, and now her clothes were nearly falling off her. Her cheeks were sunken in, causing her eyes to look like they were bulging out of her head. Even her hair seemed to be thinner. Because of her lack of calorie intake, great globs had fallen out. When Bill looked at her, he wondered how she could've let herself get to this point. He was disgusted.

Bill had no sympathy for her because he blamed Ashley for Chris's death. Even after hearing the story of what happened, and all the excuses and reasoning, he couldn't change how he felt about it. In his mind, Ashley was supposed to be watching their son. There was no excuse that would ease her guilt. It came down to the simple fact that she left that backyard without him and didn't make sure that he was safe. She was inebriated, which gave her poor judgement, and it was therefore her fault. He blamed the boy, Jake, and even Joy, too, but not the same as Ashley.

No, this was Ashley's fault. She should've been there.

. . .

HE WAS NOT PREPARED TO LEAVE HER YET. HE HAD REASONS for keeping her around. In fact, having the grieving wife at home actually helped him. It made him look better in the community and garnered a lot of sympathy from thoughtful neighbors, many of whom were women that knew just how to make him feel better. He wanted to keep Ashley right where she was until *he* was ready to change the situation, on his own terms, and no one else's.

HALF A YEAR HAD PASSED SINCE CHRIS'S DEATH. ASHLEY STILL had not left the property, but would at least go into the backyard now. She was still not herself. She suffered from excruciating headaches daily, and she often spent most of the day lying in bed, thinking of Chris. On these days, she left the bedroom door wide open, as if to remind herself she would have to leave again and couldn't stay there, no matter how much she wanted to.

Bill liked her staying at home; it was comforting to always know where she would be. He never had to worry about Ashley showing up at the wrong place, at the wrong time. He toyed with the idea of playing off her emotions to keep her upset, so that she would remain miserable for as long as possible.

In the kitchen one morning, Bill was swiping through the daily news on his iPad. His attention was caught when he read the headline: "STALKER LANDLORD SLAYS MOM OF TWO." He continued to read about Jenny Jackson's murder and what was to become of her two sons. A slow smile spread across his face as he read. He finished the article, then swiped to the next. Ashley was making breakfast while Bill sat up to the kitchen island on a barstool. Boredom soon overcame him. He sighed.

"What's wrong?" Ashley asked, not looking in his direction. She was cracking eggs into a glass bowl. She tapped one against the edge, then broke it open with her fingers. The sound of the plop into the bowl was somehow satisfying.

"I was reading this story about these boys who found their mom dead in bed with them."

"You... What?"

"Yeah, sad, isn't it?"

"Good lord, Bill." She frowned, turning back to her cooking.

"I guess she was mutilated and left there on the bed with them." He studied her, watching for her reaction. She stopped what she was doing. Her face went pale, and she stood frozen, hands wet with egg whites held out in front of her. She closed her eyes, taking a deep breath, then turned back to whip the eggs.

Bill was all innocence, acting like he couldn't possibly imagine what upset her. Ashley was fully aware of his game. He liked to see her squirm. She tried to not show him how much his words affected her, but it was a hard reaction to fight. "That's terrible, Bill." He shrugged, then turned back to the article, a sly smile on his lips.

Even though Ashley tried to hide it, Bill knew that to bring up any subject relating to kids getting hurt was a trigger for her, especially a story about boys with their mother. It would instantly bring back the pain and memory of Chris, which was unbearable for her.

He could see it written all over her face. Any time she saw a boy that was Chris's age on TV, she would have tears in her eyes or run to the bedroom, sobbing. She could never talk about other families that had lost or missing children, like the news that Bill referred to that morning, without breaking down.

Even months later, she was raw. How could he not notice her reaction? He wasn't stupid. Even though Ashley didn't think he cared to pay attention to her, Bill noticed things, and it would've been extremely hard for him to miss her running into the bedroom at any mention of a little boy.

Ashley thought she might always be this sensitive, and Bill thought so, too. He wondered if she knew what he was doing when he tried to antagonize her and decided that she didn't have a clue. Bill thought she would never have a clue and didn't think that his wife was the brightest bulb in the box, being in her current frame of mind. But Ashley did know. She fought giving him the satisfaction, but it was hard because she blamed herself, too. Ashley felt, deep down, in the end, it was her fault Chris died, and because of this, she let Bill treat her however he wanted. She deserved every ounce of torture that he wanted to dish out.

She not only suffered emotionally, but physically through her headaches as well. They came on with a vengeance, but Bill wasn't aware of them. She believed she deserved anything he gave her but didn't want to let on that he was causing her physical pain, too. For all that Bill did notice, he hadn't noticed her having them, and he didn't need to know how much he actually hurt her. What mattered was that she was being hurt at all.

6

When Ashley had her bouts of sobbing, she cried for the loss of her son, but also for her lost marriage. It wasn't a secret that it was over between Bill and herself. They were hanging on by a thread, putting on the charade. God only knew why, but one day soon, it would all be over. She didn't think Bill loved her, and she didn't love him, either.

Besides the lack of love, there was no relationship. He was hardly home to spend a few minutes with her, and she really didn't care. If he didn't show up for an entire month, she wouldn't have cared. But she wasn't sure if it was because she could no longer care about anything or anyone anymore.

They'd gotten married nine years ago; Ashley was seventeen, and Bill thirty-three when they met. Ashley was working in a library, which was where they met. Bill accidentally bumped into her while they were both in the adult fiction section. She was a librarian's assistant and had been putting books away. She had a stack in her arms, and it spilled to the floor when Bill knocked into her. He not only apologized profusely, picking the books up for her and helping her place them, but he charmed her with smiles and compliments, too.

Bill had looked at her with eyes so dark, she hadn't known if they were dark brown or black. They matched his black hair. He seemed dangerous somehow, which only drew her to him, and she'd almost instantly fallen in love. He was the stereotypical tall, dark, and handsome man that many women dreamed of, but that wasn't all.

There was something dark about Bill, besides his physical features. It was like a secret loomed over and around him, luring her into the darkness with him. Their age difference didn't bother either of them in the least. They went on their first date shortly after meeting and married within the year.

Ashley had been a little bothered by the way other women responded to him, even when they were obviously together, but soon grew used to it and learned to ignore the flirting. There was something about Bill that drew women in. He was like a human magnet that others were naturally drawn to. His looks and charm gave him a sense of trustworthiness that prevented any doubts about him from crossing her mind. She thought others probably felt that way, too; they couldn't help it.

Ashley realized women Bill's age were jealous of her because she was younger, and she was okay with that, even liked it. She felt proud to have caught such an amazing husband. She didn't care about the age gap; love was love. Plus, Ashley reasoned, he was amazing in bed, which excused a lot of things. Ashley was also a beautiful woman, which was why Bill had been drawn to her. She wasn't only beautiful, but remarkably smart and had a sense of humor that drew Bill in. They were a perfect match and had been very happy together in the beginning.

It took three years of struggle and heartbreaking loss for Ashley to finally have a successful pregnancy. Through those three years, she'd suffered three miscarriages, but had never given up the hope of having a baby. She and Bill met when she was young, but they had both agreed to start a family right away. Ashley loved the idea of an older husband, who already had an established career and was ready to settle down and start a family with her. She knew he would support her and any children that they had. To her, it was the idea of heaven, and something she'd wanted for as long as she could remember.

Through all the pain and heartbreak of infertility, Ashley held on to her love for Bill. When she had finally gotten pregnant again, and successfully gave birth to Chris, she had been the happiest woman in the world, and her love for Bill was deeper than it had ever been. Ashley was so happy that she was blind to how Bill truly felt about her and the evil he was capable of.

She had thought all along that Bill was head over heels for her, but the reality was he was head over heels for her when he first met her, and that was about it. He'd wanted a beautiful young wife who would keep him entertained and be easy to groom to his liking, and she'd fit the bill perfectly. He had pretended to want a family and pretended to be supportive.

Unbeknownst to Ashley, Bill was never faithful to her a day of their relationship. He was intensely attracted to Ashley, and lusted for her, but he lusted after many women that he came across. Ashley reminded him a great deal of a woman who he knew and loved when he was younger. Her strawberry blonde hair and gray eyes made her look nearly identical. Ashley's resemblance to this woman made him feel as though he had to have her at any cost.

He didn't love her, but he had reasons for wanting to marry her. The only thing in life that
did truly matter to Bill was his hobby.

When Ashley couldn't get pregnant or miscarried, Bill was glad. It had taken her years to get pregnant because he had been crushing birth control pills and putting them in her food or drinks. He'd been drugging her with them. Even after she became pregnant, he took steps for her to miscarry. When Bill wasn't ready for a child, he wasn't going to allow his wife to become pregnant.

She had wanted a child from the beginning. Even before they'd gotten married, Ashley told Bill she wanted children right away. She wanted him to know up front what her dreams were and was not willing to marry anyone unless they were on board with having children. Bill had agreed from the start, not really wanting kids, but knowing he needed to play a certain part in order to get her.

He had wanted Ashley, and he was willing to do or say whatever was necessary to get her. Once they were married, he talked to her about birth control and tried talking her into waiting to try for a baby. She refused, of course, and Bill found it was easier to pretend to agree, rather than to openly fight her. He could not talk her out of it, so he took matters into his own hands.

Instead of wasting his time and energy arguing with his new wife, Bill wanted to spend that time and energy on his hobby. He needed his wife to appear happy in order to do what he wanted to do. All along, Ashley thought they had fertility problems, and he went to every fertility appointment and had sex with his wife any time she wanted, whatever weird position or time of the day was required of him when he was home. He pretended to be devastated, right along with her. Bill told himself if he married Ashley to serve a purpose, he was going all the way with it and would not allow her to have a child until it too served his purpose.

When Chris was born, it was because Bill had finally been ready. He stopped drugging Ashley, and she quickly conceived. The pregnancy was full of tension for Ashley, with the fear of another loss. Bill cared about Chris, but not how a father should. To Bill, Chris was something that *belonged* to him. Chris was *his*.

There was an image that Bill strove to achieve. The image of the perfect man with the perfect family. He *needed* to be normal, with the ideal wife and family. When Chris died, Bill was grieving for the loss of something that was his. His possession. His image he'd worked so hard for. It was an inconvenience to him. He wasn't grieving from heartbreak over the death of his son. He was angry and hurt that something that belonged to him had been taken away.

It had taken years, and the loss of her son, but Ashley finally saw that Bill just didn't care about her how he should. She would never know of the unforgivable things Bill had done to her, but she did finally see their marriage was over. Seeing clearly made her feel completely and utterly alone. To Ashley, it was a matter of time before either Bill left for good and didn't come back, or before she did.

Now that Ashley's only reason for living was gone, Ashley dreamed about ending her own life. She wanted to die more than anything else. Suicide was an idea that consumed her thoughts, when she wasn't replaying that day in her mind. The guilt that weighed on her was massive and unforgiving. She thought she could never forgive herself; she deserved pain for what she had let happen to her baby boy and hated herself every day. Ashley even had a hard time looking at herself in the mirror without wanting to cause herself bodily harm. She had no appetite, and without intending to, was indeed starving herself to death.

There was something deep down that resisted the thought of suicide. It wasn't just her belief in heaven and hell, there was something more. It evaded her conscious thought, no matter how she tried to dig at it and pull it forward. It was really just a feeling that arose anytime she had these thoughts, like having something important you needed to remember but couldn't.

It was something that nagged at the back of her mind, constantly through her grief. In the end, she told herself that suicide was the easy way out. She didn't deserve to be let off easy; she deserved to suffer. She had to go on living. This was why she walked out of the bedroom, and went on living, despite knowing she was utterly and completely alone in the world.

7

TWENTY-SEVEN YEARS AGO

Sixteen-year-old William Wright was bored with his tedious life. He had a steady job as a ranch hand, where he'd worked for the past year after dropping out of school and running away from home. Living in a rural community in Montana, Bill lived a simple country life. His birthday was yesterday, and turning sixteen made him realize how unhappy he was.

Lately, he hadn't been satisfied with his life, and the boredom was making him irritable and prone to violence. He would daydream about traveling the country and having nothing in the world to tie him down. He dreamed about having a different woman every night and being in a different city every week. Bill felt that the monotony of his life was eating away at his very soul, and he knew he had to change something, or he would lose his mind.

Working as a ranch hand earned little income, however. His pay was minimal because of his age and lack of experience, and even less because he lived on the property. What little income he had, he spent on his car payment. Anything leftover got him a few beers at the local bar. Lucky for Bill, the bartender had no problem giving him alcohol, despite his being underage. Money was one reason Bill hadn't left town yet. He promised himself things were about to change. He was determined to do something big, something that would spice up his life and bring him some excitement.

The ranch that Bill worked on comprised of three live-in ranch hands, including himself, as well as three additional hands who lived off the ranch. All of them reported to Mrs. Allison Green, a forty-five-year-old widow who lost her husband about five years ago. Mrs. Green and her husband had purchased the land and, over the last twenty years, developed a prosperous ranch together. At fifty years old, Mr. Green was out in the fields alone, when he had a fatal heart attack. It had been hours before he was found.

Mrs. Green and her daughter, Willow, were left to tend the farm on their own. With the loss of her husband, Allison elected to hire a few more ranch hands to help keep her husband's legacy going. By allowing the hands to live in the barn, she could stretch her dollar a little farther. She also felt a little safer knowing the men would always be about. Allison thought that a single woman could never be too safe, especially with a daughter to protect.

When he was fifteen, Bill had been thankful to get any job, especially one that would allow him to stay out of his father's house. He was an eager worker and glad for the opportunity. But now, a year later, he'd been doing the same thing day in and day out, and he couldn't take it anymore.

Once a month, all the hands got together for a poker night. Sometimes it would be in the barn, and sometimes at one of the non-live ins' houses. On a poker night in late May, it was to be held at Kevin Barnett's home. He was an older hand who lived in town with his family. After a couple of rounds, Bill said, "I'm gonna turn in early, boys. I think I ate something bad earlier. My stomach is killin'." He was glad that poker wasn't in the barn this month, because he'd been preparing for this special night for a long time.

The boys would be occupied until early morning hours, which would give Bill plenty of time to do what he had in mind. When he got back to the ranch, all the lights in the big house were out. Before doing anything, he waited in the barn for good measure. He wanted to make sure there really was no one up and about.

Finally, around midnight, he quietly made his way out of the barn, to the back of the big house. Out in the middle of nowhere, it was so quiet that you could easily hear the smallest of sounds from a mile away. This late at night, sounds were even more intensified. Bill felt like he had to hold his breath or Mrs. Green would be able to hear him inhale and exhale from inside her bedroom, even with all the windows and doors closed.

A few months back, he had an idea that both scared and excited the hell out of him. He wanted to get into the attic and *watch* Mrs. Green. He thought that being up there would give him a completely different perspective of her, and he wondered what kinds of things he might see her doing. There was attic access in the hallway ceiling, but Bill wanted a way to get up there that was a little less noticeable.

To solve his dilemma, he placed a ladder on a back wall of the house where no one would notice. Some trees were blocking it, and if anyone asked about it, he thought he would just say he was checking on the roof since he'd noticed a few shingles on the ground. It was a crappy excuse, but no one had noticed or said anything yet.

Bill kept the ladder nearby, hidden. Since he was going to be a frequent visitor of the attic, he found it wonderfully handy to have the ladder right there, in his secret spot. Anytime he found the opportunity to go up, he would be able to easily lean it against the eves and make his way up.

Now, on this night in May, he climbed up to the roof with all the stealth of a ninja, then creeped a few feet to the spot he had prepared. A section of the roof, just big enough to fit through, was cut out and camouflaged so that no one would notice it. Bill hardly noticed it himself in the middle of the night. If he hadn't made it, he probably wouldn't have been able to find the damned thing.

He was proud of the job he'd done. The section of roof he had tampered with, was cut into a square, and he added hinges, which allowed the piece to drop. They were installed on the inside, so they were not visible from the top of the roof. He didn't have a handle, but had installed a small latch that was covered by false shingles.

Bill lifted the latch to the makeshift door before slipping down into the crawl space of the roof. There was not enough space to stand, but there was enough room for him to crawl across the beams on his hands and knees. Over the past several months, Bill had made small holes all throughout the space, that allowed him to view the occupants of the house. Each time he went into the attic, he brought a black marker with him, marking any new areas he wanted to add eye holes.

Then, when he had the opportunity to cut with no one around, he would make one, always staying neat and cleaning up any sheetrock that fell to the ground. He plugged the openings with the cutout circle, so they weren't noticeable from below. Each opening was small; only large enough for his eye to see through, and the plugs had small handles so he could open and close them with ease.

Bill had gone up to the attic on a couple of poker nights so far, but he didn't want it to be noticed that he wasn't around on game nights. There were many other nights, and days, too, that he could visit the attic. Any time he got a chance, he would go. Even on hot nights, when he almost couldn't breathe up there from the heat, he didn't mind.

He found it to be the most exciting thing he'd ever done in his life. Being up there, watching everything that happened below, made Bill feel powerful and *smart*. He was well trusted by Mrs. Green and the other ranch hands, which made him feel even smarter for fooling them. Bill was not close to the daughter, Willow, but she was friendly enough any time he saw her. Bill was confident no one suspected a thing.

One of Bill's favorite things to watch while in the attic was Mrs. Green in intimate situations. He especially loved to watch her in the shower when she had a little fun with the shower head. He'd watched her have sex with one of the ranch hands every now and then, when it suited her. Bill found it amusing how they tried to hide their relationship, when it was obvious to everyone that they were sleeping together.

His idea of spying on the household started with the desire to watch Mrs. Green, and he felt it was worth every effort just to be able to do that. Her bedroom activities entertained him, but Bill's obsession began to change when she became predictable. He began to spend more time watching Willow and less watching Mrs. Green.

Willow was thirteen years old, but to Bill, she had an old soul. Bill felt like she was a special girl. He couldn't put his finger on it, but there was something about her that drew him in. She was gorgeous, with long, straight, strawberry blonde hair and large gray eyes. She was short, with a full figure, but it was more than just her beauty that drew him.

Eventually, Bill made a hole in the ceiling, directly over Willow's shower, and would imagine himself touching her while she was in there. Since he was frequently in the ceiling before she went to bed, this was often. She stayed up late, hours past her mother. Sometimes she would watch a movie in bed, and Bill would watch with her.

Some days, he included Willow in his daydreams about living his new life. He imagined how they might travel the world together. Bill told himself, *she wouldn't even mind if I have other women in my bed*. She was an open-minded woman. Of course, she would never want another man besides himself. She would never even dream of it. They would have the perfect life together, and she would always be there for him to come home to.

His adoration for Willow grew, but it didn't change his attraction for her mother. He fantasized about both of them, together and separately. He imagined who might be better in bed, and even acknowledging Mrs. Green was more experienced, he thought Willow might hold her own. Bill's thoughts grew increasingly vivid. He found himself lost in his daydreams about having sex with Willow and her mother when he was supposed to be working. He was beginning to slack off noticeably, and he realized he needed to get it together, and quick.

8

Bill decided things were going to be a lot different from his usual watching. He was done with only watching and fantasizing with no real physical pleasure, other than from himself. Bill had scored some Ruffies and, after dissolving the tablets, had prepared two syringes. He had them carefully packed in a small bag, ready to go as soon as he needed them. After making his way up to the attic, he spied both Allison and Willow in their beds, sleeping. *Perfect.* He had thought Willow might be up still, as was her tendency to stay up late, but he was glad to see that she was indeed asleep.

This was his first time attempting to approach either of them. Even in his normal daily routine, Bill never even spoke to them without one of them approaching him first. Especially with Willow, he'd only had a handful of minutes conversing with her, over all of his time at the ranch.

Climbing down from the attic, he felt more alive than he ever felt before. He could feel his heart pounding in his chest, and he felt light-headed from the excess blood flow.

Full of nervous excitement, Bill went to Willow's room

first; it was the closest to the attic entrance. Tiptoeing across the room, he wiped the cold sweat off his brow with a shaking hand. He stood at the foot of the bed where Willow lay sleeping. Then, setting his small bag down onto the bed beside her feet, Bill took one syringe full of Rohypnol out. He took a moment to stop and just look at her.

Inhaling deeply, Bill smelled her scent and the scent of her room. There was a hint of flowers in the air. It suited her. He admired the shape of her sleeping body. She looked so peaceful, laying there, tangled in the covers. Willow had one leg out and one underneath the blankets. Her arms were wrapped around a pillow, and she had two other pillows under her head. Bill thought she looked like some kind of princess and wondered what she was dreaming about. Then, he took another deep breath before injecting the syringe into her foot that was sticking out.

Willow began to stir. Bill took a quick step back, grabbing his bag that was on the bed as he did. Holding his breath, he waited. Willow kicked her leg out, wiggled around a bit, but then settled back down. She didn't get up.

Bill breathed out a sigh of relief. He decided to give her injection a few minutes to kick in, so he made his way to Allison. The same process took place with her, except slightly quicker. Bill was less hesitant now that he'd done it once and had no desire to admire Allison's sleeping form. With Mrs. Allison Green, Bill was ready to get down to business.

With both women now drugged, Bill left Allison to let her dose kick in as he went back to Willow's room. She was as before, but somehow more still. Bill kicked his shoes off and dropped his pants to the floor. He climbed into bed with the thirteen-year-old sleeping girl and proceeded to rape her.

Bill was unsurprised to discover that she was a virgin. He felt satisfaction and pride knowing he was the first man to touch her. He'd heard some rumors from other ranch hands

The Wrong Stranger

about how she liked to hang around older high school boys, and even had a boyfriend who was a dropout. They claimed she was a little slut. Bill never believed it, and now he had proof.

After he finished, Bill was able to hide any trace that he had been in the house. The only sign left was blood between Willow's legs and a small spot on her sheets.

He wiped her up as best he could but hoped she would chalk it up to her time of the month. Bill climbed back up through the attic, out to the roof, down the ladder, and back to his small room in the barn. He couldn't stop smiling. The feeling of total and complete fulfillment encompassed him. It was more than just the sexual satisfaction he received. For Bill, it was the experience of living. He had been so scared and excited, thrilled and terrified. He couldn't remember another time in his life that he had ever felt that way. He felt no sense that he'd done anything wrong. In his mind, he hadn't hurt Willow because she would never even know what happened.

With the success of the first encounter with Willow, Bill continued to visit both her and her mother's bedrooms. He was no longer content with staying above in the attic. When he came down, he always drugged both of them because he was not about to get caught red-handed, having one of them wake up. He began raping not just Willow, but Allison, too. Most of the time, he preferred Willow, but he would trade off occasionally and even take both of them in a single night if he was particularly lusty.

The more he did it, the more his confidence grew. After that first night in May, and after all subsequent encounters, both women resumed life as normal. To Bill, they didn't seem to act any different; they were completely normal. He made sure not to make two visits too close together because he didn't want them having negative side effects from their injections. If that were to happen, he was sure they would grow suspicious.

Several months passed, and once again, Bill began to get bored. It was almost too easy for him, and although he did still get satisfaction out of his newfound hobby, he was beginning to have no fear at all. Bill had to have that thrill. He missed the feeling of nervousness and adrenaline that made him feel so alive. He needed something to bring back that feeling, so he was less careful and made visits more often. This brought the excitement back for him so much that one week in September, he visited every single night.

Then, one day Bill heard the news. Willow was pregnant. Somehow it hadn't crossed Bill's mind that this would happen. Of course, he knew the consequences of having sex. He wasn't ignorant. But he really had never stopped to think about it or think about using protection with her. He wondered if the baby was his or if she'd lived up to her reputation after all. Bill thought, *if it is mine, she's probably a little confused right about now.*

Bill may not have been ignorant, but when it came to knowledge about reproduction, Willow was. She knew nothing about sex, despite her unkind reputation. Willow watched movies where men and women kissed, and then suddenly, they were waking up together in the morning, naked and smiling. She thought it must be something pleasant, but she also thought she would *know* when she actually did it. Shouldn't it be something you were aware of doing? Especially if it felt so good, wouldn't you know what was happening? Willow didn't remember having sex with anyone, and for someone who knew nothing about human reproduction, it took her quite a while to figure out that she was, indeed, pregnant.

Willow was utterly confused and worried, once she finally figured it out. She'd been dating an older boy and thought back to some of their times together. He'd kissed her and touched her, too, but she knew there was something else to it besides that. She felt so stupid not knowing anything about it. Willow thought she was surely the only thirteen-year-old in the world who was clueless.

She wondered if he'd done something to her when she was sleeping. She fell asleep in his truck a couple of times when they were out late and wondered, *would I have slept through something like that? Would he have really done that to me while I was asleep?* She didn't fully understand, but thought that had to be the answer. What else could have happened?

She was an emotional wreck, trying to figure out what had happened and what to do. She was just a kid. How could she take care of a baby? Especially, when she didn't willingly have sex with anyone. Why should she have to pay for someone else's lust? The worst part was that her mom didn't believe her. When she'd finally worked up the nerve to talk to her mom, after she figured out she was pregnant, Willow asked, "Mom, can we talk?"

"Sure." Allison was distracted, only half listening.

"Well, you know I've been really sick for a while now," Willow said, wringing her hands. Both her body and voice shook. Her mother stopped what she was doing and looked at her now. She eyed Willow up and down, seeming to know already.

Without Willow actually saying anything about being pregnant, her mother asked, "Was it the boy from school?"

Willow began to cry. "I don't know!"

That's when her mother began yelling, "You don't know? How do you not know? Are you a whore, Willow?" But Willow was too distraught to explain. She didn't know how to explain to her mom that she'd never even had sex. She was a virgin, for heaven's sake! Willow was so confused and scared, but she was crying hard and couldn't get the words out.

At one point, her mom slapped her across the face, trying to get Willow to stop crying, but of course, it only made her cry harder. After that, they hardly spoke to one another at all. A week went by, and Willow thought she might be able to stay calm enough to explain things properly.

So, she tried to approach her mom again. "Mom, I need to explain—"

"Don't bother." Allison walked away.

Willow called, "Mom, please!"

Her mom turned on her. "I don't want to talk about it, Willow. Don't bring it up again."

"Mom!" Willow couldn't help but try. "I never even had sex." She said the truth, but her mom didn't hear.

Willow didn't understand the reality of what had happened to her. She had been raped, and even if it was from her falling asleep in a boy's truck, she didn't understand the full impact of what it meant. Willow didn't grasp the concept of consent or know that what happened to her was wrong in every possible way. She did not stop dating the boy and, instead, went on to have consensual sex with him. She did not tell him she was pregnant until she was beginning to show.

Because of Mrs. Green's reaction to Willow's news, there was a rift between them. Word about what happened quickly got around the ranch. Bill found Willow in the yard alone and crying one day. He sat down beside her, trying to lend a listening ear, which was when she explained how terrible her mom had been.

"She won't let me explain," Willow said through her tears.

He was uncomfortable, but eager to speak with her.

"What does she say?"

"She calls me a whore and won't listen to a word I have to say."

Bill didn't know what to say to that. He never wanted to make her life hard. He was falling in love with her and wanted to take care of her. Bill thought about proposing, but Willow barely knew him and would probably laugh if he tried. There was nothing that Bill hated more than a bitch for a mom. He had his own share of that and understood how painful it could be. He decided, right then and there, he would teach Mrs. Green a little lesson that she wouldn't forget.

After a pause, Bill said, "Sounds like she needs to learn how to listen. I'm sorry she's treated you this way." His presence and words comforted her. She gave him a small smile, appreciating his efforts. She thought he was kind to listen to her complaints when he probably had something better, he could be doing.

After that conversation, Bill began to visit Mrs. Green, and not Willow, when he made his secret trips through the attic. He also stopped injecting Willow. He grew curious about how she and the baby were progressing, so he still devoted time to watching her from in the attic. Bill would watch her until she fell asleep, then climb down to visit her mother. He had developed a protective feeling toward Willow and the baby, thinking of them both as *his*. He was going to protect them from that bitch.

As Bill was walking through the yard one afternoon, months later, he saw Willow laying in the grass under a large pine tree. She was rubbing her growing belly, talking to it in a low and loving voice. "Hi, my little Daisy," she cooed. "I've decided to name you after my favorite flower. I want you to have a happy name, baby girl." Bill wondered how she knew it would be a girl and if there had been an ultrasound, or if she was just guessing. He thought Daisy was a fine name, though. The next day, he left a bunch of daisies on the front porch for Willow to find.

A different kind of desire was building up in Bill. He wanted more from Willow than just physical pleasure. He wanted to speak with her, to start a relationship. Bill began attempting to converse with her anytime he saw her, but only if she was alone. Unfortunately for Bill, this was a rarity, which made starting a relationship nearly impossible.

Willow was seldom alone. Her mother had been keeping a tight rein on her. She was forbidden to speak to any of the ranch hands, or any man or boy, for that matter. Willow went to school and came home, and that was it. She seemed to be withdrawn and only a shell of her former self now; she had developed a dazed look in her eyes, as if she were far off in another place. The only time she was even remotely happy seemed to be when she was talking to her baby.

Bill blamed the change in Willow on Allison and swore he would make her pay.

Realizing that a relationship with Willow would not happen, that October, Bill put in his resignation. He informed Mrs. Green he intended on traveling for a while before settling down in a big city. Everyone wished him the best and bid their farewells. Bill put on a great show, having no doubt that everyone was convinced he was leaving town. In reality, he sold most of his belongings and had the rest in his pickup. He kept it parked a couple of miles away, in a safe location so it wouldn't be noticed. After parking the truck, he walked back to the ranch, expecting to be camping out in the Greens' attic for a while.

It didn't take long until Allison, too, became pregnant. It was early December, and Bill had been watching her when she took the pregnancy test in her bathroom. She'd looked at it and instantly gone pale, looking like she would faint. Bill thought it was hilarious. He nearly laughed out loud before he caught himself.

All the time he'd been in the attic, never once had she said a kind thing to Willow. She'd never been supportive of her or willing to listen to her in any way. He thought, *if the bitch would've just listened, Willow would've explained that she thought she'd been raped*. Well, now she was seeing the situation for herself with eyes wide open.

Seeing that Allison hadn't been having any men in her bed for the past few months, Bill wondered how she would react to suddenly becoming pregnant. He thought she might panic, but it seemed he was wrong. It seemed Allison Green was getting some action from someone, and that someone hadn't been to the house.

Bill was intrigued by the thought. He decided to let things simmer for a while, to see what she would do about the baby. He thought now Allison might at least talk to Willow about what she was going through. Instead, Allison did something wholly unexpected.

Just before New Year's, Allison informed Willow that Willow would be giving her baby up for adoption and did not have a choice in the matter. Willow was shocked and dismayed at the thought of being forced to give up her baby. She protested, crying and begging her mother to listen to her. When that didn't work, she screamed and threw things across the house. She wanted to keep her baby. She already loved it, even though it had been unplanned and initially unwanted. Willow acknowledged she was young, but also believed she would make an excellent mother. She would give her heart and soul to this baby. But now, that chance was being taken from her.

Willow was inconsolable. She told her mom, "Joe is going

to marry me. He's going to take care of us." She was going to be fourteen in a few months, and Joe already talked about getting married. He was making good money, and she'd have her own home to provide for the baby.

"Don't be an idiot. He can't marry you until you're sixteen."

Willow hadn't thought of that. Did Joe know? "It doesn't matter. He's going to take care of us anyway, and when I'm old enough, he'll marry me then."

"Well, until then, you're my responsibility. I will not hear another word about it!"

"You can't make me do this." Willow was devastated but held out a stubborn hope that she would somehow be able to keep her child. She vowed to run away if that's what it took.

Bill overheard the entire conversation. He was both shocked and angry to find that Willow was seeing someone and that she would consider marrying him. It was *his* child she was carrying. He struggled with what to do next. Bill thought about how much he cared for Willow and how he had dreamed of starting a life with her. He wondered what would happen if he told her *he* would marry her. Did she love this other guy, or was she just in need of someone to take care of her?

He'd been bored for so long and wondered if starting a family at this age was really the smartest thing for him to do. How soon until he was bored again? Bill imagined coming home to a screaming toddler every night and grimaced. He'd fallen in love with her, and as much as it pained him to think of her with another man, he was beginning to think he would let Willow follow her own path. He decided he would help her; it was the least that he could do, and he'd vowed to not let her witch of a mom win. One thing was for sure: he would not allow Allison to force Willow to give up the baby.

On New Year's Day, Bill came down from the attic one

last time. He went into Allison Green's room and used some rope to tie her hands and feet to the bed. Bill did not inject Allison this time because he wanted her to be fully awake; there was no need for secrecy anymore. She began to stir as soon as he touched the rope to her skin and was awake within moments. Allison's eyes opened wide in surprise and recognition. Before she could scream, Bill shoved an old cloth in her mouth to gag her.

He smiled. "Hello, Mrs. Green." She tried to talk through her gag, but he ignored her. "Now, just sit back and relax. There's no need to talk."

Bill took a step back from the bed, looking at Allison objectively. She was bound at the wrists, arms reaching up on the sides of her head and then tied to the headboard. Her legs were spread wide, tied at the ankles to the corners of the footboard. She was in the same blue silk nightgown he'd seen so many times before.

She was twenty years older than him, but God, he was so turned on. Seeing her like this, and actually awake, was an excitement he didn't know if he would feel again, but hoped so. It was totally different from when she was sleeping. It was so much *better*.

The look of terror in her eyes and knowing *he* was the one in control, nearly made him lose himself. Bill looked away, getting his thoughts together. Then, turning back to her, he pointed to one of his holes that he'd made and left unblocked. Her eyes followed his finger to the ceiling. A look of confusion crossed her face.

"I've been around, Mrs. Green. The attic is quite cozy this time of year." She looked at him, still seeming to not understand. Then, it dawned on her, and her face went as white as a sheet. Bill laughed. "That's right." She tried to wiggle out of her ties, bucking her hips and shaking viciously. But her struggle only made him more excited.

Bill slipped off his shoes and dropped his pants. Without saying a word, he climbed onto the bed and raped her. She was crying and trying to scream through her gag the whole time. When Bill was done, he got off the bed and got dressed again.

He'd used protection this time and took a minute to clean up any evidence he might've left behind. Then, he walked over to the dresser where he'd left a twelve-gauge shotgun leaning. Bill took the shotgun and walked back to Allison. Her eyes were wide again, eyebrows to her hairline, but she didn't make a sound. She glanced at her stomach, as if to say, "I'm pregnant." Bill knew. He didn't care.

"Oh, by the way, it's mine. And Willow's is mine, too." He rested the barrel of the shotgun on her nose. He took a breath then pulled the trigger.

There was a deafening blast as Allison Green's head exploded. The explosion from the gun blew chunks of her all over the room, including on Bill. He'd known that the sound would be loud, and it was exactly what he wanted. That feeling of adrenaline coursing was as strong as ever. Bill didn't stop to relish it, though, he figured he could do that later. At the moment, he was getting out of dodge.

He grabbed the shotgun and ran for the front door. Not stopping to look back, he blew through the door, out back, where the trees would provide him with cover. Bill ran as fast as his legs would carry him. His truck was parked two miles away, and he ran the entire way. Reaching the truck, he was panting for breath and nearly dying of thirst, but he didn't stop. He didn't look back. With the keys already in the ignition, he started it up and drove away, making sure to drive the speed limit.

9

After Bill left the ranch, he had an unquenchable thirst for his newfound hobby. He constantly thought about being back in the attic, able to observe Allison and Willow in their most private moments, all while remaining unnoticed. It had been like nothing he'd ever experienced in his life. He thought about the power he'd felt when he could climb down from the attic and do whatever he wanted to either of them without them ever knowing.

He didn't understand how they could be so stupid as to not know something was off. They'd not had one iota of a suspicion that a person working for them could possibly be raping them in their sleep, which was ultimately why he was able to go so far. That sense of power that Bill felt was still coursing through him, and he was high off it, even though he was long gone from the ranch. He felt like it wouldn't be long before he was desperate to find someone else to watch again. This couldn't be the end.

Bill thought about pulling the shotgun trigger. He not only thought about how it made him feel, but how it had looked and smelled, how the room had sounded, and the look on Allison's face before her head exploded into tiny bits of meat. He smiled to himself, remembering every detail, and the smile slowly turned into a grin. Bill could only describe it as an amazing experience. He'd killed no one before, let alone shot anyone's face to pieces with a shotgun. Remembering the violence and blood, the climatic release and power that he had felt, and was still feeling, caused Bill to be instantly addicted. Without a doubt, he had no choice but to repeat the experience again.

He traveled the country for a long time, working odd jobs, trying to decide on a course of action. Bill needed to find a career. He wanted something that would enable him to live a life he wanted, and easily practice his beloved new hobby when he wanted. Bill didn't want to be like most people, and he didn't want to become bored with his life. Boredom came easily to him. He needed something that would hold his interest.

When he turned eighteen, Bill made his way out to California, deciding to get his commercial truck driver's license. Until the age of twenty-one, he would be limited to working within the state, but it was a big enough state to keep him entertained for a few years. When the time came, he could travel the entire country.

Despite being relatively new to stalking and murder, Bill made careful, well-planned choices. He was both smart and lucky, never getting caught, and never even suspected of anything illegal, because he always appeared completely normal. He had a regular strain of "normal-looking" girlfriends and tried to make his life seem completely ordinary to the outside observer.

Appearing ordinary was a motto he lived by, and it generally served him well. Because he was trying to look normal and unsuspicious, and because he was confined to the state for work, he limited himself in regard to his hobby. He could travel anywhere and pick a target outside of work, but Bill thought it would be too risky. He liked to have plenty of time to watch his targets and wasn't into picking up hitchhikers yet. Besides, things were much more convenient when he had his rig.

So, Bill limited himself. This meant two things. It meant he could spend a longer amount of time choosing the perfect target, and it also meant he could spend a longer amount of time watching them. When he looked at it that way, he didn't really mind. The first year he was in the state, he only found one target. Over the following two years, he progressed to two and then three targets until finally, he turned twenty-one and was ready to go long haul.

The day of Bill's twenty-first birthday, he applied for a long-haul driver position within the company he was already working for. Normally, insurance would be an issue for a driver his age, but they were willing to cover the cost since he'd been an excellent employee for years. That year, he felt as if the invisible chains had been cut loose. A sense of freedom filled him, and he nearly threw his "always appear normal" mantra out the window.

The year he turned twenty-one, Bill went through six targets. It was a staggering amount, considering it was double the amount of the previous year. Anxiety ate away at him, telling him he'd gone too far and lost control. He thought for sure he really had done too much, and he'd be caught any day. But even though it was far more than he'd ever done, it was not enough for Bill to get caught. He had covered all his bases.

All of his targets had been in different states, far apart from each other and not connected in any obvious ways. The investigators hadn't even linked them all to a single killer.

Bill's anxiety and worry over being discovered transformed into confidence every time he got away with something new. He reminded himself that he still needed to keep a healthy sense of caution. Arrogance would be his downfall if he didn't keep himself in check.

Throughout the years, Bill learned the best practices for his hobby. He learned the best places to find targets and the easiest ways to pick them up. He was awed by how many idiots were out in the world. They were so trusting. It was almost too easy. With the world being what it was, he was mind-blown at the stupidity. Most of these people were desperate, or kids, or both, but that still didn't give a good excuse to be so damned trusting.

Even the women he watched, who had little interaction with him before he revealed himself, gave away personal details about themselves without even thinking. They would tell another woman in the checkout line what road they live on. They would tell the clerk at the counter their kids' names and school they attend. They were willing to give out so much information about themselves to complete outsiders. People knew what could happen to them. It was everywhere. TV, the papers, radio, literally anywhere you turned there were stories of people getting killed because they trusted the wrong stranger.

Bill was like a wolf in an all you can eat sheep buffet. He was picking them off one at a time, but they didn't notice because they were too stupid. He felt as if he could keep snacking on them any time he felt like it, until there were none left. He loved it, and yet in later years, there were times he wished there was a little more challenge in it for him.

Throughout the years, Bill learned that if he didn't want questions asked at work, about what he was doing, or the timeline he was sticking to, the best thing to do was to work for himself. After getting plenty of experience, he started his own trucking company. He started rolling in the money, and the more he brought in, the more he could invest back into his side interests. More money also meant a better chance of not getting caught. By the time Bill met Ashley, he had over fifteen years of experience under his belt as a truck driver, and ran a successful trucking company, with other drivers working under him.

When Bill had first seen Ashley working in the library, he'd almost mistook her for Willow. She looked so familiar; it was astounding. Seeing her had caused him to lose his breath for a moment, which was something that never happened to him. Bill had to find out more about her. His initial thought was that she could possibly be his next target. He began to do his homework, taking her on dates while watching her and taking in every detail. There was something different about her he couldn't write off. It took Bill careful consideration before finally deciding what to do.

He'd been thinking about a wife for a while, at that point, for years even. He had kept thinking about how a thirty-three-year-old man, who was still single, did not appear normal to most of society. Bill had a stereotypical image in his head, of what "normal" looked like, and that's what he strove to achieve. He'd been fighting the idea of marriage because he did not want to be tied down. He wanted to be free to do what he wanted, when he wanted. At the same time, Bill was paranoid about standing out from the crowd and drawing attention to himself. He had the idea that if he remained single, he would somehow stand out.

He had been going around and around with himself, arguing for and against marriage, and after finding Ashley, the answer was simple. He had to have her. As long as she remained ignorant, he could continue on with his hobby, like nothing happened.

PART II

10

PRESENT DAY

Although Bill had a love of watching women targets in their home, he also had another passion. He loved to pick up hitchhikers. Not knowing who a person was, or how likely they were to be missed, excited him almost as much as watching. As a truck driver, Bill saw hitchhikers all the time. He preferred to plan his encounters, but if he already had a playroom picked out and was just waiting to find a target, he didn't hesitate to work with what he was given. The way Bill saw it, if it fell into his lap, he was not about to look a gift horse in the mouth.

His current target, Roxy Wilson, he had picked up off highway seventy-five in Tulsa. He frequently visited Tulsa to make deliveries and hadn't picked up a target there yet. He noticed Roxy hitchhiking along the highway when he was on his way back from a drop off. She was a pretty, young thing, who looked to be in her late teens or early twenties. His mouth watered just looking at her. Her black hair was cut short. She had been wearing tight black skinny jeans and a low-cut top that showed the top of her breasts. She was walking along the highway in high top black sneakers with a pink Jansport backpack.

Roxy was walking with her arm and thumb hanging out to her side; Bill slowed to get a good look as he passed her. In his semi, it would've been impossible to stop at this stretch of highway. Liking what he saw, he pulled over and parked in a Home Depot parking lot. He was in the far stretches of the lot, far enough away from the store that no one would be around. He was only a short way from where she had been trying to catch a ride along the highway, knowing if she kept walking, she would see him in a matter of minutes. The highway had a sidewalk on the side of it in this part of town, and it crossed right next to where he was parked. Bill was confident she would be approaching.

He'd become an expert over the years, knowing what they would do before they did; he knew what would happen each step of the way. Sometimes it became tedious for Bill because he liked to be excited. Sometimes he was pleasantly surprised, but not for very long. In the end, it didn't matter. Even though he ultimately knew how it would work out, he still enjoyed the punishment he gave. No matter what, he enjoyed that.

This time with Roxy was like other times he'd encountered hitchhikers. Bill had driven by slowly enough to see her. He knew the best places to pull over to catch the target's attention, but at the same time, not appear to be a questionable figure. If he offered them a ride, it was totally different from them asking him first. After parking, Bill hopped out of the truck, making himself look like he was busy checking the tires.

Sure enough, not five minutes after parking, Bill heard footsteps approaching and looked up. The young woman from the highway was waving at him and smiling. He stood and looked around, as if he was unsure that she was waving to him. Seeing nobody else, he smiled and gave a hesitant wave. Now she was next to him and giggled at his surprised reaction.

"Hi there, mister," she said in a friendly way that made him smile.

"Hello there, ma'am," he drawled in his friendly truck-driver accent that had been practiced and mastered. Bill knew he was attractive and knew the effect that his smile had on women. It drove them wild. It didn't matter how old he was. If you were good looking enough, age was just a number, especially to these screwed up girls that were running away. One day, he probably would be too old to play the game, but that day wasn't here yet.

She responded in the usual fashion, blushing and fidgeting. "C-c-could I b-b- bum a ride off you? I-if it's not too much trouble?" she stuttered. Funny how she now seemed almost shy when she had been forward enough to approach him. Once she'd gotten a good look at him and his smile, she was done.

He had to resist grabbing her right then and there. Bill took a breath and arched an eyebrow, giving an apologetic smile. "Sorry, ma'am, we're not supposed to give rides. I could get in real big trouble with my boss." This was a bold lie, as he had no boss. He *was* the boss, but she didn't know that. When they had to beg for it, it seemed more like it was their idea, not his. It garnered more trust. Plus, he loved to hear women begging for him.

The begging of a stranger made him feel powerful. It was that feeling of power that he wanted. It came in so many ways with his hobby and was one of the primary reasons he couldn't stop. Looking down, Roxy frowned. Then, after a pause, she looked him right in the eyes, and said, "I'll do anything. Please, mister, no one will ever know. I gotta get out of here."

He gave her a look that said, "I want to help, but you're really not worth getting in trouble for."

She took a step closer, and she was so passionate, begging for his help that she was no longer shy and stuttering. Bill was laughing inside. "I'll kill myself if you don't help me!" She cried as she clung to his arm, gripping with full force. He wasn't expecting that one, but he almost laughed out loud at the irony, since she would be dying anyway.

Normally, this was the point where the woman would offer sex or money or drugs, or all of the above. What a piece of shit human being to put her life on him like that. Who the hell did she think she was? What if he was just a normal guy? A normal fucking truck driver, minding his own damned business. She comes waltzing up and expects his help and puts it on him that she'll commit suicide? His blood boiled at the thought. He gritted his teeth in anticipation of what he was going to do to her. Bill pitied any man who'd come into contact with this bitch previously in her life, thinking, *what a manipulative little slut.* He ground his teeth together, trying to get his anger under control. She'd lit his fuse, which hadn't been expected.

A few moments later, he was cool again. Bill was used to the anger; he had a short fuse, and when it lit, he burned hot. But he was also used to not showing it. If he let his temper slip, she would slip away, too, which was something he wasn't about to let happen. Still playing the part, he looked at her with his eyebrows raised and mouth open in shock. He said in a calming, placating voice, "Now, now, there's no need for all that. Whatever trouble you're in can't be all that bad, can it?" It was better for her to believe she had the upper hand. It was always better.

"Yes! It is!" Now she had tears running. *Fake,* he thought. He didn't want her yelling to cause a scene.

"Alright then, I'll do it. But please, I'm begging you, don't tell anyone that I helped. I can't lose my job! I'm not even going to tell you my name, so you're not tempted to give me any credit."

"I won't tell!" she agreed eagerly, tears now gone. "Anything you want, I just need to get the hell out of here. I don't care where you're headed, either!" She went to the passenger door without him giving any kind of word or assistance. She opened it and stepped up. "By the way, my name's Roxy."

"Nice to meet you, Roxy," Bill said, closing the door behind her. He didn't think this was her first rodeo, and he was glad. It would make things a lot easier for him. He looked forward to letting his anger have free rein as soon as they got to the playroom. As he drove away, Bill smiled.

11

Ashley's friends were worried about her. She was home alone ninety percent of the time and refused to answer the door. They had to stalk the house to wait for Bill so they could hound him for information on her status. He told them about how she never left their bedroom, but gave some song and dance about how she had phone appointments with a therapist. They accepted his story at face value, but after six months of Ashley still not leaving the house, her friends decided to try to do something about it.

Ashley met her small group of friends at a neighborhood barbecue when she and Bill had first moved into their home after getting married. Stacy, Tabby, and Joy hosted a neighborhood women's jogging group. It was a tight-knit neighborhood, all on one long street that stretched for several blocks, ending in a cul-de-sac.

Many of the families would get together for barbecues, dinners, and just good old-fashioned hangouts. Three days a week, they got together on mornings to walk or jog. Over the years, Stacy, Tabby, and Joy had been there for Ashley's struggles with infertility, pregnancy, and birth of her son.

Now they were there for his death, too. They were her best friends and were put in a difficult position when Ashley lost her son, wanting to comfort her and wanting to give her space at the same time.

Joy hadn't been able to handle the guilt of her son killing her best friend's son. She told herself over and over that it was her fault. Joy attempted suicide a few days after Chris's death. Her husband found her when he came home. She had been lying in bed with a bottle of pills open on the bed beside her, all gone but the few scattered on the sheets. Unlike with Chris, the paramedics who came to help Joy, were able to resuscitate her. She was admitted to the hospital under suicide watch then to therapy.

Ashley was disappointed the attempt hadn't been successful. She found it ironic that they could save Joy, who *wanted* to die, but not Chris, an innocent child.

Joy spent a couple of months at an institution, then upon her release, she and her husband listed their house for sale. They moved and spoke not a word to anyone else. Joy's decision to not say goodbye to Tabby and Stacy had cut them deep. They knew what she was going through and heard that Joy's son, Jake, was going to therapy sessions, too. They didn't understand how she could leave without saying goodbye, though. Stacy and Tabby sent emails and texts, all unanswered. They couldn't do anything else to help Joy now, but they still had Ashley in their lives and were determined to not lose two friends over this terrible tragedy.

Eating dinner together on Tuesday evenings became something of a habit for Tabby and Stacy. Since it was just the two of them now, until Ashley healed enough to leave the house, they liked to have at least one night a week to relax together and have a nice dinner that they didn't have to cook, with a cocktail or two.

They still went jogging in the mornings, but didn't really

talk at that time. They met up, jogged down the road and back, and said their goodbyes. There had been so much tragedy and stress going on in the neighborhood that it felt like everyone was disconnected from each other and distanced. Even though the suffering did not directly happen to them, it had still indirectly affected them, and both women felt it was just nice to pretend for one night a week that all was normal.

This week, Stacy and Tabby opted for Mexican food. They sat on the outside patio at Don Juan's, each sipping on a margarita with a little umbrella poking up from the glass and snacking on tortilla chips with salsa and guacamole. It was a warm evening, and even the shade of the patio was not enough to keep them cool. But the women didn't seem to care. The only thing on their minds at that moment was their friend, Ashley. Ashley, who had undergone a terrible loss. Ashley, who wouldn't leave her house. They had to help her.

Swallowing a bite of salsa laced chip, Stacy asked, "Have you brought them anything to eat this week?" They were terrified that Ashley was going to wither away into nothing. Bill probably wasn't cooking for her, and if he was, it couldn't be anything of substance. Did the man even know how to cook? Both women doubted it.

Tabby said, "I brought a lasagna over yesterday. Bill answered the door, so I didn't get a chance to talk to Ash."

Stacy frowned, feeling anger rise to her cheeks. "He should want her to see us. What did he say?"

"He said she was sleeping." She shrugged, adding, "I didn't think it would do any good to argue with him." It was true, Stacy knew. Bill was a stubborn man, and of course, he had gone through a loss, too. But somehow, it was different with him. The women weren't exactly crazy about the man, but he was their best friend's husband, and they were determined to give him the benefit of the doubt. He had just lost his only son, and they knew well that everyone grieved differently.

On the one or two occasions they had visited with her, Ashley had looked half dead. Her hair was greasy, as if she hadn't showered in days, and her eyes were always puffy and swollen from crying. According to Bill, she never got dressed anymore, wore nothing but sweats. To Tabby and Stacy, it seemed like Ashley's clothes were all too baggy, and her arms that peeked out of her sleeves, seemed to be nothing but bones with skin on them. They both agreed that Bill could do more to help her and he was gone from home far too often, but they didn't think there was much they could do about that, other than complain to him. After all, it wasn't his fault that Chris died.

What the women didn't know was, every time they'd visited, Bill had been prepared and staging the scene for their benefit. Being polite friends, they liked to call and leave a message before they came over. They had tried to text Ashley, but she never responded anymore, so Stacy and Tabby had gotten in the habit of calling a day or two ahead, saying they'd be dropping by. This gave Bill the perfect opportunity to drug Ashley, mess up the house, and make things look how Bill *wanted* things to look.

He could do this if he was home, but if he was on a trip, he had a doorbell with a camera and speaker outside the front door. If Bill was on the road, which he mostly was, he could access the camera and speaker through his cellphone and pretend to be in the bathroom or otherwise occupied. He made sure he was alerted instead of Ashley. He had them drop their goodies on the doorstep and leave.

Bill didn't feel comfortable with Ashley's friends knowing too much about their lives, knowing when he was home, and knowing her condition. Let them think she wasn't better at all. Let them wonder if he was home taking care of her.

The server brought over Tabby and Stacy's meals, sliding the chips over on the table to make room for the large plates. "Can I get you ladies anything else?"

They both smiled politely, responding, "No, thank you." They sat in silence, neither of them eating or drinking, both just thinking. The soft restaurant music played through their silence.

Finally, Tabby spoke. "So, what to do?"

"Yes," Stacy agreed. She lived the closest to Ashley, just a couple of houses down.

Tabby asked, "What about when you and Dan go on your trip? Can't you ask her to do something while you're away? Or some kind of favor?"

That made Stacy perk up, and she was so excited that she exclaimed, "Yes! Of course!" She blushed and ducked her head slightly, looking around at the other eyes glancing her way. "Oops," she whispered, "didn't mean to be that loud." Tabby laughed, and Stacy laughed with her. They were both pleased at the promising idea.

Stacy and her husband would be gone for two weeks on their vacation to the Bahamas. Part of Stacy felt guilty for letting her friend go for so long without help. She also felt guilty asking Ashley to do anything at all, considering her state of mind. But the other part of her was determined that if she could just get Ashley out of the house, it would be a start. She would hire a therapist herself, if she thought there was any chance Ashley would see one. God only knew why Bill hadn't gotten a better one for her.

"I'll ask her to house-sit while we're gone. What do you think, Tabb? I'm worried it will be too much." She'd been excited, but now worried that it was a crazy idea. Ashley wasn't even leaving her bed, for heaven's sake. Why the hell would she agree to house sit?

Stacy really wouldn't need a house sitter, everything

The Wrong Stranger

would be taken care of and covered already, but she would pretend to need one. She would pretend like she was desperate, with no other options. Stacy thought this was probably the only way she could help Ashley and was determined to do something for her friend. Even if Ashley said no, which she probably would, it was worth a shot.

Tabby shook her head. "No, it's not too much. She needs this, Stace. And besides, if it's really too much, she'll just won't show up." She shrugged.

The food and drink seemed to taste a little better now that they had a plan of action. Both women had been trying to come up with some way they could help Ashley for weeks. But now, they had something relatively easy, something safe, and something simple enough to just get her out of the house and into the world.

They finished their meal in good humor, spending another hour chatting and enjoying the cuisine. Just having the idea seemed to relieve so much tension for the both of them, and the rest of the night was delightful. They shared an Uber home and didn't have another thought of Ashley or their plan to help her until the following morning.

STACY RANG THE DOORBELL AT THE WRIGHTS' HOUSE. IT WAS A beautiful and sunny morning, around eleven, but the shades to all the windows were still drawn. She normally called ahead of time, but this time she hadn't. Stacy shook her head in disappointment. After no answer came, she knocked, calling, "Ashley, it's Stacy!" A few minutes later, she heard footsteps approaching

Ashley opened the door with a tentative smile. "Hey, Stace. How are you?"

Stacy pasted a huge grin on. She was overly positive on

purpose, hoping to be happy and bright enough that a little of it would rub off on Ashley. "I'm just great! Can I come in for a bit?" She inched her way forward as she asked. Ashley looked a little better than the last time Stacy saw her. It gave Stacy a little hope. But despite Ashley looking like she'd at least had a shower, she still looked like she hadn't been eating. Her face was gaunt with sunken cheeks, and her eyes looked dull.

Ashley didn't look like she wanted Stacy to come in at all.

Hesitating a moment, Ashley said, "Sure, Stace, come in," Ashley didn't really feel like visiting, but this was one of her best friends in the world. How could she turn her away? Ashley held a hand to her head that was beginning to ache, as she led the way to the living room, which Stacy was surprised to see was tidy. "Do you want something to drink? Some water?"

"No thanks," Stacy smiled again. "I've actually come to ask a favor of you." Ashley frowned. She felt anger begin to rise and fought to push it back down. Ashley's headache grew worse. It was like someone pounding on her temples with a small hammer. She couldn't believe her friend would come over here and ask something of her after everything she was going through.

Ashley was a mess and knew it had to be obvious. She let her friend into the house, thinking she was there to visit. She thought Stacy had been worried about her and wanted to catch up a little. At that moment, Ashley wanted her friend to die. Violent images flashed through her mind of her friend being burned alive. She was surprised by such an intense reaction. Ashley tried to calm down, but it was hard to focus with the pain in her head.

As if her thoughts were written on Ashley's face, Stacy flushed, rushing to add, "I was just hoping for you to check on the house from time to time, maybe every other day, or so."

"And here I was, thinking you came to check on me and visit. Low and behold there's an ulterior motive."

Stacy's blush depended. She was ashamed, even though she did want to visit and check on her friend. She deeply cared for Ashley's wellbeing. The only reason for the so called "favor" was to try and help. She was ashamed of how she'd approached the situation and the awkwardness she now faced. Stacy was screwing this up already and dreaded losing her friendship with Ashley, which she felt was barely hanging on by a thread.

"Oh, Ash, I'm so sorry!" She reached to grasp Ashley's hands. They were cold and limp, but Stacy held on. "Ashley, you have to know how much I care. Girl, I've been trying to get ahold of you for so long. Every time Tabby or I stop by, Bill tells us you're in bed. I want to visit with you so bad, but I thought you didn't want to be bothered. I thought if I didn't have a specific reason to be here that you wouldn't see me."

Ashley thought for a moment. Bill hadn't told her that her friends had been coming by to visit. Her anger began to turn toward her husband. God, her head was pounding.

Trying to think back, she remembered she'd seen him at the door a couple of times, but he had played it off as being a delivery man or the takeout that he'd ordered. He'd been so casual. There'd been food brought by regularly, and Bill always said it was from members of the local church. Bill and Ashley didn't attend the local church, but she hadn't thought it was weird for them to be bringing food by. She just thought that's what churches did for the community and was grateful.

There had been no doubt in her mind that her marriage was on the rocks, and probably past that even. But for him to do this was unforgivable. Why did he care if her friends came to visit? Was he jealous because he didn't have close friends like she did? Ashley was so mad now that her face was red. She clenched her fists together. It was starting to be hard for her to even see straight. Her eyes watered from the pain in her head, and Stacy thought she was crying. Closing her eyes, Ashley asked, "Was it you and Tabb bringing the food by?"

Stacy was growing more concerned by the minute. Seeing Ashley as mad as she was, almost made her a little afraid. Stacy was confused, too. Did Ashley not know that they'd been stopping by? "Yeah, it was us. We've been taking turns, every other week."

Ashley gave a slow nod. "I didn't know it was you. Bill told me the food was from the local church. Thank you." Stacy couldn't believe it. How could Bill be that way? She was in shock with disbelief. Before Stacy could say anything else, Ashley asked, "Are you going somewhere?" Stacy blinked in confusion.

"You wanted me to check in on the house."

Stacy perked up. "Yes, it's our annual trip for the Bahamas in a few weeks. We'll be gone for two weeks. I'll text you all the details; just fresh food and water for Wiskies and water my flowers in the kitchen, maybe a couple other things."

Ashley couldn't believe it was already time for Stacy's Bahama trip. It seemed like she just went. How time flew. She thought about the time they had all gone together—Bill and her and Chris with Dan, and Stacy. A tear dropped out of her eye, onto her cheek. She quickly wiped it away, hoping Stacy didn't notice, but of course, she did.

Concerned, Stacy said, "I'm so sorry, Ash. If it's too much to ask, I'll find someone else, of course. I didn't mean to upset you, love. Shit, I'm really screwing up today, aren't I?" To hell with her plan to pretend to be desperate for help. Her plan had backfired anyway. Now it was time to just make it out with her friendship still intact.

Ashley shook her head, giving a weak smile to reassure her friend. "No, Stace. I know you mean well. I was just thinking about the trip we all went on together. It's not your fault."

Stacy felt so stupid. *Of course*, Ashley would think about the time they had all vacationed together. It was the last vacation that Chris had been on, and they'd all had such a great time. How could she not have thought of that? She felt like such an idiot, but there were so many memories with Chris, it was going to be hard to avoid bringing up the past.

The guilt swelled up inside her, and now she was the one who almost cried. "I'm so sorry, Ash." She went to her friend and embraced her. It was long and much needed on both sides. Neither of them wanted to pull away. When they finally parted, both of their eyes were brimming with unshed tears, and they seemed to communicate without speaking.

They sat side by side on the couch for a few minutes and then finally Ashley spoke. "Sure, Stace, I'd be glad to watch the house."

Stacy took a deep breath. She wasn't sure if she *had* really won this battle, because it didn't feel like it. She hadn't known how damned hard it would be to do this. God help her. She couldn't even begin to imagine the pain her dear friend was going through. Even after all these months, it was unimaginable. She did know one thing, though. She knew it was for the best for Ashley to get out of the house. If she was only going a few doors down, for a few minutes, at least it was something. She told herself maybe this would lead to more.

12

Bill had known for weeks that Dan and Stacy Hill were taking their annual trip to the Bahamas. He also found out that Stacy stopped by the house unannounced and asked his wife to house-sit. It was damned irritating. The nosey bitch always called before showing up, and now she decided to drop by out of the blue. Bill enjoyed having Ashley at home, right where he knew she would stay. He needed her to stay that way as long as possible. But that meddling friend of hers couldn't keep her nose in her own business to save her life.

This was just the first step. Once Ashley started leaving the house again, it wouldn't take long for her to become her old self. He thought that once she was back to herself, she would probably leave him for good. Bill could see in the way she looked at him that she was done. He would try to hinder her in any way possible, but he was rarely home and didn't think there was much he could do. If he tried to prevent her from helping her friend, she would push back. It could backfire.

Ever since the day Stacy stopped by the house unannounced, there had been something off about Ashley. He couldn't put his finger on it, but felt it. He hadn't gotten away with his hobby for years without being an observant man. It was her attitude and behavior. She'd already been in a mood over Chris, but that was different. Now she seemed to be turning to ice.

Bill figured, in the end, his wife would probably wind up having an accident of some kind. She would probably off herself out of guilt and grief. As a grieving widower, Bill would still appear normal and have the community's trust for a time, until he was expected to re-marry. It was better than divorce. If she left him, the marriage would have been for nothing. In Bill's mind, his image would be worse as a divorced man than if he never married at all. No, he'd much rather be a widower than a divorcee.

With the upcoming Hill family vacation in mind, Bill was planning to bring Roxy to the Hill house once they left for their vacation. They had a basement that would be perfect for his needs. It had a soundproof room he'd been itching to use. Dan told him all about the kinky shit that he and Stacy were into, and Bill had a raging hard-on just thinking about the fucked-up shit he was going to do to Roxy.

Ashley would now be house-sitting the Hill house, which was an annoyance, but he didn't think it would be much of a problem. It was more of an irritation that just meant he had to keep a closer eye out. Bill reluctantly admitted to himself that having Ashley house-sit was better than having someone else do it, someone he didn't know.

Each time Bill told Ashley he was headed on a run for work, she would ask about his load and destination, taking a polite interest in his work. Even when she locked herself in their bedroom for half a year, she would at least say goodbye or nod or *something*. But this time, she acted like she didn't hear him say a word at all.

"I'm headed to Seattle tomorrow. I'll probably be gone for about a week."

He'd casually mentioned it as she was moving about the kitchen. He was sitting on the couch in the living room, but they could still see and converse with each other.

Ashley hadn't looked at him. She kept moving around, getting some food on a plate, warming it in the microwave, moving dishes around, and generally making noise.

Bill watched her, waiting for her to say something, but when nothing came, he asked, "Did you hear what I said?" Still no response.

When he looked at her, she didn't look angry. She looked blank. He could see her clear as day, and she could see him, too, if she would look. She was ten feet away, and there were no hearing issues. Bill was not concerned; he was annoyed and growing irritated. He was a man who did not like to be ignored, and there was no reason for Ashley to be a bitch to him at the moment.

Bill yelled, "Ashley!" Still, she didn't acknowledge him. His face turned red. Bill thought, *what the fuck is she trying to do?* He took a moment to think. Bill took a calming breath, asking in as cool a voice as he could manage, "Ashley, do you hear me talking to you?" He watched her closely. If she didn't answer him, he was going to get up off the couch and help her have that little accident he'd been daydreaming about. Forget everything else, he would just have to move his timeline up.

But she did answer him this time. She'd been reaching into the open cupboard to grab something, and when this final question was asked, she stopped to turn toward him. Now, her face didn't look blank, but confused. "Bill? Did you say something?" The expression on her face was so believable, that Bill thought, *My God, she's losing her shit. That accident really might be an accident, after all.* He stared at her in wonderment. Now it was her turn to be irritated. "Bill?"

"I was just saying that I'm headed out to Seattle for a week or so."

"Alright."

"Will you be okay?"

"I'll be fine. When are you leaving?"

"Tomorrow."

She nodded her acknowledgement.

"You really didn't hear me the first time?"

"No, I'm sorry. Microwave must've been too loud."

It wasn't. Their microwave wasn't loud, and it hadn't been on the entire time that he'd been trying to talk to her. The TV hadn't been on, either. She would've been perfectly capable of hearing him, just like she was right now. Bill decided to let it go, though. If she was losing her marbles, it was okay with him. He liked a little excitement, and his wife going bat shit might not be such a bad thing.

The next day, Bill got up early and went through his usual long-haul prep routine. He packed an overnight bag of clothes, packed an ice chest with snacks and drinks, got some other things together, then headed out. His black duffel was already in his Ram, waiting in the driveway. Everything he did was his normal, standard routine.

Bill wasn't really about to head to Seattle for a week, but he didn't want Ashley to know that. She might have a screw loose at the moment, but Bill didn't want to risk her seeing anything that she wasn't supposed to see. He wanted her to believe he was really gone.

Leaving the house, Bill climbed into his lifted truck and started it, knowing Ashley would hear the exhaust and recognize him leaving. His rig was parked at the building he leased for work, about twenty miles away, and he drove all the way there, putting all his supplies in his rig and making his safety checks. It was important to go through the entire process, spending the exact amount of time it would normally take. He was meticulous in his routine for a reason. It was all about timing.

Bill wasn't going to Seattle, but he did still need a place to sleep at night, and that place was his rig. It was a sleeper, which meant there was a bed, a small fridge, and even a table in back of the driver and passenger seats. It was as good as a travel trailer, and even better, in Bill's eyes. There was a curtain for privacy, which was beyond perfect when he picked up his targets.

Once the rig was all ready to roll, Bill headed out of town, about a hundred miles, to a very specific truck stop. It was a rural location with not much around, but it was a hot spot for other truckers. Bill parked his rig, grabbed his black duffel, and got out. He scanned the parking lot, then headed toward the white Honda Civic he kept there.

The Civic was one, among several other cars, that Bill kept secret. Neither his wife nor anyone in his acquaintance was aware of him owning these other vehicles. Being able to switch between vehicles allowed Bill to remain unnoticed when he did research for his hobby. He kept the knowledge of them private, since the whole point was to go unnoticed.

Once Bill selected a target, he regularly watched and researched. If he was always in the same vehicle when he did his stalking, Bill knew he would have been recognized or suspected of something insidious quite quickly. He especially didn't want his semi recognized, so he'd invested in his own small fleet of normal-looking, average-American cars, all of which would fit into the back of an empty semi's trailer.

Originally, he'd started out with just one other car to switch to but had learned that the more he had at his disposal, the easier his hobby would be. He kept them all registered to his company name and would explain them as a business necessity if they were ever discovered by his wife. There were a variety in order to fit in a variety of situations and types of neighborhoods.

The white Honda that Bill parked at the truck stop was newer and spoke "middle-class." It was something that one of his own neighbors would have driven and would blend right into his neighborhood. Parking it at a truck stop a hundred miles away was all part of the game. He got in and headed back toward home. Bill could park and watch Ashley from the street unnoticed. She had the front curtains pulled back, and through their large front windows, he could see her, clear as day.

Bill was parked closer to his own home than the Hill residence because he'd wanted to watch Ashley while she was inside. Living in this neighborhood for nearly ten years, he was comfortable believing no one would bother him if he sat in the parked car for a while. Besides, this was his hobby. This was what he did and had done for years. It was his jam.

Now, Bill had the driver's seat leaned way back, so that he was almost laying down, and was using binoculars to get a better view of Ashley.

The windows on his sedan were tinted enough to hide him from a passing glance. Someone would have to get up close to the car and stick their face right up to the window in order to get a good look at him. He was also using a special device that allowed him to hear her from inside the car. It made Bill feel as though he was back inside the house with her. Only he was invisible now.

Watching from the outside allowed Bill to observe Ashley differently from when he was home with her. It was the same way with anyone. Over the years, Bill had observed that when a person was alone, something inside was set loose, and they were somehow more free to be their true selves.

This was one reason that watching others fascinated Bill

and always had. When he watched a target, he watched her while she was both inside and outside of the home, and sometimes the differences in behavior truly amazed him. Some people could be polar opposite when in public places versus the privacy of home.

Bill saw that Ashley's posture was visibly more relaxed than he could remember seeing in a long time. She was humming to herself, which was something she hadn't done since before Chris died. When Bill heard her, he double checked his equipment to make sure it was picking up Ashley and not one of the neighbors. No, there was no mistaking her voice. He could see her through the front window, walking about the living room, back and forth, like she was picking up. Bill's brow furrowed. He wondered, *what is she doing?* The house was picked up already when he left a few hours ago.

There was nothing to pick up. Ashley bent over, reaching for something he couldn't see, then stood back up. She turned back the other direction, took a few steps, and reached over again. The realization finally dawned on Bill. Ashley was humming a lullaby that she had sung to Chris when he was a baby. She was walking around the living room like she was picking up his toys.

Now, he could hear her saying, "Oh, Chris, why won't you pick up your toys for me?" She was using that soft, babying voice that used to drive him crazy. She gave a gentle laugh. "Oh, it's alright, baby. I'm just glad you're having so much fun."

Holy shit. She really is losing it, he thought. He had his suspicions that his wife was a little cracked after their son's death, but now there was no doubt. Especially after the incident yesterday, and now this. Bill had to catch himself from laughing too loud. "The woman is going fucking bat shit," he said to out loud. He had never seen someone lose touch with reality before, and to see it happen now, was both amazing and somewhat hilarious.

He wondered how bad it really was, and if this was just the tip of the iceberg, so to say. Bill also wondered if maybe this behavior was something temporary from grief, or if it was something more permanent. While he watched her, he wondered about what exactly this meant for *him* and how he could use it to his advantage.

After what felt like hours, the alarm on Ashley's phone went off. Bill saw her look at her phone. She seemed to almost transform before his eyes. Ashley turned off the alarm and stood more rigid, almost instantly. Her smile dropped from her face. She didn't frown, but looked forlorn. She took the hair tie off her wrist and put her hair back up into a messy bun that sat on top of her head. She glanced toward the front door, then after a pause, she moved to get her shoes and keys. Bill saw her walk out the front door a short while later.

Despite where he was parked, he could still watch Ashley walking down the street and up the front walk of the Hill house. She seemed to be hunched over now, walking fast, not wanting to be seen. It was a warm day, but she had a sweatshirt on with the hood pulled over her head. The hood was shaped like a cone at the top, from where her hair was bunched up in a bun. Once Ashley entered the house, he timed how long she took to go about doing whatever she was going to do. Then finally, he watched her leave and go back home.

BILL SPENT FOUR DAYS WATCHING ASHLEY'S HOUSE-SITTING routine. Each day he would watch her for a few hours before she left for the Hill house. She'd only had that one episode, which Bill referred to as her "bat shit incident." Every other day that Bill watched her, she spent time watching TV, reading on the couch, or doing various other mundane things. He'd been curious about how far her insanity ran and was beginning to think it may have been a one-time thing. Maybe the stress of him leaving her alone set it off.

He couldn't stop thinking about it. He was frustrated, trying to think of ways that he could find out more. Bill thought about if she was aware of this behavior or if it was unconscious. Regardless of his curiosity about his wife's state of mind, he was confident enough that Ashley wouldn't be a problem for Roxy or himself while they were at the Hill house.

Based on Ashley's routine, and the time she seemed to normally check on the house, Bill decided he would make sure to bring Roxy to the Hill house later in the afternoon or early evening, when the time came, and all would be well. Ashley only ever spent a few minutes at the house, and always under twenty- minutes. It wouldn't be a problem. She had a daily alarm set, and she'd been sticking to it.

Bill decided he would pick Roxy up in about three days, after Dan and Stacy had been gone for about a week. This way, if somehow one of the neighbors heard Roxy or himself, they would just assume Dan and Stacy were back early from their trip. Bill didn't think anyone would hear them anyway, because of the soundproof walls in the basement, which was his reason for going there in the first place. But it didn't hurt to be extra safe. The Hills' neighbors tended to be nosey, just like all neighbors, but he counted on the time of the day to work to his benefit. *Thank God for the predictability of suburbia*, he thought.

13

As planned, Bill brought Roxy to the Hill residence in the afternoon. Arriving at 2:33, Bill made sure there was no sign of Ashley before he led Roxy down to the basement and into the secret room, that wasn't so secret. She'd been an unplanned target, picking her up off the side of the highway. He knew almost nothing about the woman, but couldn't wait to find out more.

He'd wanted to use Dan's sex room for a long time now and had realized that a rare opportunity would present itself when the Hills went on vacation. Bill couldn't pass on Roxy, even though she made her appearance a little too early for his plans. He also didn't want to risk the possibility that he wouldn't find another target in time to use the room, so he stored her away, saving her for the right time. He'd been keeping her in a storage unit, gagged and drugged.

He had to drug Roxy to keep her sedated and kept an IV running into her arm to keep her hydrated. He kept her fed, in between when he was observing Ashley and actually working. Besides this, Bill refrained from touching Roxy. He felt like he was saving her for "the big day," the same way a person might save an expensive wine for a special occasion. When he thought about what he was going to do to her, he nearly salivated with excitement.

It was beyond tempting to have her within arm's reach and not do the things he wanted to do. But dammit, he really wanted to use that room. To keep busy, Bill told himself he still needed to make money, so he'd been doing smaller local jobs over the past couple of weeks when he was done watching Ashley. He knew himself better than anyone; if he didn't keep busy, he was going to give into temptation and have his way with her right there in the storage container. It wouldn't be the end of the world, but it would complicate his clean-up process, and it would mean he had to go another year without using that room.

Since she was weak from being sedated for so long, Bill wanted to give Roxy plenty of time to recuperate and get her strength back. He wanted her to have a little fight in her; it made things much more interesting. He took her off the drugs for a few days, only giving her a mild dose right before he transported her to the Hill house.

She was able to walk assisted, but still looked like a drunk, zoning out in her own little world as they headed downstairs. She tried to speak, but anything she said was mumbled. The only thing he could make out was, "Please." Upon entering the room in the basement, Bill tied her hands and feet to the four bedposts, then went back to the truck for his bag of goodies.

Bill could hardly stand the anticipation. Everything had worked out perfectly for him so far. It had been hell keeping himself from touching Roxy for so long. She'd been right there, just an arm's reach away. But he'd maintained his self-control, and now he had earned his opportunity to play.

He enjoyed being this excited and forcing himself to wait for gratification. It was one reason he so often observed his targets instead of jumping into things right away. Of course, he also reveled in instant gratification, the way any man would, but there was something extraordinary about delaying it first. It seemed to intensify the pleasure for Bill, and this time would be the same.

He loved for his targets to see what he was doing to them. Sometimes he loved to sedate just enough to where they were lucid, but still not fully able to fight. Sometimes he just used muscle relaxers, and sometimes he didn't drug them at all. Normally, he would tie them up, but not always. He did like a bit of a struggle, just not too much of one. Sometimes he loved to hear them scream out in agony, and sometimes he preferred a quieter experience. For Bill, it was all about spontaneity. Too much of the same thing would grow dull. More than anything, Bill treasured the excitement and the adrenaline rush. He wanted to feel alive.

With Roxy, Bill had chosen not only to tie her up, but to gag her as well. Initially, he had been so enthusiastic about the basement room being soundproof. It was the main reason he was desperate to use this location, but after thinking about it, he changed his mind. He thought he might remove the gag later on but wanted to start things off on a quieter note.

He took a pair of socks, rolled them up, and shoved them into Roxy's mouth. Then, he added a strip of duct tape on top for good measure.

Once she was all set, Bill had his tool of choice selected for the afternoon. Today, he chose a simple pair of scissors. These were extra sharp so they would do the job he needed of them.

Bill stood at the edge of the king-size bed, knees touching the side of the mattress, and stared down at Roxy. He traced her body with his eyes, scanning her from the top of her head down to her toes. He reached out to touch her foot. She flinched away. He wasn't surprised. When he looked into her eyes, he saw the familiar terror reflecting back at him. It made him smile, and she whimpered when she saw it. Laughing, he said, "Don't worry, love, you'll enjoy it, too." Confusion mixed with the fear in her eyes.

Bill undressed her. He went slowly, taking his time. She was already tied up, and he wasn't going to untie her, so he took the scissors and cut away her pants and shirt. He wasn't in a hurry and enjoyed making her wait to see what would be next. He snipped the scissors slowly, methodically. The anticipation for the both of them was what he loved. Once he finished cutting away her top, Bill set down the scissors, unsnapped her jeans, pulled down her zipper, and reached a hand down between her thighs.

Roxy gasped and wriggled in protest. Bill chuckled and then pulled his hand out and grabbed the scissors again. Roxy became deathly still, staring at him unblinkingly. With a serious face, he looked her in the eye, holding the scissors up high, as if he was going to plunge them down into her. He waited, hovering. Then, he slid them down into her pants, poking a hole through the crotch, from the inside out. He continued to push them, cutting the inseam all the way down her left leg. Once that leg was finished, he moved to the other side, then slid the leftovers out from under her.

The entire time Bill was cutting her clothing, Roxy had lain utterly still. The adrenaline pulled her out of her drug-induced haze. She didn't want to wiggle and cause him to cut her. The thought had been automatic, but stupid, because he obviously meant to hurt her anyway.

She had no doubt in her mind that he was going to rape her. Roxy wasn't wrong. Bill was definitely going to rape her, but there was so much more in his playbook than just that. He'd removed her shirt and jeans, but so far, left her underclothes.

The Wrong Stranger

Laying in her bra and panties, Roxy shivered with the adrenaline coursing through her. Now Bill used the scissors to snip the front of her bra. It opened and her bare breasts fell out. He tugged the bra out from under her and tossed it to the floor. Then, he reached under her panties and ripped them from her body. "Now that's much better," he drawled.

She had tears streaming down her face but didn't make a sound until he removed his clothes. Her eyes dropped to his erection. She wriggled and moaned in protest. She tried to speak through her gag, to beg him to stop. Bill smiled at her again, amused. "Now, now, doll. Tsk, tsk."

With the scissors still in his left hand, Bill kneeled in front of her. He had to climb on the bed when he undressed her and stayed up there to undress himself.

"Make all the noise you want, love."

She thought, *why did you gag me, then,* but she only had a moment's thought before he laid down on his belly and put his face between her legs. He began to lick, kiss, and suck at her tender skin. He pushed two fingers inside her, sliding them in and out, adding pressure from his thumb. She had started off by trying to struggle against him, but her struggle weakened and then stopped all together as he continued.

The body's reaction to pleasure could be traitorous. This wasn't just a torture on her body, but on her mind, too, which made it even better. To be completely unwilling and taken by force against her will was one thing. To have a man bring your unwilling body pleasure that made your body, if not your mind, want more and more, was another thing.

Now she was not struggling for him to stop, but urging him to go on. She was panting for more and moaning in pleasure now, instead of fear. Bill reached up and pulled the gag from her mouth, but she seemed to not even notice. Her hips rocked against him, begging for more. He rose up and thrust inside her. He pumped into her fast and deep. Her legs were already spread wide, but he pushed them even farther.

At the moment of his release, Bill reached with his left hand and used the scissors to slice deep into Roxy's thigh. Her moans of ecstasy changed to screams of agony. He switched hands, reached up, and stabbed down into her other leg as hard as he could. The scissors plunged to the handle in her flesh, and Roxy screamed so loud that Bill's ears rang. She was wiggling violently, tugging at her bonds with every ounce of energy she had. Blood gushed out of her legs, onto him and all over the bed. Blood was pouring out of her and was all over the both of them. He was still hard as a rock and nowhere near done with her.

Bill grabbed the roll of socks and shoved them back into Roxy's mouth. She was still screaming, so it was easy for him to push them back in. She wasn't expecting him to do it and didn't even try to bite. Bill reached back between her legs and rubbed her again. He knew that even through pain and bleeding, pleasure would win. The need for release would make her body betray her brain and want him.

He reached up to play with her breasts, licking and circling her nipples with an expert touch. She tried to scream through the gag, crying and fighting as best she could. Tears rolled down her face, with snot, too, and she seemed to be almost snarling at him. But Bill kept working her until she responded more favorably to his touch.

Roxy began to rock her hips once again, panting and aching for climax all over. He kept going, wanting her to be consumed by pleasure, but denying her the final release. Instead, he waited until her mind was fully fogged over, then he opened the scissors, pushed against her skin, and sliced a slow, deep cut in the side of her torso, from breast to navel. Hot tears sprang from her eyes anew as she let out a high-pitched wail through her gag. She squirmed violently.

Although she was tied tight, she nearly bucked him off. Bill laughed and then, without warning, he pushed himself into her. He pumped hard and came fast. Roxy stopped struggling now, and her eyes were closed, as if she were sleeping. She lost a lot of blood, but her face was still flushed. Bill slapped her cheek with one hard hit, forcing her to open her eyes. "We're not through yet, love."

He repeated the pattern of pleasure and torture. Even without her making a sound, he could easily tell when her body broke past the barrier of free will and gave into the ecstasy. This was the point he would stab or cut her with the scissors. She was covered in cuts and holes, leaking blood everywhere.

Finally, Bill saw she was getting too weak from pain and blood loss. There was a point where pain did override everything else, and no matter his efforts, she would not feel the pleasure anymore. He tried to take things relatively slow at first, to extend the fun, but in his eagerness, he stabbed too deep in a few places, and now the game was almost over. Bill was finally about to wrap up the party when he received a surprise.

He had been in the middle of thrusting into Roxy for the last time and had the scissors raised, ready to end her. Bill saw movement in the corner of his vision. When he looked up and saw a figure in the doorway, he froze. He was shocked to his core. Roxy seemed to come back to life; her eyes grew wide, nearly bulging from their sockets. She tried to scream through her gag. She was so weak that her efforts to pull at her bonds barely made them move at all.

Bill was so surprised that he couldn't think of a single thing to say or do. He just sat there, still inside Roxy to the hilt, with hand and scissors still raised in the air. The figure stared at him, studying him. He stared back, trying to see who it was, but for the life of him, couldn't tell.

The lights were dim, and the doorway was dark, preventing him from getting a clear view. For what seemed like forever, they stared at each other, unmoving. Roxy even quieted and stilled, waiting to see what would happen. Finally, the figure took a few steps out of the dark doorway and into the room, where Bill could then see who it was.

Once she began to move, she didn't stop. She walked right up to Bill and took the scissors from his hand. He gave them up with no protest. She held them like a vice, raised them high in the air, and then plunged them down into Roxy's throat, with one violent swing. She looked Roxy right in the eyes as the girl gurgled and choked on her own blood. When Roxy took her last breath, the woman turned to Bill. He still hadn't moved a muscle, but now he was grinning like a fool in love. He said, "Hello... Jessica."

14

Ashley was running late that day. She was committed to getting out of the house before noon so she could be back before anyone had a chance to spot her and stop her. There was nothing she dreaded more these days. She didn't want to see the pity in their eyes or hear about how sorry they were for her loss. Ashley also didn't want to listen to them asking her how she was feeling.

She felt like she could rip her hair out, thinking of all the hypocritical assholes, and said a silent prayer that she wouldn't run into anyone, every time she left. It had been a week that she'd been checking in on the Hill house. She had an alarm set every day, to get her out of the house when she'd wanted to be out, and so far, things had been fine.

Today, though, she hadn't been able to keep to her schedule. She hadn't even woken until noon. Ashley forced herself to take a shower, where she had spontaneously cried for nearly an hour. She sat at the bottom of the shower with the water running over her, envisioning what had happened to Chris. Water seemed to trigger these episodes. It was one reason she'd been avoiding showers and baths as much as possible.

Often, when she had an episode, she would black out. She would lose time, not realizing it. She'd been having the worst headaches of her life lately, too. Many times, she would sit down in the morning, glance at the clock, then when she looked again it would be much later in the afternoon, and her head would be pounding. She wasn't sure where her mind went and didn't really seem to care. All she wanted these days was for the day to be over so she could go back to sleep. She'd decided to live, but living still sucked.

Ashley pulled herself together and cleaned up. She finally made it out of the house before four o'clock. Glancing at the time on her way out the door, she gritted her teeth with the feeling that she was for sure going to run into someone she knew today. Just having the thought brought on a headache, and she put a hand to her temple in an effort to soothe it.

Because the Hills lived just a few doors down, she decided to walk over. She had a bike but didn't want to even think about using it. Riding bikes was something she used to do with Chris all the time. They'd loved riding together, up and down the streets, cruising and waving to all the neighbors. Ashley hadn't touched, or even looked at, the bikes since he was taken from her.

She made her way down the block, attempting to be invisible in her hoodie. She slumped her shoulders and looked down, trying to keep her face hidden. Nobody approached her, and she was able to make it to Stacy's door without incident.

Punching in the security code, she entered through the front door and went about her chores. She watered a couple of plants then went to feed the cat. It only took her about ten minutes, same as always. Today, though, the house seemed off somehow.

The Wrong Stranger

Something gave Ashley the urge to walk around and check all the windows to make sure they were sealed. She normally didn't do this because of the security alarm, and she assumed it would take care of the issue if one arose, but today, she had the oddest feeling. It was some kind of intuition, deep down in her gut, that was making her feel slightly anxious. Her gut hadn't steered her wrong yet, and so she decided it would be no sweat off her back to double check everything was locked up tight.

Ashley walked through the upstairs rooms, re-opening, closing, and latching all the windows. She even did the tiny bathroom window that only a child could fit through. She made her way downstairs to the main floor and did the same thing to those windows. Then, she opened the door to the basement stairs. She tried to look down them, but it was dark, and she would have to take a few steps before she could pull the light string. Ashley was fully aware of what Dan and Stacy did in the basement and really didn't want to go down there.

It was common knowledge throughout the neighborhood, even though Dan and Stace swore up and down that it was a secret. If it was a secret, why did they blast the info to everyone? Ashley didn't understand it, and she didn't understand why they even needed a secret sex room with kinky shit.

Why couldn't they just do their thing in the bedroom? She didn't want to think about it. Ashley didn't care about their sex life and had no desire what-so-ever to find out any more information than they already forced on her. She tried to remember if there were even any windows down there but couldn't think. Peering downstairs, the basement looked so dark to her she didn't think there were any, but couldn't remember for sure. She sighed thinking, *May as well check.* Then, she made her way slowly down.

At the bottom of the stairs, Ashley saw blackout curtains covering two windows, and headed toward them, glad it wasn't a waste of time going downstairs, after all. After checking the windows, she headed toward the closed door that led to what she believed must be the "sex room." Ashley had never been in the room before and had no clue if there was a window or door leading to outside the house. She questioned if it was really worth checking into. She still had that feeling in her gut and knew she needed to check, even though she had absolutely no desire to walk into the room.

If someone robbed the Hill's blind, she would have even more guilt laying on her shoulders, and she wasn't sure she could handle that. What would she tell Stace? *"Sorry, I checked everywhere but your sex room because it was too weird for me?"* It wasn't that she was a prude or grossed out. Once upon a time, Ashley and Bill had a great sex life of their own. The problem for Ashley was, she felt exceedingly awkward being a witness to other people's sex life. She felt it was a private matter between two lovers and didn't need to be shared with the rest of the world. She didn't like to know or see what other people were doing to each other, and forcing the information onto her, made her feel weird and uncomfortable.

Ashley sighed. She told herself it was no big deal. All she was doing was opening a door, checking for a window or door leading outside, and then turning around and going home. Nothing to it. She was about to open the door, but hesitated. Ashley heard what sounded like a low, slow, groaning coming from the other side of the door. It was faint, and it was hard to tell exactly what it was. She stopped and waited. Leaning forward and putting her right ear next to the door, she focused on trying to make out what the sound was.

She closed her eyes in concentration, listening to the muffled sounds. To Ashley, it sounded like someone having sex. She blushed scarlet. She thought, *this is what I wanted to avoid!* She supposed they'd left on some kind of porn. She was exasperated with her friend, thinking, *who forgets to turn their porn off when they're going on vacation for two weeks?* She wondered how that happened. Then, she wondered if she was supposed to turn it off for them or just leave it.

Now Ashley heard a higher pitched, feminine voice that was moaning but not saying any words. A deeper, gruffer, what she assumed was a masculine voice, was grunting in quick succession. The voices were definitely in sync with each other. She heard what sounded like flesh pounding against flesh. Ashley blushed even more hotly, now thinking that this was starting to sound super real. Maybe it wasn't porn at all.

The sounds were getting louder and sounded too real to be from something recorded. Suddenly, she felt she was definitely intruding on something private. Stacy and Dan had been known to get freaky; Stacy had loved to fill her in on details that Ashley really hadn't been interested in. From the sound of it, they were home from vacation a week early and forgot to tell Ashley about it. Feeling embarrassed and a little angry, Ashley was about to step away and leave them to it, but then she heard the masculine voice again—this time it spoke.

Ashley could have sworn it was *Bill's* voice, and she had an instant moment of panic. A cold sweat broke out on her forehead as anxiety flooded her veins. She clenched her fists, trying to hear better and think, but her head was beginning to ache again, which made it impossible. Panic launched through her whole body like a lightning bolt. Starting from her heart, she could feel it shoot through her torso, down her legs, and out her arms. It gripped her like a vice, and she began to feel dizzy and lightheaded. She'd only barely heard his voice, but was nearly certain that it was him.

For a long time now, she had suspected Bill of cheating. Even before Chris died, she had the feeling that something just wasn't right with him. After Chris, though, she really didn't care about anything at all. She had no sex drive herself, and almost couldn't blame her husband for looking elsewhere to fulfill his needs. *Almost.* It was obvious to Ashley that their marriage had been in an awful place, and neither of them had been working very hard to save it. She knew Bill blamed her, at least partially for what happened to their boy, and thought it could be part of the reason for his lack of interest or care recently. But did she deserve *this* kind of betrayal? After all that they'd been through, and all of their years of marriage, did she deserve *this?*

She was now pressing her ear hard against the door. Ashley listened with every ounce of her concentration. The man's voice was giving encouraging words. She heard him say, "Yes," then, more grunting. Then, heard clearly, "Mmm, yeah, baby, that's perfect," and then more grunting as the feminine moaning was getting louder. Tears pooled in Ashley's eyes and dropped down her cheeks. It was him; there was no doubt. They'd been married how many years, after all. If she didn't know her husband's voice while he was screwing, there was something wrong with her.

Ashley didn't know what to do. Should she walk in and interrupt? She imagined what his face would look like, being caught in the act. Would he ignore her and keep pounding away? Or would he look at her with a guilty face and try to give some lame excuse? Should she go home and confront him there? Ashley thought if she did that, he would deny it all. No, it would take catching him red-handed, and even then, something inside told her he would still make it out to not be his fault.

The idea of Bill fucking another woman, in her best friend's house, right under her nose, made her want to crumple up and die all over again. He was doing this to her, *and* after their son just died. Why should she let him get his happy ending?

She felt like the walls of the basement were closing in on her; she could barely breathe. The feeling of panic that shot through her moments before was now squeezing her in its grip. She kept asking herself how he could do this, especially now, and then she wondered if it wasn't just something new. How long had he been fucking around behind her back? This could explain a lot. It could explain why he hadn't been there by her side, grieving for their dead son.

It only took seconds, but once her train of thought started going down this road, Ashley started to feel less broken and more pissed.

The anger grew and fed itself with each new question that ran through her mind. She grew more infuriated with each breath she took. Within seconds, the feeling of anger had grown into a fury. The pounding in her head was now so intense that her vision was growing blurry, but she hardly noticed. The rage within her reached deeper, spreading through her chest and belly. She felt it pulsing, like a monster within that was trying to break out. She closed her eyes for only a moment to gather her thoughts, then her world went black.

15

SIX MONTHS AGO

Despite his lack of interest in being a family man, his son's funeral was a difficult experience for Bill. He did not cry, but it was also not very hard for him to play the part of the grieving father. He'd been fond of his son, and although they didn't have a magical relationship, the boy was *his* and had been taken away from him without warning.

The loss had angered Bill, more than hurt, but after seeing the boy in a casket and being lowered into the ground, he clenched his jaw not just in outrage, but also to fight the slight ache he felt. He would not allow himself to feel anything but ire, and Bill vowed that somehow, someway, he would make Ashley, and everyone else that was responsible for this theft, pay dearly.

After the funeral, there was a reception held by some friends and neighbors. Ashley only stayed for the funeral service, choosing not to attend the reception. Attending the funeral had been one of the hardest things she had ever gone through in her entire life, and for her to then attend the reception and be forced to sit through the talk and seeing the looks on everyone's faces... it was something that she could not bear to endure. Of course, everyone understood. No one would hold it against her for not attending the reception. Bill, however, was not as understanding as everyone else.

He didn't understand how she could just go home and not be there at all. He felt that she should have made more of an effort. She was being self-centered and rude to everyone who was showing their support. She was going to make their family seem *abnormal*. He had feelings of annoyance, and even irritation, toward his wife for a long time, and then she'd been careless with their son. Bill couldn't understand. She'd wanted a child. *Why* didn't she take better care of him?

After Chris's death, Bill's feelings towards his wife transformed into a deep disliking. Now, though, she was showing a disrespect that he couldn't stand for. This was not about *her* losing *her son*. This was about something being stolen from *him*.

The entire situation with Chris being killed was a slap in the face. The lack of respect that it took for Ashley to be so neglectful, to *allow* their son to be murdered, was inconceivable. Now she was even more disgraceful, not even having the nerve to follow through with a funeral reception.

Bill thought Ashley had to hate *him*. Yes, that was it. Ashley had to hate his guts to allow this to happen. To allow this to happen, and then to not even come to the reception. She was trying to snub him; she was trying to make him look like a fool.

That none of what he was thinking made any sense at all, never crossed Bill's mind. It wasn't logical, but that didn't matter. He was trying to place blame on someone, trying to make sense of the situation, and was pinning it on the easiest person who it would be to punish. He was taking the facts surrounding Chris's accident and twisting them into a situation that never existed.

He was a man with little emotion and little empathy. Part of him was purely incapable of understanding what it truly meant to love another person with your entire being. He didn't understand it and was a little jealous of the relationship that Ashley and Chris shared, although he would never admit it, even to himself.

The internal dialogue began once Ashley left the funeral service and continued through the hours he was at the reception without her. Bill split his conscious mind into two parts. Externally, he played the role of the grieving father. He held polite conversation with acquaintances and shared memories with those who knew Chris. He felt like he was performing in exactly the way a grieving father was supposed to. Inwardly, though, he was thinking about his dearest wife. At the same time he was conversing and fully functioning in a public situation, the other side of his mind was droning on and on about what a selfish bitch Ashley was.

By this time, Bill had worked himself up into such a rage that he'd been almost shaking. She was the one person in his life who could force him to lose control like this. He prided himself on *not* losing control of his anger, which only served to infuriate him further when he did lose it.

For the past several hours he'd been thinking to himself about how much he hated Ashley, how much everything was her fault, and what he was going to do to her to make her pay. He'd played with the idea about killing her off now, too. He'd thought about it so many times. Ironically, he'd dismissed the idea almost immediately because he still felt that she was necessary.

He had never physically hurt Ashley before, despite wanting to. In all the years they'd been married, there had been a few times he had to hold himself in restraint, but never once had he let his anger get the best of him. His hobby had always been an outlet for any temper that Bill possessed, and if his wife pissed him off, he would take it out on his targets instead. He thought that by doing this, he was being smart, and again, staying under the radar.

Everything he did was all about his image. Bill thought if the news came out that he was a wife beater, then he would find himself under a big spotlight, which was exactly what he didn't want. People rarely trusted a man that beat his wife, and it was of vital importance to Bill that he was trusted.

He realized, of course, that with his particular occupation, he traveled the country and there was no way for strangers he met to have any idea of his reputation. But in the back of his mind, it didn't matter if they knew. There would be a stench that would follow him wherever he went. He felt it down to his bones that this was true, and therefore, above anything else in his life, Bill worked toward maintaining the image of normalcy, including not beating his wife when she made him angry. The day of his son's funeral was the one day of his life that he'd been unable to keep control.

Chris's funeral took place in the late morning, and luncheon was served during the reception. The morning and afternoon were busy, and Bill and Ashley spoke only a handful of words to each other the entire day. When Ashley left for home immediately following the funeral service, she was suffering from another of her agonizing headaches. Her pain was so excruciating that it gave her another outlet to focus her attention on. She zoned into it, feeling every ounce of agony thrumming through her skull. During the service, she welcomed the pain, making no outward sign that she was in physical discomfort.

She sat silent and still, while listening to the priest give his sermon and to the people who stood to give kind words. All the while, Ashley felt like a demon was beating relentlessly on her skull. The pain Ashley was experiencing was not in one particular spot, like a normal headache, on the forehead, temple, or behind their eyes. Ashley's headache was all-encompassing. She was in anguish from her forehead up and over the entire back of her head, down to her neck. From one ear, up and over, to the other, she felt a constant pounding, pulsing, hammering pain. Ashley grew so sensitive to the light that even closing her eyes wouldn't help. She had to put sunglasses on while still keeping her eyes closed in order to block it out.

Ashley welcomed the physical torment because she believed it was the only thing keeping her from an emotional breakdown. Once the service was over, though, she didn't see any reason to put herself through any more torture. She wanted to go home, take the strongest painkillers that were in the cabinet, close all the curtains, and sleep for the rest of her life. Sitting next to Bill, she leaned over to whisper that she was going to leave when the service was over. She gave no explanation, feeling surely it was obvious, and she shouldn't have to explain herself.

When Ashley whispered, "I'm going home when the service is over," Bill gave her a look that only lasted for a split second but frightened her to her core. He'd never looked at her that way before, as if he could murder her right then and there. She stared at him, hearing him grind his teeth in a clenched jaw. She nearly backed away from him, but he put a hand on her arm. When she felt his grip, she almost jumped out of her seat, she was so startled by his reaction. But looking back into his face, he'd schooled his features into a look of polite understanding.

"Of course. Whatever you need," he said. Did he sound sarcastic? Ashley couldn't quite tell. She eyed him, but her head hurt too much for her to think or do anything else. "Thanks." She couldn't nod or she might pass out, and talking was also out of the question, so she'd said as little as possible. As soon as she had the opportunity, Ashley left without saying a word to anyone else. She figured she was probably being rude, but didn't care. If people couldn't give her a pass at her son's funeral, then they could go jump off a bridge for all she cared.

At home, the only pain pills she had on hand were some extra strength Tylenol. She took three, closed all the curtains, and got into bed. While she laid down, she felt her head pulsing. The pressure felt like her skull would burst open. Through the pain, Ashley thought about Chris. She replayed images in her mind of when he was a baby, nursing from her. She remembered how small he was, and how bald, too. He'd been the most precious thing she'd ever seen.

Ashley thought about feeding Chris spaghetti for the first time and what a mess he'd made. God, how he loved it, though. She remembered the smiles and laughter and all the love that they'd shared. He wasn't just her son; he was her best friend. They had done everything together, and every new experience that he went through, she had been there. Ashley remembered when Chris turned three and got a tricycle for his birthday. In her mind, she watched him riding it up and down the sidewalk and saw herself chasing after him, trying to prevent him from steering into a tree.

Ashley played memory after memory in her mind's eye. With each one, new tears fell. She was lying on her side, hugging a pillow, when she noticed the side of her face was wet, and she could barely see through her swollen eyes. The pillow was soaked through. She tossed it to the floor, grabbed Bill's pillow and the box of Kleenex that was on the night table, and laid back down.

Her mind was consumed with thoughts of how fast her boy had grown. Everyone always said it went by in the blink of an eye, but you didn't even have a clue until you experienced it for yourself. She felt like she really had blinked, and he'd been six years old. Where had the time gone? It really didn't matter now, because he was gone. She let go of everything else and focused on remembering until her world faded, and she fell unconscious.

16

Dan and Stacy Hill gave Bill a ride home from the funeral reception. They were the last to leave and stayed to help with the cleanup. Others offered to take Bill home earlier, telling him not to worry about a thing and to go be with Ashley during this difficult time, but Bill politely declined them all. For one, he didn't want to go home and be with Ashley, and two, according to his warped sense of normalcy, he thought it would seem even more out of the ordinary for both himself *and* Ashley to leave early. So, he stayed through it all, until the very end.

He was still battling with his temper and the internal debate on how best to handle Ashley. He was afraid of what he would do to her when he saw her and thought that delaying it would give him time to calm down. When they pulled up to the curb to drop him off, the Hills had taken his silence for grief. Stacy got out of the car to give him a hug.

"Hang in there, Bill. We're here for you both." Bill gave a tight smile and nod as she got back into the car. Dan drove away while Bill plodded up the front walk.

Normally, Bill was an observant man. It was not unusual

for him to notice the most minute details; it was essential for his hobby. He was a man all about the details. Coming home from the funeral, though, his mind was too occupied with his anger to notice much.

He failed to notice that the car wasn't in the driveway. When he had to unlock the front door and turn off the security alarm, it didn't register in his mind that the alarm shouldn't have been set. The question, "If Ashley was home, why would the alarm be set," did not cross Bill's brain until several minutes later.

After getting inside, turning off the alarm, and slipping off his shoes, Bill headed straight for the bedroom. The door was wide open. He was expecting to see Ashley asleep on the bed, but the bed was empty. The covers were crumpled like she'd been laying on top of them and one pillow was on the floor. He checked the bathroom, but she wasn't there, either. That's when the thought "If Ashley was home, why would the alarm be set?"

finally registered. *"Fuck!"* he yelled. What was she doing out of the house? Bill felt his control slip.

He tried texting Ashley, but there was no response. After several minutes, he tried calling, but it went straight to voicemail. Her phone was turned off. Bill cursed again. He threw his phone down onto the bed. It bounced to the floor, but he left it. Bill walked out to the living room to sit on the couch, thinking about what his options were while he tried to calm down.

Taking a deep breath, he told himself, "Whatever she's doing, she's doing it out of grief. She's probably lost her mind a little, that's all." And saying these words seemed to work. He liked the idea of Ashley out there, driving around like a crazy woman. Maybe she'll get into a nasty accident and take a few others out with her in a fiery blaze. This idea was something he held on to while he stayed on the couch, waiting for her to return. He turned on the TV and stayed there waiting, until it grew dark outside, and he fell asleep where he sat.

Bill was startled awake when he heard the front door open. He jerked, then sat up, blinking against the lights that were still on. Ashley stood in the entryway, staring at him. Something was off about her, but Bill was too groggy to put his finger on exactly what it was.

There was a moment where neither said a word. They each were perfectly still, staring at the other. Finally, Bill asked, "Where were you?" She continued to look at him without responding. Bill stood up and started toward her.

Before he could take two steps, she said, "Well, Bill, it's about time we met."

He stopped walking. Now fully awake, it was obvious what was different about her. The woman standing in the entryway was Ashley, but somehow, wasn't her at all. She had her hair down, instead of pulled back, and it seemed to be somehow shinier because the light was reflecting off it. Ashley's hair was always pulled into a tight bun on top of her head. It was never down, and if it was, the only thing shiny about it was the grease. This woman's hair looked like it had just been pampered at a salon.

Her hair wasn't the only difference. She seemed to have a whole different aura. Looking at her now, he was seeing a completely different woman than he saw that morning. Ashley was no longer hunched in baggy clothes with the feelings of death and depression emanating from her. She stood strong and straight, was dressed in a knee-length dress that Bill had never seen before, and she was standing up straighter, emitting many emotions—confidence among them. She seemed to be almost completely opposite of her normal self, and if Bill wasn't mistaken, she seemed to be speaking with an English accent.

"What the fuck are you doing? What the hell kind of game are you playing at?" Bill's anger from earlier in the day came roaring back. He didn't allow Ashley to respond. Instead, he continued walking to her, reached back, and slapped her across her cheek. She reeled back in shock, holding a hand against her cheek that was now turning bright red. She stared at him with wide eyes, saying nothing. When he saw she wasn't afraid, Bill slapped her again, even harder, this time on the other cheek. Her head flung back, and her feet staggered to keep balance.

There was a drop of blood that leaked from one nostril. "Answer me, goddammit!" He raised his arm to slap her a third time, but she stopped him.

"Hit me again, and you're going to fucking regret it." When she spoke, her voice was cold and hard, and it was her tone more than her words that caused him to stop.

"Are you going to—" He stopped when he finally got a good look at her eyes. They were a different color. Ashley had gray eyes, but now they were ice blue. He grabbed hold of the sides of her face, pulling her to him, so they were almost nose to nose. He studied her, trying to see the outline of contact lenses, but could see none. Somehow, she'd changed her eye color.

He took a steadying breath, but now it was her turn to speak. "There is no game here, Bill."

"I don't understand what you're trying to do."

"I'm not trying to do anything."

"Then, what the shit is going on! Your eyes are a different color, for Christ's sake!" Bill was shouting now, but she was speaking in a voice that was cold and collected.

"My eyes are my own now, not Ashley's."

"And what is that supposed to mean?"

"Are you so stupid that you can't figure it out?" In all of Bill's adult life, no one had ever spoken to him this way.

When he was a child, his parents spoke to him similarly all the time, but when he grew into an adult, he swore to himself he'd never stand for that treatment again.

He wanted to slap her again, or better yet, do something more painful. In fact, what if she had that long-awaited accident within the next couple of days? It would be the perfect opportunity for a suicide, right after Chris's funeral. Forget the idea that he needed her. He didn't need anyone. He would start the prep work tomorrow.

"I'll sleep on the couch tonight, Ashley. Just go to bed."

"Jessica."

"What?"

"You said Ashley. I'm not Ashley; I'm Jessica."

"Goodnight, *Ashley*." He turned and went back to the couch to lie down. He turned off the lamp on the end table and covered himself with a throw blanket. Ashley was playing a game, and it would be too easy to let his temper get the better of him. Bill imagined that Ashley had come home from Chris's funeral before leaving to go shopping and get her hair done. It explained why she'd been gone. As for the eye color, she probably did have contacts on, and he was just too tired to see them.

She was trying to screw with him somehow. The idea only infuriated Bill more. He didn't understand *why*. He considered perhaps she was doing this to cope with the loss of Chris, but, it was too much. He didn't like being messed with. Not at all.

17

The morning after Chris's funeral, Ashley woke up alone in bed. She was cold because she'd fallen asleep completely naked on top of the covers, stomach down, ass in the air. Her face hurt, and she felt like she did after a night of sex but the last thing she could remember was lying on the bed, crying herself to sleep.

Ashley didn't remember taking her clothes off, not even to change into sweats. She racked her brain, trying to remember what else might've happened. She might've been a little delirious from the headache yesterday but was almost positive she hadn't seen Bill for the rest of the day. She was surprised that Bill wasn't in bed with her now, though. She was disappointed at the thought of him leaving her to grieve alone.

She began to cry. Still cold, Ashley got up to get dressed and then got back into bed, underneath the covers. She spent the next several hours in a cycle of crying, blowing her nose, thinking of her son, and then crying all over again. Finally, she cried herself back to sleep for a few more hours. When Ashley got up for the second time, it was afternoon. As soon as she opened her eyes, the memory of her loss hit her, drawing fresh tears all over again. She didn't want to get out of bed, but she needed to know where Bill was.

Ashley went into the bathroom first, which was when she saw her reflection in the mirror. She gasped at the sight of her face. Her eyes were red rimmed and swollen, but she also had the start of a black eye. Her cheeks had dark bruises on both sides and seeing herself this way made her want to cry all over again. *She thought, what in the holy hell happened?* Ashley closed her eyes to replay the memory of yesterday over again, concentrating as hard as she could. No matter how much she tried, she could remember nothing happening that would make her look like this. Waking up naked was one thing, but this was totally different. Her face looked worse than it felt, which was good she supposed, but she was beginning to feel like she was losing her mind.

Ashley left the bathroom, then bedroom, expecting to see Bill in the living room watching TV per his usual. She was not disappointed. As soon as she opened the bedroom door, she could hear the soft sound of the television and saw the back of Bill's head, leaning against the arm of the couch.

"Bill? You didn't come to bed last night."

Bill sat up and turned off the TV. He seemed to study her every detail.

He noted the bruises but made no outward sign of guilt or regret. He noticed her eyes, too, not just the state of their health, but their color. They were back to gray, and he made a mental note to search the bedroom for the contacts.

When he said nothing, just stared at her with those dark eyes, she asked, "Why not?" Bill blinked. Too focused on how she looked exactly like her normal self and not a bit like she did last night, he had to think about what she was asking.

"Don't you remember?"

Ashley blushed, thinking they must've made love. She

couldn't remember doing it, though. How was that even possible? She had taken no drugs that she could think of. Surely, the over the counter pain killers she took wouldn't cause memory loss. She wondered, *could my headache have put me that out of it?*

"Did we... you know....?" She raised her eyebrows suggestively. Then, she cried, feeling immense guilt at the idea of being alive while her son was buried six feet under.

Bill didn't seem to notice her tears. He smiled, remembering the night before. After he'd lain back on the couch, trying to ignore her, she'd come over to him and tugged his pants down. She stripped naked right there, then sat on him. She rode him with her shirt off and breasts bouncing, just the way he loved. It had been amazing, and after they were finished, they'd moved into the bedroom for some more. They had stayed up late, spending hours in there together. Bill wouldn't exactly describe it as making love. It had been better than they had in years.

When Ashley had fallen asleep, he left her laying naked on the bed. His anger was cooled for the time being, but he still didn't like the game she was playing.

"Yeah, something like that." Bill had a self-satisfied smirk now, and to Ashley, he looked extremely boyish and adorable. She couldn't remember thinking that of him in a long time.

She sniffed. Wiping her eyes, trying to stop crying. "Why don't I remember?"

Bill was completely honest when he said, "I don't know."

Ashley took him for his word, not understanding and frustrated at her lack of memory. Okay, so they *had* made love. But... "What happened to my face? I don't remember that, either."

His smile faltered but didn't completely fall. He felt sorry, but not for hurting her. The regret that Bill felt was more for putting himself in a difficult situation. "We got a little rough."

Ashley thought about it, and she decided not to question it. Never in their entire relationship had she woken up with her face like this. It made little sense, but nothing seemed to make sense this morning. Maybe she rolled off the bed and hit her face on the ground or something stupid. She let it go because it didn't really matter anyway. The only thing that mattered was that Chris wasn't there.

After that interesting night, Bill wasn't quite sure what to think anymore. His anger was eased, but it was still on a low simmer, waiting in the dark. She was probably coping with losing Chris in her own way, even though he couldn't understand it. Ashley claimed to have no memory of her behavior, and he didn't know if he really believed that or not. She was definitely back to her normal self, seeming to drop whatever game she'd been trying to play at the night before. He didn't know what to think of it. He'd let his temper get the best of him and was angry with himself for his lack of control. He was a man that prided himself on control, and he'd not only hit his wife, but had let serious thoughts of killing her take over. Bill vowed he would look at the situation rationally now and wait to make his final decision about how to handle her.

Bill waited for Ashley to make a repeat act, but after months of nothing but living in bed and crying all day, he'd seen nothing of her odd behavior again. He wasn't home very often, but when he was there, she barely spoke to him. She was too consumed with grief. The night of Chris's funeral, she had told him to call her *Jessica*. Bill remembered it clearly, and over the months, he waited patiently for her to play the game again. He thought often about the name change. He liked it and wondered if it had a special meaning or if she knew someone with that name.

He thought for her to have gone through all that trouble to come up with another identity, it must be disappointing for her not to use it. The longer that Bill was forced to wait, the more he thought she really hadn't been playing mind games. He felt more and more that Ashley had just been trying to cope with the funeral and their loss. Maybe she felt if she became another woman, she would be a woman who hadn't just lost her son.

ONE DAY IN NOVEMBER, ABOUT FIVE MONTHS AFTER THE funeral, Bill had just got back into town from a cross-country haul. He was gone for four days and decided to take a day off at home. It was dark outside when he pulled into the driveway, well past ten o'clock at night. He got out of the truck and walked up the front steps, the same as he always did. He moved automatically from memory, not really thinking. It was a rare night that he was too tired to think. He didn't think about Ashley, just bed and sleep.

Because of the nature of his hobby, he got very little sleep, not nearly enough. Sleep was of vital importance for Bill, not only as a driver, but because his body needed it in order to function. Some people could fully function on minimal hours of sleep and some just couldn't, no matter how hard they tried to train themselves. Bill was in the latter group, and despite all his efforts to make it work, he was incapable of sustaining himself for more than a day with so little sleep.

Ashley was always in bed, crying or sleeping. It wasn't something he thought about; it was just a fact. Keys in hand, Bill unlocked the door. When he stepped into the dark entryway, he nearly jumped out of his skin. The house was pitch black with the outside light shining through the doorway. Bill flicked on the entry light to see Ashley standing right in front of his face, staring at him. He jolted backward, almost falling out the door.

He was wide awake and alert now. It took a lot to scare him, and Bill was not happy about it. He did a double take, looking more closely at Ashley, who was still a statue in the middle of the entryway. She was unmoving and unblinking. Bill thought she was staring at him, but now realized she was just zoned out, staring into space and not anything in particular.

Her eyes were like solid emeralds. They looked glazed over, like she had cataracts. He'd never seen them look that way before, and it scared the shit out of him. It wasn't the ice blue that he'd been expecting. Then, he thought, *more contacts.*

Bill closed the front door and walked around Ashley. He turned on some of the house lights, so it didn't look so damned creepy. Then, he went back to her. She looked like a ghost, standing there in her white nightgown and almost translucent skin. "Ashley?" She didn't flinch. He tried a little louder. "Ash?" But still nothing. Then, he put a hand on her shoulder and without warning she let out a guttural, ear-splitting scream.

Again, Bill was startled, stumbling back and covering his ears. She began wailing, "Don't touch me! Don't touch me!" He could tell she wasn't really seeing him. She was still in her own world, seeing someone else, or maybe no one at all. He recognized if he tried to talk to her, she wouldn't hear him, but it might set her off in some other way.

After days on the road, he was beat. During this period, Bill was particularly tired because he'd not only maxed out his driving hours, but he had been doing recon for a new target as well.

While on the road, he was religious about pulling into a rest area, climbing into the back of the truck, and sleeping for as long as possible. He was aware of his body's needs, but this downtime was also the only available time to spend on his hobby. Occasionally, he would forego sleep to do other things that needed to be done. If he went too long without sleep, he would start making mistakes. Even minor mistakes could be costly.

It had been a hard week on Bill. Despite every effort to not overdo it on the recon, he was helpless to stop himself. It had been the perfect opportunity to do a few needed things, and he'd gone for it. The result was him being dead tired now and wanting nothing but to hibernate for twelve hours.

He was also a man who did not enjoy being startled. Surprised—yes, but not startled. All he could think was, *nope. Not doing it.* He didn't have the energy to deal with this. Ashley was still emitting her deafening cries but hadn't moved an inch from her spot. The only move she made was to put her hands between her legs, shielding herself. Bill turned and walked away from her. He left her there in the entryway while he went to the bedroom. He could still hear her fifteen minutes later when he closed his eyes for sleep.

When Bill woke up the next morning, Ashley was in bed next to him, sound asleep. When she finally woke, he asked, "How'd you sleep?"

She was hesitant. "Like a rock."

He nodded. "Hey, do you know anyone named Jessica?" He watched her closely to gauge her reaction, but she didn't look guilty. She looked the same, as if he asked what the weather was like.

"Jessica who?"

"Just anyone with that name. No particular last name."

"No particular last name?" She thought for a moment, then said, "There was a girl at my high school named Jessica."

"Anyone else?"

"I don't know. I don't think so. Why?"

"You said that name in your sleep." This was a lie, of course, but Bill was dying to know where she'd come up with her other persona. He wanted to see what she would say. The previous night, she'd been different from the night of the funeral. He didn't know what was going on with her, but he had a good idea that she was no longer trying to screw with him.

18

PRESENT DAY

When Ashley opened her eyes, she was in her bed with the covers pulled up over her shoulders. The curtains were closed, but she could tell it was dark outside because there was no light shining through the spaces between them. Her head was throbbing again. She reached an arm up to her head and put a little pressure against the ache.

After a moment, she sat up and looked around the room, feeling like she was missing something. She was still in her nightgown, which was really just an old baggy t-shirt.

With a feeling of being off kilter, she looked at the clock on her night table. It said "9:30" in big red numbers. She was confused, and with her throbbing head, she wondered if she had slept the entire day. It wouldn't be the first time it had happened. Wasn't it her day to check in on Stace's house? Did she remember to go over there? For the life of her, she couldn't remember if she had or not.

She got out of bed and went into the bathroom. She looked at herself in the mirror, scrutinizing every detail of her face. There were shadows and circles, lines that hadn't

The Wrong Stranger

been there a year ago. God, how she had aged. She began to cry, thinking about Chris again. This was going to be another bad day. She felt it. It was one of those days she didn't really want to leave the bedroom, just stay there all day and wallow in her own misery. No matter how much she wanted that, though, she couldn't let herself go back to being that woman. She had to move on.

Her head hurt so damn bad. She'd been having stress headaches and migraines for months now. They plagued her constantly. After using the toilet and popping a couple of pain pills that wouldn't help, she padded down the hall to the living room. Bill was in the kitchen, fixing himself something to eat. He had the TV on in the background and glanced up from fixing his meal as she approached. "Hey," he greeted her, turning the volume on the TV down.

Ashley gave a weak smile and a return, "Hey." She went to sit on the couch, and he joined her. She was silent for a minute before asking, "Are Stace and Dan back?"

After a few seconds, he said, "Not that I'm aware of. They haven't stopped by. Aren't they supposed to be gone for another week?"

Ashley nodded and then put a hand to her head from the pain that the movement caused. "God, my head is killing me."

"Did you take anything for it?"

"Yeah. I could've sworn they were back. I thought I heard them."

Bill smiled. "You've been in there sleeping all day. No one's been over. Maybe you heard the TV." He shrugged.

She pursed her lips, trying to think. "I guess I was dreaming." Ashley leaned her head back on the couch. They watched television in silence. Then she realized he should be out of town. "Bill?"

"Yeah?"

"Aren't you supposed to be gone for work?" She was so

confused. This wasn't the first time her timeline was off, and she hated when it happened. Ashley held a hand against her head to put pressure against the pain.

"I got back while you were out of it."

"Oh," Ashley said, not really caring anymore. She didn't want to think about anything, just wanted the pain in her head to go away. They continued watching television together before heading to the bedroom to go back to bed.

They each lay separately, untouching, on their own sides of the bed. They hadn't made love since Chris's funeral, and she still didn't remember that time, so it seemed like even longer to her. Ashley had no libido, and if she even thought about it, the guilt was too much for her to bear.

At first, Bill understood, and then he had some colossal problems with it. They had fought and argued over it. Bill had made her feel so guilty for not "thinking of his needs." And then, finally, he stopped trying altogether. Part of Ashley was relieved. She hated the fights and hated how it made her feel, but the other part of her thought if he wasn't getting it from her, he was definitely still getting his needs met somehow.

When she had those kinds of thoughts, she would push them into the back of her mind to get them out of the way.

Bill was snoring within minutes, and Ashley lay awake for hours, thinking. She tossed and turned with the guilt and anxiety eating away at her. It was a silent torture she had to endure every night. She didn't feel tired, but she felt drained. Ashley had no energy to do anything. She'd been sleeping all day and still had no energy. She should get up and do some chores or *something*. Ashley didn't *want* to do anything, though. She didn't even want to exist, but here she was. When the dark thoughts in her mind finally consumed all that was left of her, she blacked out with tears streaming down her cheeks.

PART III

19

After years of enjoying his hobby alone, Bill decided to take a different direction. There was only one way to both simplify things and solve the problem of Jessica. Bringing Jessica on, as something of a partner, would be the most exciting thing he'd done in years.

Seeing her kill Roxy had done something to him. He'd been so excited that he could hardly see straight. Bill remembered feeling the blood rushing through his veins, mouth dry with anticipation, and being frozen with excitement.

From the start, it had always been about the adrenaline. The excitement, the rush, and the thrill of feeling his blood pump in overdrive were what he craved. Because of this experience with Jessica, it was easy for him to decide that he wanted her around again and again. He wasn't sure how much he could really trust her, but keeping her close at hand would solve that problem. Keep your enemies close and all that, isn't that what they said?

He had a deep down *need* to watch her again. She was unpredictable, and Bill had a strong intuition that seeing

Jessica in action again would be even better than the last time.

It took little convincing on his part to get her to agree to work with him. While in the Hills' basement, they had sex on top of Roxy's bloody corpse. Afterward, Bill popped the question, "So, how would you like to work together?"

She'd smiled and laughed, "I hope your wife won't mind." Jessica didn't help him clean up the mess. She'd taken a shower with him before she left. On her way out the door, she said, "I'll have a target in mind for you, when you're ready."

Bill smiled at the memory. He liked her having a little sass. It was so different from what he was used to, and he really liked a woman who kept him on his toes. Bill was attracted to Jessica in a way that reminded him of when he'd first met Ashley. He looked forward to being around her more often, but still didn't understand what made her appear the way she did.

He couldn't help but compare her to the current Ashley.

Ever since they'd lost their son, and even before that, Ashley had been a weepy, boring mess. When he married her, she was attractive and exciting, but after so many years together, and especially after their mutual loss, he no longer cared for her. He still didn't know where the Jessica persona came from, but he couldn't get enough of it at the moment. If he had to put up with "Ashley" at home, then so be it, if it meant that he got "Jessica" to play with.

About a week after Roxy, Bill encountered Jessica again. He'd been sitting at the local diner, having breakfast for dinner after a long couple of days driving. It was late for dinner, but he didn't care. He was eating alone because

Ashley still wasn't ready to leave the house to join him, and he'd needed to get out. Now, he was enjoying his meal while he thought about Jessica. He wondered when he would see her again and thought about how it would be best to draw her out. He was ready to get the ball rolling on the next target.

Finished eating, Bill got up from his booth and headed to the men's room. The small bathroom had one urinal and one stall, both empty. He stood in front of the urinal, and just as he finished with his business, the bathroom door opened. Bill wouldn't normally look up, but he heard the sound of the door lock. He glanced at the door; the surprise made him smile. It was Jessica.

"Did I scare you?"

"Of course not." But she *had* startled him. Not that he would admit it. "What are you doing in here? I'm sitting over by the window if you want to join me."

Jessica smirked, but said nothing. She walked toward him, reaching for his zipper. She pressed her hand against him. Rubbing slowly, she looked up into Bill's face and, with her other hand, pulled him down to kiss her. Neither one said a thing after that. For the next several minutes, the entire restaurant was quiet, except for the sounds coming out of the men's bathroom.

When Bill and Jessica left the diner, Bill led the way, with Jessica right behind him. "Let's go for a walk," she said when they were outside. The town was small, but there was a sidewalk that wrapped all the way around it, and if they followed to the left, it would loop past a small park, and eventually, back to the diner and their vehicles.

When they were down the street a way, Jessica gave a quick glance around. No one would be around at this time of night, on a weeknight in a small town, but it didn't hurt to be careful.

"So, I have someone in mind," she said.

"It's not someone that you know, is it?"

"Why? Does that matter?" Jessica frowned.

"Hell yes, it matters. Look, it has to be a total stranger. Someone who couldn't be linked back to you in any way. That's the only way we stand a chance of not getting caught, and if you can't live with that, then this partnership is over." He looked her in the eyes to make sure she understood how serious he was.

"Don't worry," she huffed, "It's just some lady I came across while running errands."

"Normally, I pick targets that are farther from home." He was hesitant. Picking someone too close was dangerous, and the potential to be linked to that person could be much higher.

"Normally? Is this something you do all the time?"

"Let's just say, I've done it more than once, and I do things a certain way for a reason."

"This is the one I really want." Bill looked into the distance. He was considering if it was really worth arguing about. "What's so special about her? Didn't you just say that you ran into her randomly?" And since when did she start running errands again? It wasn't a mystery. She was hiding something.

Jessica nodded. "It's the profile. I've been waiting for a woman who looks this exact way, and finally, I found her. Besides, she isn't too close. I was shopping at the mall, and you know that's an hour drive from here. And if you've never picked someone that close before, it couldn't hurt, could it?"

Bill was quiet again, thinking, *she must've been planning this for a while if she's been on the lookout.* Did he trust Jessica enough to believe this woman would be a legitimate target? He suspected she wasn't being entirely truthful with him. He would have to do his own research on the woman, but he'd planned on that anyway. Bill was still hesitant about the close proximity.

He enjoyed his adrenaline rushes but did not like the idea of prison time. There was a difference between being exciting and being stupid. He enjoyed his freedom and was not prepared by any means to go down yet. On the other hand, Jessica could be right. He'd never had a target that was closer than a two-hour drive, so if he just did one, maybe it wouldn't hurt. He could do this to please her. Next time, he would be the one to find the target.

Finally, Bill nodded, "Okay. Let's do it."

Her face lit up. "Thank you, Bill."

He could see it in her eyes that this meant a lot to her. "Alright. But I need you to agree that next time you'll let me pick the target. Give me a list of what you're looking for, and I'll find someone." She agreed instantly.

"So, what's the profile?" He already had a good guess going but wanted to hear her confirm it.

"I was at the mall when she walked past me. She's a woman in her thirties. She'll be slender, and tall for a woman. Around 5'9 or 5'10, at least. She's blonde, but a particular shade of blonde, not platinum, white, or that fake orange looking shit. A natural medium blonde. More than that, she's got a certain look about her. She's sophisticated without trying. She has a natural classy air about her. Some women just have that look about them. You know what I mean?"

He nodded. He knew what she meant. And he knew exactly the type of woman she was describing. He stopped himself from feeling pity. "Is that all?"

Jessica shook her head. "One more thing. Her nose. This is very important. It's Greek—that means straight with no bumps or humps."

Bill nodded. "I know what a Greek nose is."

She looked into his eyes. "This is important to me, Bill. It's why I agreed to do this with you. It's like an itch I'm dying to scratch."

Bill knew all about itches that needed scratching and sympathized with her. "This is my itch now, too. Don't worry, we're gonna make this happen."

Bill wanted to ask about how she changed back and forth to Ashley. He wanted to know how it all worked; did she remember things? There were so many questions. He didn't want to scare her off, though, because he didn't know how to get her back if she disappeared. Bill left the interrogation for now. There would be time enough for that later.

20

Bill realized right off the bat, what kind of woman Jessica wanted. He was looking for a woman who looked identical to Joy Carter. The woman whose son drowned his. That's where Jessica's mind had instantly gone; how could it not? He wasn't surprised until he pulled up to the address she'd given him. Through the front window, he could see a woman walking around. Bill slammed his fist down on the center console in his car. Ashley hadn't just found a woman who looked identical, she'd found Joy herself.

Joy and her family were living in a two-story house, about twenty minutes from their local mall.

When they moved away after Chris died, Bill could've easily tracked Joy down, but he chose *not* to because he would've been too tempted to do something to her. He stayed away on purpose, not willing to push his luck. If one or all of the Carters wound up dead, there was no way in hell that the police wouldn't be looking in his and Ashley's direction. If he and Ashley didn't have a motive, he didn't know who would.

Now Jessica had found their address for him, despite his wanting to stay away. He sat in one of his cars, parked on the curb outside of the Carters' home. For a moment, Bill succumbed to the fantasy of what it might be like to get a little revenge. He leaned back in his seat and pictured the house at night.

Bill would make his way into the backyard before finding a way into the house. A smile formed on his lips as he thought about dragging the boy downstairs by his hair and drowning him in a bowl of water. They didn't have a pool anymore, so he would have to make do.

He would like to do something creative with Joy. Maybe he would drag her outside and tie her up first so she could watch her son drowning. *Yes, that would be better*, he thought. How painful would it be for her to see him suffocating in a few inches of liquid? Then, he would stab and slice until there was nothing left. He would leave the husband alone; he was innocent, after all. Bill played his imagined actions through his mind, reveling in the thought of how sweet revenge would feel. Then, he came back to reality. It was impossible. At least for now. He thought, *Jessica isn't going to be happy.*

She said she found her target at the mall, and maybe that was true, but maybe it wasn't. More likely, Jessica had tracked Joy down and conveniently the mall was close by. Well, Bill could use the damned mall to his advantage, too. He vowed to find the perfect target that was nearly identical to Joy. A woman that looked so much like her that Jessica would have to do a double take.

There was a moment where he asked himself why he should go through the effort just to please Jessica, but deep down, he already knew the answer. She intrigued him. He wanted her to be pleased so she would continue to please him. He *wanted* to work with her, to *play* with her, and if she was kept happy, he thought things would work out just fine for the both of them. Besides, having a target who looked just like Joy Carter would be pretty nice.

Bill spent the next month dedicated to the hunt. He didn't just limit himself to the local mall, he branched out to other areas, too. His aim was to find a target who was not only perfect, but had a nice routine that would be easy to follow. If he could get the routine down, it would be a piece of cake to bring Jessica along. He had his list of criteria, and after three weeks, Bill found her- the perfect woman for Jessica's first target.

PAMELA ARNOLD WAS A THIRTY-TWO-YEAR-OLD WOMAN WHO was married to a successful attorney. Her husband had been trying to go for partner in his law firm for the past several months. This meant that he was doing anything necessary to impress his associates. His efforts included, taking harder cases, putting in more hours at the office, going on undesirable business trips, and asking his wife to host dinner parties for his colleagues.

When Bill finally saw Pamela for the first time, her husband had just asked her to prepare for one of these dinner parties. Pamela went to the mall to get a new outfit and some new table linens, along with some other accessories for the dining room. She didn't like to use the same decor more than once or twice when hosting a party, and she'd already used her current decor last month.

When Pamela went to pay for her items at Nordstrom, Bill didn't just stop at spying Pamela's name on her credit card. He followed her out of the store, all the way to her parked Mercedes. He took a picture of the license plate while she was loading the trunk. It was lucky for him that their cars were parked in the same parking lot. Bill made his way to his own car, but by the time he pulled out of his parking spot, Pamela was already gone.

He was determined to follow this woman.

Bill pulled out his phone and dialed 911. "I just saw a woman break into a white Mercedes in the mall parking lot. She took off like a bat out of hell. I have the license plate number," he informed the operator. Then, he provided the details and told her he preferred to remain anonymous. After hanging up, he continued driving. It didn't take long before he heard sirens, telling him which way to go.

Bill laughed at the look on Pamela's face while he waited for the police officer to finish speaking with her. She looked like she was about to blow a gasket when he pulled her over. Despite this, she wasn't yelling or making a scene for the officer, and Bill admired her self-control. When Pamela finally continued on her way, Bill followed.

She led him straight home. Bill took down the address. This was the exact type of neighborhood that Joy was from, as he'd suspected. An upscale, suburban neighborhood with large two-story houses and built-in swimming pools. He imagined the backyard parties and barbecues that surely happened every summer, just like the Carters used to have..

When Bill took the opportunity to find Pamela again, it was to begin watching. It looked like they were having some sort of party because there were several cars parked in the driveway and along the curb in front of the house. Bill brought out his handheld listening device and put on the connected headphones. He pointed the satellite-like cone toward the house and listened.

After sitting in the car for an hour, Bill picked up enough information to know that Pamela and her husband were hosting an office party, and they seemed to be a bunch of lawyers. He also picked up that the husband was going to be on a business next month.

He came back to the house a few more times but didn't want to be recognized by any of the neighbors, so he set a limit for himself. He went to her husband's work and also followed Pamela out on some errands. The rest of his watching was done from inside their home. Once he was comfortable with her routine and *positive* that she was the one, he brought Jessica into the loop.

SINCE BILL HAD NO SUREFIRE WAY TO CONTACT JESSICA directly, he had to wait for her to appear. He was finding that she appeared more often when Ashley was pissed off or in a stressful situation. He'd been trying to experiment with different ways to bring Jessica out, and this was the best that he'd come up with so far. When Jessica made her next appearance, Bill confronted her about Joy.

"What kind of shit are you trying to pull?"

She was all innocence. "What do you mean?"

"You told me she was just some woman you saw at the mall. Did you really think I wasn't about to do my homework?"

Jessica turned away, unable to meet his gaze. She'd known he would find out, of course she'd known. She'd hoped that he would've just set everything up, and by the time all the effort was made, he would just allow it. Jessica was not passive like Ashley; she had fire in her, and when she was pissed, she made sure Bill knew about it.

"Why the hell can't I have her? There's *no* reason good enough!" The fire in her eyes was nearly burning a hole into him. If looks could kill, he'd be long dead.

Bill could feel how much she needed to hurt Joy, but he

couldn't allow it. "Look, I tried to explain it before. It's going to feel good as hell—"

"You're damned fucking right!"

He held up a placating hand. "But! It's going to be short-lived when you wind up in jail for the rest of your life. Trust me on this, woman. It's far better to take your revenge out on someone else, someone *unconnected*. You won't get caught, and one day, many years down the road, you'll finally be able to get to Joy."

"What if I don't care about jail? Let me rot for all I care."

Bill didn't like the question. Jessica might not care, but what about Ashley? There was no love lost on his side, but it still didn't sit right with him. Besides, it was more of his own ass he was worried about. "If you go down, how hard do you think it will be for them to connect me to it, too?"

Jessica knew he was right. Dammit, she knew. She didn't like it at all and didn't want to accept it. She wanted to scream her frustration. "How are they going to catch us if we make it look like an accident? And there are ways of causing pain that leave no physical evidence. I would be good with that!"

"Goddammit, Jess! I'm done with this. Stop being a child. I will not be a part of it." He was growing more impatient by the minute. After she stopped talking, he waited to make sure she was really going to shut up. Finally, he said, "Now, I found an alternative target that won't disappoint. I know it's not what you want, but I've already done the legwork. Are you interested?"

This seemed to grab her attention. She hadn't known what to expect of him, but really hadn't been expecting him to find someone else and so soon. "Who is it?"

"Her name is Pamela Arnold. As soon as I saw her, I knew she was the one for you."

"How did you find her?"

"Ironically, I found her at a mall." He smirked. "I followed her into Nordstrom, and when she paid at the register, I was close enough to make out her name on her credit card. Even if I didn't see her name on the card, the clerk said, 'Thank you, Ms. Arnold, have a fantastic day!'"

"Great customer service." Jessica rolled her eyes.

"After that, I followed her home, and the rest is gravy."

"Wow, it's really that easy?"

"Yup. Usually is."

"Bill, that's kinda scary."

He laughed. "You'd be surprised."

21

By the time Pamela's husband was ready to leave for his business trip, Bill was ready to pick her up. He had a rural location secured about twenty miles out of the city. There was an abandoned barn on an old farm that would work well for their needs. He had a feeling that Jessica was going to want to hear some screaming, which meant that he needed to make sure no one else would be around to hear it. The stage was all set. Really, his only question was whether Jessica would show up on time or make him wait.

WHEN SHE OPENED HER EYES, ASHLEY WAS IN AN UNFAMILIAR place. She looked around, blinking in confusion. At first, she thought she might be dreaming because she was sitting in the passenger seat of a car. Then, she felt the familiar pounding in her head. She knew if she was dreaming, she wouldn't be feeling the pain. *How did I wind up here?* she wondered. She couldn't remember leaving the house.

Ashley looked out the window to see a large two-story

home. Glancing at the other houses nearby, she realized she was in an unfamiliar neighborhood. Ashley was beginning to be frightened. The frequency with which she was winding up in places, not knowing how she got there, was increasingly happening and starting to concern her. She imagined she might be doing things in her sleep, like a sleepwalker.

Ashley wondered who'd been driving the car. She didn't know what kind of car it was, but didn't think that she knew anyone with one like it. Was she supposed to be waiting for someone? Ashley was about to get out to look around when she saw Bill walking down the sidewalk. He had his arm around a woman's shoulders. She looked like was stumbling all over and might be hurt. Ashley rolled down the window and called out to him. "Bill?"

It wasn't the concern in her voice that made him jump; it was her voice itself. Ashley's soft melodic voice sounded completely different from Jessica's huskier tone. As soon as he heard her, he realized Ashley was back. He'd known it was a possibility for Ashley to show up, but somehow, didn't think it would happen. Jessica always seemed so in control. He would have to have a chat with her later about how she did things.

Bill came around to the back of the car to put Pamela in the back seat. She'd already been given a sedative, and as soon as she hit the seat, she passed out. Bill racked his brain for something to tell Ashley. He got in and drove. "Bill, what's going on?"

"What do you mean?"

"What are we doing with that woman? Why am I here with you and not at the house? Why the hell don't I remember leaving the house?" She took a breath. "Whose car is this? Do I need to keep going?"

"What do you mean you don't remember leaving the house?"

"Exactly what I just said! I. Do. Not. Remember." She was steadily raising her voice as she lost her temper.

Bill was trying to confuse her, upset her, anything to raise her blood pressure. He needed Jessica to come forward again because this was damned awkward. "Look, you're being really weird. The lady in back is Joe's wife. You remember Joe from work, right?" He said it with a condescending tone that he hoped would grate on her nerves.

"Why is she passed out?"

"What?" He glanced in the rearview mirror. "She's not."

"Bill, that woman is asleep." Ashley looked at Pamela again, studying her.

There was nothing else for it. Bill was done dealing with Ashley. This was happening today, and he wasn't about to let her get in the way. He pulled over to the side of the road. When the car was stopped, Bill threw it into park. Ashley began to ask another question, but he didn't give her time. He reached back and punched her with his full force. There was a sickening crunch and for a moment, he feared he broke her nose. Her head whipped back, and she passed out from the single blow.

Bill squeezed the steering wheel in frustration. This was the second time he'd hit her now. He felt like he was losing control. He thought, *this damn woman.*

He hadn't wanted to hit her, but it worked. She was out cold, and if she woke up as Ashley again, at least he would have some time to think. He would make sure Jessica was back before he got started on Pamela, but Bill needed to be able to drive without all the questions. He reached into his bag for some sedative and injected her. Then, he put the car into drive and continued on.

Bill's black semi was waiting in front of the old barn with the empty trailer attached. Part of the plan involved Bill driving his sedan into the trailer. If the police were looking for a car that fit its description, it would be out of sight. If anyone in Pamela's neighborhood had seen him drive away, he would be a target. Bill had extra license plates waiting to be switched out, too. Everything was ready in the trailer. With both women sedated, he had plenty of time to prepare their workspace, get the women out of the car, and move the car into the trailer.

When Ashley's sedative wore off, Bill didn't have to wait long for Jessica to show up. When she opened her eyes, it was Jessica's icy blue ones that looked back at him. He gave a thankful sigh of relief. "You want to tell me what that was about earlier?"

She looked annoyed. "Look, I don't have control all the time, okay? I don't need you giving me shit."

"You don't need me giving you shit?! Woman, I'm the one who has to deal with the repercussions."

"I don't know what else you want me to say. I can't control her all the time." She was done talking about it. "Are we ready to roll or what?"

He let it drop. Now wasn't the time, but he would have to address it again later. He needed some answers. "Yeah. Everything is ready, and she's waking up."

"Excellent."

Jessica had a look of eager excitement in her eyes. She was fired up and ready to get started. Bill laughed with pleasure, seeing her like this made him just as eager as she was. Although Jessica had been present for Roxy and finished her off, she hadn't been there for the entire experience.

She confided in Bill that it had been her first time taking a life. He wanted to take things as slowly as she needed this time, to nurture her passion and creativity. He had already given her an idea of what he would do with Pamela, but he was giving the reigns to Jessica this time, since this was her target. Jessica was fully aware that today, it was in her hands. Bill would be on the sidelines, watching.

Inside the old barn, Bill had prepared plastic sheeting on the ground, with Pamela tied, laying in the middle. She wasn't moving yet but was just beginning to wake up. Her wrists were bound with rope, and her legs were also tied together at the knees and ankles. Her feet were bare, but she was otherwise fully dressed. She was on her left side with her knees slightly bent. Her mouth was left ungagged.

Gloves and other supplies and tools, including a gag and roll of duct tape, were laid out neatly on the ground next to the plastic sheeting for Jessica and himself to use as desired. He'd left Pamela without a gag, thinking Jessica might enjoy the sound of her suffering, but in case he was wrong, it was better to be prepared. He had a chair set up for himself to sit in and observe. It was placed so that he would be sitting near Pamela's feet, looking up the length of her. There was enough plastic laid out, that it would catch any bodily fluid that was flung, sprayed, splattered, dropped, or otherwise spread over the course of the next few hours.

Jessica looked down at Pamela, lying unconscious on the plastic sheeting. Her breath caught as she realized just how much the woman looked like Joy. Bill had chosen well. She glanced at him; he nodded, and then she turned toward the instruments that he'd arranged for her. Everything was very basic, and mostly everyday things that you might find around the house. But each item could be used as a tool to inflict pain, if looked at with imagination.

Kneeling, Jessica selected a metal nail file to start with. She picked it up and sat on top of Pamela. Holding onto her bound wrists with one hand, Jessica used the other to drive the fingernail file underneath Pamela's right index fingernail. She forced it in as deep as it would go, and then pulled it out and jammed it in again as hard as she could.

The Wrong Stranger

Blood began leaking out, and Pamela was wide awake now. She began to scream when Jessica drove the fingernail file in for a third time, prying the fingernail off. She tried to wiggle and buck Jessica off, but the adrenaline coursing through her was not strong enough to overpower the drug Bill had used as a sedative. Pamela was awake, yes, but still weak.

Jessica only laughed and moved onto the next finger. She used all the force she had in her to continue driving the fingernail file from finger to finger, until all the fingernails on Pamela's right hand had come off. Her hand was soaked in blood now, and Jessica continued onto Pamela's left hand.

She was using so much force, that a few of the fingernails came off with just one blow. But her aim wasn't to just take her fingernails off. It was the pain. She wanted to cause Pamela as much pain as possible, and the more Jessica continued to ram the fingernail file into her, the more violent and enthusiastic she grew.

Picking up a common household lighter, Jessica raised the bottom of Pamela's blouse up and tucked it in under her chin. Pamela's voice was hoarse from screaming and crying, but she croaked out the expected, "Why are you doing this?" Jessica ignored her, holding the ignited lighter to her midsection. Pamela cried anew, using everything she had to try to get away. The smell of burning flesh wafted in the air.

Jessica drew back with her free hand and slapped Pamela across the face, over and over again, still holding the lighter with her other hand. With a low growl, she said, "We're just getting started, bitch."

Jessica rolled Pamela over so she was lying on her stomach, face turned to the left, so that she didn't suffocate on the plastic. She had Bill assist with holding Pamela down while she then took two lengths of rope and stretched them to two of the open beams in the barn. She untied Pamela's legs and spread them wide. Then, she re-tied each of them to the longer lengths of rope, as tight as possible, so that she was spread wide and couldn't force her legs shut no matter how hard she tried.

Bill was surprised that Jessica wanted her in this position and was excited to see what would come of it. With the legs taken care of, Jessica took a final long length of rope and fastened it to a beam that was closer to Pamela's hands. She didn't spread them, but left them bound at the wrists. Now that Pamela was attached to the beams, Jessica didn't have to sit on top of her to hold her still, and Bill returned to his chair to watch.

Reaching for a tool belt, Jessica picked up the hacksaw, holding it in front of Pamela's face. This got an even more violent reaction from Pamela. She couldn't move an inch, but she thrashed her head around and tried to move her hips and butt, but instead, made it look like she was trying to hump the plastic sheeting. Jessica cackled. Pamela wailed and pleaded, begging for Jessica to stop, praying to God for mercy, and telling Bill that she would pay anything he wanted if he would just make this crazy bitch stop.

Both Bill and Jessica were amused by the howls and wails, but otherwise ignored her.

Jessica moved down to where Pamela's legs were spread wide. She took the hacksaw, placed it against Pamela's inner thigh, and began cutting away. The saw ripped through the material and into Pamela's sensitive flesh, tearing away both her meat and her jeans. Jessica was not slow and gentle, but moved the saw back and forth viciously with a madness that consumed her. When she finished with one leg, she moved to the next, until finally what was left of the pants fell off. Both women were covered in blood and chunks of flesh.

When she was done cutting, Jessica positioned herself so that she had maximum leverage. She began to swing a hammer high and drive down as hard as she could. She pounded the hammer over and over again until blood was flowing once again. Then, she turned the handle around and used the hammer's claw to rip away at the inside of Pamela.

Jessica took her time, enjoying every scream, every cry, and every ounce of pain that she drew. Bill was right to not gag Pamela. Her cries of agony only made Jessica want to do more and more. She ground her teeth together and snarled when Pamela howled for her to stop. She moved onto using scissors and knives, and she also used other instruments that she could stab with, but might not go in quite as nice. Her favorite was a pair of tweezers. The tips on the tweezers were blunt but slanted. When Jessica positioned them in her palm, she slammed them down into Pamela hard enough to just break through the barrier of her skin. They weren't long enough to go very deep, but the blunt tips caused more pain than they would have if they were sharpened.

At one point, Jessica took a towel and held it over Pamela's nose and mouth. She yanked her head back by the hair with one hand, and with the other, pushed the towel into her face. She glared into Pamela's eyes as she suffocated. Pamela's eyes grew wide with the lack of oxygen. She could not move or fight; she was completely helpless as Jessica held her still, watching the life leave her. Jessica wanted her to feel it. Wanted her to be afraid. Wanted her to feel what Chris felt. She finally let go just before Pamela was about to black out.

Once she began, Jessica was in her own world, and the only two people in it were herself and Pamela. But Jessica wasn't seeing Pamela. She was seeing Joy. She'd nearly forgotten Bill, who was still in his chair, watching. He had been so turned-on watching Jessica, that he'd taken himself in his own hand before she was finished, but was still not sated. He was beginning to think that he almost loved watching her as much as he loved doing it himself.

She was so passionate, and the anger that flashed in her eyes was pure evil. Bill recognized it and related to it on a deeper level than expected. He thought that the look in his own eyes was probably very similar to hers. He hadn't been sure on what to expect from Jessica. Bill initially thought that she might back out or be too nervous to perform, but then he remembered how she had handled Roxy. No, he knew deep down that she was meant for this. It was a part of her. She was born for it, just like he was, and she wouldn't let him down.

Although Bill had no desire to get up out of his chair or end the night, Their time in the barn was limited. He'd been keeping a close eye on his watch, allowing Jessica several hours to play while he enjoyed watching her. Even when Jessica didn't notice that Pamela was already dead, and no longer crying out in agony, she continued her effort to cause pain. Bill didn't interfere. He let her do her thing.

Only when the time on the clock was running low, he got up from his chair and stopped her. He'd left plenty of time for sex and was glad that he did, because they were both hot and ready. Ignoring the mess, Bill took her standing up against an open beam in the barn.

The entire time that they'd been there, Bill had a nagging feeling in the back of his mind that Ashley would show up again. He was nervous for the first time in a very long time, and it both annoyed and excited him. He never had to worry about his wife before, but now with Jessica, things were different. Eventually, the excitement overruled anything else. He decided that if she *did* show up, it would be no matter because he would just kill her. He didn't want to, and hoped it didn't come to that, but he would do what was needed if push came to shove.

But she didn't come back. It was just Jessica, Pamela, and himself until Pamela passed on, and the two lovers were left alone. They agreed that Bill would find the next target while he was working and would watch for a few months until making a move again.

22

EIGHT MONTHS LATER

On the last Saturday before Halloween, Maggie Harris looked out the window of her apartment, experiencing the Pacific Northwest weather phenomenon. She was from out of state, moving to the Seattle area three months ago to attend school. Being in the region for only a short while, she was poorly prepared for what the day held.

She smiled at the sunlight pouring through the window when she started the day. Maggie had already learned that sunshine could be a rarity in Washington and was immensely enjoying it. When she stepped onto the balcony, the sun shining down was comforting and warm.

She left her apartment, and by the time she was down the stairs to the parking lot, the sun was already gone. Maggie had left her sweatshirt upstairs. She had an internal debate about running back up to grab it but finally decided against it since she was already running late.

As Maggie got into her car, she felt her phone vibrating. Looking at the caller ID first, she answered, "Hey, girl."

Her friend Maya, who shared two classes with her, cried, "Bae! Where you at?"

"I'm getting in the car now."

"'Kay. I'm early for once!" She laughed. "I already picked up Erica, and we're about five minutes from the farm."

Maggie laughed, too. "Look at you! Okay, well you're gonna be there way before me, then."

"No worries. You've waited on me plenty of times! We'll hang out at the giftshop and grab some cider."

"Okay. I'll try to hurry. Is traffic bad?"

"Nah, not too bad."

"'Kay, see you soon!"

MAGGIE HUNG UP. SHE TURNED HER CAR ON AND DROVE toward the pumpkin farm where she and her friends planned to meet for the afternoon. Maggie drove separately because she had work scheduled for later in the day. She planned on spending the morning and afternoon at the farm, then heading to work straight after. The farm was an hour away from her apartment, and as she was on her way, the weather began to make a dramatic turn.

She was about halfway to the farm, on a rural highway, when drops of rain began to splat on her windshield. It was light at first, but intensified within minutes. It didn't take long before Maggie had her windshield wipers on full blast, but the rain was still pounding her windshield so hard that she couldn't see through it. The sound of the downpour was so loud that it drowned out her radio. She could barely hear herself think and couldn't see a thing through the windshield.

Growing flustered, Maggie turned off the radio, then slowed down. She was in a hurry to meet her friends, so she feared slowing down too much. Guilt clenched in her gut as she thought of Maya and Erica waiting for her in boredom. *The weather was supposed to be sunny today,* she thought. She shivered as the temperature fell. Her heater wasn't working; she'd been meaning to get it fixed before winter. Maggie was beginning to worry that they would all be forced to turn right around and go back home because of the rain. Her mind was racing with emotions, and although she had slowed the car down, she hadn't slowed nearly enough for the present conditions.

Maggie had a thought that Maya might try to call her again, but with the volume of the rain, there was no way she could hear the phone. Her small backpack she used as a purse was sitting on the front passenger seat. Thinking her phone was inside, Maggie reached with her right hand. Slowly, she wiggled the zipper up and over to the other side, creating an opening for her hand to reach through.

The highway curved as she climbed in elevation. She reached into her bag for her phone but didn't feel it. Her brow furrowed in frustration. "Where the hell is that damned thing?" She continued to feel around for it for a few seconds. Still not finding it, she picked up the bag and pulled it onto her lap. Maggie felt the bumps from the tires getting too close to the side of the road. She looked up and swerved as she almost drove right off the edge of a cliff.

She corrected the steering wheel just in time, panting from fear and nerves. Maggie had the idea of pulling over to wait out the rain, but again checked the clock. She was already so late. She looked down into her bag, now on her lap, and clearly saw that the phone wasn't there. Out of the corner of her eye, she noticed it sitting in the cup holder. There was enough time for her to think, *Seriously,* before her car plowed into the three-hundred-pound deer that jumped into the road when she'd been looking down.

Maggie wasn't driving fast, but it was fast enough. The

buck's antlers punched through the windshield, straight into Maggie. It was like hitting a brick wall with spikes attached to it. Maggie screamed with surprise and pain. The front end of her Geo Metro scrunched up like an accordion, and the back window blew out. Since she wasn't looking at the road when her car hit the deer, she didn't apply the breaks or try to turn the car away. The buck was now attached to her car through the windshield, but his side was also mutilated and fused with the front of it.

The car came to an abrupt stop. Neither Maggie nor the buck were dead. For a brief moment, the world was still. Maggie and the buck both panted with fear and pain, not completely sure of what just happened. Maggie has been stabbed by the buck's antlers in her right arm and shoulder. She was in agony with blood steadily leaking out of her. She heard nothing but her own heartbeat in her ears and the distant sound of rain on the car.

She began to shiver from shock and cold. The rain has let up a little now, not pouring down anymore. She turned her head to look at where the antler pierced her skin. Grimacing, she clenched her teeth and attempted to pull the antler out of her arm. Maggie was following her first survival instinct: to get free. She wasn't thinking about the antler still being attached to the deer's head or wondering if the deer was still alive. She was lucky to be alive herself, and the first thought that went through her mind was, *Get out of the car.*

When Maggie pulled on the antlers, it set the buck into motion. He began to thrash his head in all directions, violently kicking his legs and twisting his body. He was trapped on top of the demolished car, unable to free himself. With each move that he made, his antlers ripped into Maggie's flesh, drilling and tearing away. She let out a guttural cry. Maggie was unable to free herself from the deer. She was pinned to him like a piece of meat at the end of a stick. She tried pushing back in her seat, but it did nothing. Her cries of agony did nothing but scare the deer more. She reached for the door, thinking if she could just get out, she could get free, but the deer's legs were kicking right where her door was. If she fell out of the car, the deer would probably kick her to death, although she thought it could still be better than being stabbed to death by his antlers.

Maggie pulled the door handle, trying to push the door open. She was pinned, with the deer still going at it, so movement of any kind took an immense amount of effort for her. Maggie could push the door open with her left leg, but had to hold her foot at the base of the door to keep it open. She reached with her left arm, trying to grab for anything, so she could pull herself free.

As she was doing this, she heard the air horn of a semi-truck. Panic washed over her anew. Filling her mind was the image of a semi plowing into her tiny, smashed car. She heard the air horn a second time, this time much louder. She reached out toward the door, grasping at nothing but air. Her heart was racing, and she was crying, all the while the deer was still ripping into her. She was able to reach her left arm up and hold on to the roof of the car. Finally, she could pull.

She was still holding the door open with her left foot when she began pulling herself free. The buck's legs pounded against the window of the door. She was sweating with effort, and when the air horn blared for a third time, she was scared half to death. It was right behind her. The sound startled both Maggie and the buck. Her foot slipped from the door, and when he kicked against it again, the door slammed onto her hand. Maggie howled as she felt the bones in her hand snap. With as much strength as she could muster, she kicked back at the door to free her broken hand. She looked at the damage. She couldn't bend her hand. Her fingers felt tingly. There was also a deep gash on the outside of her hand where the edge of the door had pressed into her skin.

Feeling more trapped now than ever, Maggie closed her eyes and cried out, "Please! Get me out of this!" There was a gunshot. Her eyes flew open. A man was standing outside the car, holding a smoking pistol. He had shot the buck in the head, stilling it. Maggie began crying even harder, now from relief instead of hopelessness.

She heard the man saying, "Hang on! I'll get you outta there!" He pulled the door open and freed her from both the antlers and her prison. "We gotta get out of the middle of this road." Dazed, Maggie agreed.

They were on a rural highway, at least twenty minutes from the nearest town. There were no houses close by, that she could see. The only thing she did see were endless trees and a massive black semi. The highway had some mild curves and hills, making it even more dangerous because of the blind corners for oncoming traffic.

The man handed her a cloth. "For your arm." He grimaced at her mutilation. She took it with a shaking hand. She was in shock, but still knew that she needed to stop the bleeding. Maggie's whole body was shaking; she felt so cold. The man said, "Lucky I was sittin' high in my rig, or I wouldna seen ya." She was too shaken to speak to him, but nodded her understanding. Maggie stood back while he used his truck to push her car off to the side of the highway.

The deer was still lying on top, lifeless now. Maggie was in a trance, staring at the creature that was so majestic and yet caused so much damage. She saw the cuts and broken glass in his fur, the blood draining out of his body, and she saw how he was caught in the car. Pity filled her heart. Despite her injuries and pain, she felt guilty for hitting him and ending his life. No wonder he'd been thrashing about. The poor animal had been suffering as much as she was. She didn't blame the deer for the accident. He was just in the wrong place at the wrong time.

The semi driver finally climbed out of his cab and walked back to Maggie. They were a ways out, but she was expecting to at least hear some distant sirens by now. Surely, he'd called 911 when he first came upon her, hadn't he? Glancing each way down the road, she saw that there were no other cars in sight. As if he could read her thoughts, he said, "It'll be faster if I take you to the hospital. Waitin' on an ambulance'll take too long."

Maggie was relieved that this stranger was being so kind. She knew that truck drivers had schedules to keep, and for him to help her like this was not just a relief, but also a blessing. This man had saved her life, and now he was going to go out of his way to take her to a hospital. Maggie was indebted to this man. She vowed she would send him a thank-you card every year for the rest of her life.

The driver helped Maggie up into the passenger side of the truck. "There's a bed in back, go ahead'n lay down. You look like you're freezin'."

Still shaking, Maggie started, "Oh no, I couldn't," but he had already walked away. When he got in on the driver's side, she was sitting in the front passenger seat in excruciating pain.

He started the truck, then looked at her. "You'll feel a lot better if you have a lay down."

She was afraid. For one, Maggie didn't know if she could stay on the bed while he drove, and the thought of falling off made her cringe. She had never been in a semi before, and looking at the bed in back, she didn't know how anyone could sleep back there at all, even if the truck wasn't moving. There was a small cupboard and fridge, which might prevent her from falling out of bed, but she thought at the very least, she would hit them while the truck bounced around.

The Wrong Stranger

Maggie was in so much pain that the thought of being tossed around back there frightened her.

And two, Maggie was afraid that if she fell asleep, she wouldn't wake back up. She felt weak from blood loss. Maggie swore she remembered watching a documentary about people that had significant blood loss or other major injuries being told that they weren't supposed to go to sleep. Her mind was muddled, though, and she couldn't focus on her thoughts.

She didn't know how long it was since she watched that stupid show and thought she might have her information confused. Maybe it was head injuries where you weren't supposed to go to sleep. Maybe sleeping didn't matter at all. Now she didn't know what she remembered or what she knew. She didn't want to look like an idiot, on top of everything else, so she didn't mention her concern.

Instead, she said, "Won't I fall off the bed while you drive?"

He gave a full belly laugh at that. "No. Trust me, you won't even notice the truck movin'." By now, he had already begun driving. Sitting in the front, Maggie was surprised at how nice the ride was, and she began to believe that sleeping in back might not be so bad. Never being in a semi before, she hadn't known what to think, other than thinking that a big truck had to be pretty bouncy.

"Okay, I'm going to lie down until we get to the hospital. Thank you so much for this. And thank you for saving my life." A tear fell down her cheek.

"I'm just glad to a showed up in time to help."

Maggie maneuvered her way into the back, but it was hard in such a small space to move as little as possible and not bump herself. As she was navigating her way back, the driver said, "There's some bottled water in the fridge, if you're thirsty." Until hearing the word "water," Maggie hadn't realized how thirsty she actually was. Now she felt her dry throat and lips. She swallowed, feeling the sting of a parched throat.

"Thank you, I really appreciate it." She opened the small fridge to take out a water bottle. She twisted the lid open, not noticing that the safety seal had already been broken.

Suddenly, Maggie felt as if she was dying of thirst. She chugged the entire bottle, then sighed in relief. The driver laughed again. "Thirsty?"

"Not anymore." She smiled as she laid down. She was resting on her left side with her injured left hand raised above her head. Maggie felt her eyelids droop but fought the urge to pass out. She thought she was as comfortable as possible for the moment, which was a good thing, but she still had a gnawing feeling that she needed to stay awake. The longer she fought the feeling, though, the harder it was. She began to feel not just tired, but loopy, too. It was like she couldn't think straight. She felt drunk.

Out of nowhere, she remembered her friends. How could she have forgotten them? The idea of Maya and Erica waiting for her at the pumpkin farm hit her. "Oh! I need to call my friends. They're waiting for me." The sleepy feeling began to overtake her. She barely had the energy to keep her eyes open.

"Don't worry, Maya and Erica will have fun without you."

When she processed what he said, alarm bells went off in her head. "How did you kno—" but it was too late. Maggie crossed into nothingness.

Bill continued driving on the abandoned highway. He was not headed toward a hospital, but farther into wilderness. About an hour away, there was a cabin in the woods where Jessica was waiting. When Bill pulled his semi off the highway into the hidden driveway, he drove farther into the trees, which hid both the truck and any evidence of a human presence.

Maggie was still sound asleep, so he carried her into the cabin. There was no one around for miles and miles. No one heard Maggie's cries of terror and anguish or the sinister sounds of a man and woman laughing at every scream. No one heard the power tools that were used to sever limbs or the sounds of a couple having sex with both each other and their victim while they tortured and mutilated her body. And no one heard or saw that couple clean up and leave the property, to continue living normal lives as if nothing had happened at all.

23

SIX MONTHS AGO

Federal Agent Dan Sumner had been the lead investigator on a missing persons case for over a year. It was really more of a missing people case because it involved the disappearance of four women, three teenage girls, and two little boys, across eight states that they knew of. Some of these people had been missing for much longer, but their cases had only been more closely examined when a special task force was created.

He was on that special task force, working in conjunction with the local police for each individual missing person. There was evidence to suggest that all of these missing people were kidnapped and taken by the same person or people. Some on the task force suggested the incidents weren't related, as there wasn't enough evidence to support it. They implied it was a waste of time trying to connect all the cases. But Dan didn't believe that and neither did his superiors, which was why the task force had been assembled.

There were too many similarities between the cases to just be coincidences. For instance, all four women had told a friend or family member that there was a strange car parked on their street for a period of time before they went missing. The cars were all different, but that didn't deter Dan. The minors had all been runaways. In all of their cases, the last known location was either at a gas station, a rest stop, or along a highway.

Ordinarily, runaways would not be included on a special task force, especially with no bodies found. But in this instance, there had been a body found. One of the teenage girls was found in the same county that one of the little boys was last seen. In another of the teenage girl cases, a white Toyota was seen picking her up, and a white Toyota was seen also in one of the missing women's neighborhoods. They were all linked, and it was Dan's job to fit the pieces of the puzzle together.

Most of the evidence linking the victims was circumstantial, but Dan had a gut feeling. He was good at what he did, and he *knew* these cases were all tied. Someone out there was smart, and probably had a lot of money to work with, but Dan was determined to get him. The detective in him also didn't think that any of the other missing persons were alive, despite only finding one body so far. He ran things as if they were looking for bodies, not live individuals.

In a digital age, where endless information is available at the touch of a finger, Dan often liked to do things the old school way. He felt like sometimes too much information was a bad thing. He wanted to get inside the head of a serial kidnapper/murderer to get a better picture of what move he might make or have made next. There was a profiler on the task force that had been working with the team, but Dan still liked to do his own profiling, too. He thought it couldn't hurt to have more than one of them looking from that angle. Dan didn't like relying so heavily on another person on the team.

He had been an investigator for ten years, but this was his first potential serial killer case.

His idea was to brush up on serial killer psychology at the local library. Dan thought that if he stepped away from the case and found some books by actual PhDs who knew what they were talking about, not an internet blogger who might say anything, he would get a better picture in his head. After a year of working on this case, he was willing to try anything to get a step ahead. All the leads had been running cold, and this guy wasn't leaving them much to work with in the first place. Dan figured that sitting down for a day or two in a library couldn't hurt.

He sat down at a table with an arm full of psychology books. Spreading them, he took up the entire library table with open books and notepaper. Across from Dan's table was the children's section of the library. Each time he glanced up from a book to think, he saw the area full of children's books and toys.

WHEN SHE OPENED HER EYES, DAISY FELT LETHARGIC AND disoriented. She felt like she'd been asleep for years. When she reached her arms out to stretch, she hit something hard with her left fist. "Ow!" She was sitting in a car. She didn't remember getting into a car and didn't know whose car she was in.

Her blood ran cold as she began to hyperventilate. This wasn't the first time that she'd woken up in a strange place without remembering how she'd gotten there. "I need to get some help," she whispered between breaths. With that thought in mind, she was able to calm herself down a little. She told herself over and over, "It's okay. I'm going to get help. It's okay, I'm going to get help."

The Wrong Stranger

Daisy looked through the window, seeing she was in a park and ride parking lot. Nothing looked familiar. She had no idea what city she was in, so she pulled up the GPS on her dashboard. She was only a few miles from her old home, where she'd grown up. *Why am I back here again?* It had been years since she'd run away, and the last thing in the world that she wanted was to go back.

Looking around the car for a cell phone, she fumbled through the center console and glove box. When she found it, she started a quick search for local psychiatrists. When she finally made a choice for a Dr. Jason Barnes, she made the call. The phone rang, then an automated voice came on, "If you think you're having a psychiatric emergency, hang up and call 911 or go to the nearest hospital." Daisy tried to think if what she was having was an emergency before anyone answered the phone.

As she considered it, the idea rooted that if she was having an emergency, this doctor's office wouldn't help her. The recording had just told her to hang up and go to a hospital. She hung up the phone. Daisy thought that yes, it was an emergency—not remembering how she wound up somewhere, but was it *enough* of an emergency to go straight to the hospital? She didn't think so. It wasn't exactly a life and death situation.

She didn't *want* to go to a hospital. Fear crept in. Her palms turned sweaty, and her hands began to shake. She felt her heart race and knew that a panic attack was setting in again. They were so easy to come to her; it seemed like anything could set her off. She was eternally anxious.

Daisy tried to breathe through it. She closed her eyes, telling herself she was so stupid for panicking over nothing. "You are not having a panic attack. You got in the car to go for a drive. You remember. You remember. You remember. You remember." She would not go to a hospital. If she was having an emergency, she would help herself through it, like she always did. She would not go. If a psychiatrist didn't want to help people with emergencies, then she would help herself. She thought about what would make her feel better.

Her favorite things in the world, when she was a girl, had been her dolly and her book. She wondered if she could find a toy store. The thought of holding a doll again made her smile. It had been a long time. Those two childhood things were what got her through some of her toughest, loneliest times. Daisy got back on the GPS, searching for a toy store, but there were none. "Okay, what now?" She kept taking slow, deep breaths, trying to stay calm. Her head was starting to ache, and that was always a bad sign. She'd been plagued by headaches as far back as she could remember. She kept breathing slow, deep breaths. Then, another idea came. Daisy would go to the nearest library.

When Daisy was a girl, there was nothing she wanted more than the love of her parents. She owned a single book, and every now and then, she would get her mom or dad to read it to her. It was seldom, but when one of them would finally sit down and read, she remembered feeling so happy and loved. That little book, along with her dolly, got her through a tough childhood. They kept her company when she felt especially lonely, and they gave her an escape into a magical world. One of the best ways for her to cope with her panic attacks was to escape into the world of her book. The nearest public library would surely help her now.

At the library, she found the children's section. It was right across from the work center where tables were spread out, occupied by people reading, doing research, or working on various projects. It wasn't very busy, but there were still

The Wrong Stranger

some people scattered about. In the children's section, Daisy was the only adult that wasn't with a child. She didn't seem to notice, though. A little girl was playing with some toys while her older brother was picking out a book with the help of his mom. The girl gave Daisy a shy smile.

Daisy smiled back, then turned away before her head really started to ache. She was beginning to think about what she would've done to have a mom that would've taken her to the library, to spend time with her, to love her like that woman loved her kids. But it was thoughts like these that brought on the headaches. She couldn't think about it. Couldn't remember. If she did, her head would hurt until it exploded into darkness for who knew how long. It felt like she'd been in the dark for so long, and she dreaded going back. If she did, that was when she would wake up somewhere else. Somewhere that she didn't remember going to.

Daisy looked through the selection of children's books, pulling some from the shelves and making a small stack in her arms. Her favorites were the ones with bright colors and cheerful faces. If the book had a family on it, it was a plus. She took her time meandering through the choices until her stack had grown too heavy to carry with one arm. She took her stack and sat on the circular floor rug that was placed in the middle of the children's section. Then, she lay on her stomach and began to read her chosen books.

She paid no mind to anyone else in the library. As Daisy read, she was immersed in a whole new world, with no worries. She smiled and laughed out loud, enjoying every moment of each children's story. She laughed so much that other people began to stare. Some looked at her with understanding, and some with annoyance, but no one bothered her.

Dan was deep in thought, reading a textbook that seemed

to apply to his exact investigation when the sound of a woman's laughter broke him out of his trance. When he looked up, he saw a woman lying on the ground in the children's section. She was rolling with laughter, clapping her hands with mirth.

He smirked, thinking never in a million years would he be able to enjoy himself so much in a public library. Dan couldn't even remember it as a kid. He smiled but tried to ignore her, turning back to his book and trying to let his thoughts drown out the sounds of her laughter. Dan began to read again, but kept losing his place. Each time he started over, her laughter would ring out, making him want to look at her. She had such a pleasant laugh that sounded almost musical. Dan glanced at his watch. He sighed, then closed the book.

He got up from his table, deciding to approach the crazy lady who was having a party for one in the middle of the library. Standing next to her, he cleared his throat. She didn't seem to notice him. She didn't look up, and he suddenly felt awkward like he was looming over her, so he kneeled down. As he did, her laughter stopped, and she finally looked at him. Her face grew sober as her startled emerald eyes met his.

Dan's breath caught when he finally saw her face. She was the most beautiful woman that he'd ever seen. She had a natural beauty that Dan thought was extremely rare. Her cheeks were flushed pink from her laughter, long strawberry blonde hair was tousled, and freckles stood out on her pale skin. Her eyelashes seemed to go for miles. He had to clear his throat again after forgetting what he'd come over to say in the first place.

Daisy gave a wary smile at the man who kneeled beside her. He was ruggedly good looking, with dark hair and the

The Wrong Stranger

brightest blue eyes that she'd ever seen. She realized she may have been enjoying herself too much, and now he was going to ask her to shut it. She blushed, embarrassed at what she must look like. But instead, he surprised her by smiling back at her.

"Mind if I ask what you're reading? It seems to be something good." Her blush deepened. She looked down, trying to hide it. While she looked down at the floor, she held the book up toward the man.

"I'm sorry." Her voice was so low that Dan could barely make it out. It was also cracking, as if she was fighting back tears.

"Oh, no! No, I'm sorry. I didn't mean- I—" He felt like an ass. He didn't mean to make her cry. "Shit. I'm sorry. I didn't mean to offend you. You have such a nice laugh. I couldn't resist coming over to say hi. That's all. I'll leave you alone."

When he turned to walk away, she looked up in his direction. "Wait." She stood up, grasping his hand for support when he offered it. "I'm overly sensitive. Please, just forget this whole thing ever happened. I'm so embarrassed. I really didn't mean to disturb anyone."

"No, I'm an idiot. I didn't mean to make you uncomfortable. What you must think, having a stranger approach you like this." Now he was the one blushing. God, what was he thinking? He was wasting his time putting his foot in his mouth when he should be doing research.

Daisy snorted. "What you must think seeing some lady laughing and rolling around on the library floor."

Dan laughed. "All I saw was a beautiful stranger that I couldn't resist talking to. Look, can I buy you a cup of coffee?"

Daisy was shocked. Her jaw dropped from surprise. No one had ever asked her to coffee before. At least, not that she remembered. She didn't know what to do or how to behave. Was he playing some kind of joke on her? She felt the cold hands of fear working their way up her chest again, tightening around her lungs.

Her head began to ache so badly, all she wanted to do was lie back down and take a nap. The pain was pulsing behind her eyes. She willed it to pass, knowing that if she gave in, she probably would never see this man again. Daisy saw darkness creeping into the corners of her vision. She fought it back, refusing to give into the panic. She wasn't ready to say goodbye to this stranger yet.

Dan saw her face going pale and wanted to punch himself. What was it with this woman? He couldn't say a damned thing right. He wanted to make things okay with her. He didn't feel right about this encounter but was starting to think it would be best to walk the hell away. She would have a hell of a story to tell her friends, and they could all laugh at the idiot who tried flirting with her in the library.

He started to apologize again, but she spoke before he had the chance. "What's your name?"

"Dan. Dan Sumner."

"Well, Dan, I'm Daisy. And yes, I would love to grab some coffee." She sounded confident, but was terrified and shaking inside. The smile he gave her, made her want to *be* that confident woman. Any thoughts of it being some kind of cruel joke fled her mind. She trusted this man. Daisy *wanted* to trust him. She was tired of panicking over everything and always being afraid. She wanted to see where this would go.

After exchanging numbers, they left the library together. They agreed it was pointless to go to coffee another day when they were both available then. Daisy was eager because she was afraid of blacking out again and unknowingly missing their date. Her blackouts were sporadic, but she thought that if she could just be happy for a while, maybe she would stay in the moment and *not* blackout.

She was trying to keep from having an attack, but it almost backfired. The anxiety and fear of going out with a complete stranger, an attractive one, was nearly enough to trigger a blackout. Daisy had to fight to push the darkness away, but when she finally began to feel comfortable with Dan, it eased away on its own. Before she knew it, she wasn't fighting at all.

Their coffee date went so well that they began seeing each other regularly. Dan explained his work life to Daisy. She was impressed that he was a real FBI agent, and a little intimidated, too. He was a little older than her, but not by that much. As they grew to know each other, their bond grew.

To Dan, the best part of their relationship was how understanding Daisy was about his work. He found that most other women that he'd dated over the years had become demanding about his time. They didn't like the number of hours he put in or the odd hours that he worked. Daisy seemed to be perfect, though. He could call her at odd hours, in the middle of the week or weekend. It didn't seem to matter. She was an amazing woman that he was falling for, and falling hard.

During the months they'd been seeing each other, Dan hadn't gotten any farther on his investigation. He had thought that reading those psychology books in the library would help him get an inside view. Maybe they did, and maybe they didn't, but either way, it didn't seem to make much of a difference in the case. There was a new body that turned up in recent months, and just last week, Dan received a call from a detective in Seattle who had another victim to add to the list.

Dan was growing more frustrated, which meant he was distancing himself from Daisy. He didn't do it consciously, but he was pushing her farther to the back burner. With the small amount of evidence available in his case, he'd been forced to get out in the field to do more interviews and hands-on work.

Being left alone was a place that Daisy was very familiar with, and as Dan pushed her to the back of his priorities more and more, her anxiety came back with a roaring ferocity, along with her headaches. The blackouts had never stopped, but the frequency that she had them was increasing again, the more that he was gone. She tried to tell herself that she didn't mind being alone all the time, but she was lying to herself.

She hadn't told Dan about the blackouts yet and still hadn't seen a therapist. Daisy was afraid of what a therapist would say to her. She didn't want to be medicated, and she was afraid that they might not take her seriously. Being called crazy was something she didn't think she could handle. The same went for Dan. If she told him, would he think she was nuts? She wasn't sure and wasn't willing to risk their relationship. Besides, he'd been far too busy with this investigation recently to even broach the subject.

Daisy was in love with Dan, and although they'd never told each other about their feelings, she believed he loved her, too. She loved not just him, but the relationship that they shared. Daisy loved that Dan was dedicated to his work but still found time to spend with her. He actually talked to her and *listened* to what she had to say. She was head over heels. The distancing that she felt from Dan was worrying, though, despite her confidence in his feelings toward her.

She told herself that he was busy with this case. She *knew* it was the case because it was all he talked about these days. She'd seen the stacks of files in his living room. It really didn't matter that she knew, though. There was a little part of her, in the recesses of her mind, that would always doubt.

She would doubt his affection for her, she would doubt their relationship, she would doubt herself. The more she hid her doubt, trying to ignore it, the larger it grew. It was like a shadow feeding on her fear, crawling up the walls of her mind, growing, all the while whispering in her ear and watching.

24

PRESENT DAY

Bobby winced, remembering the memory of his latest beating from his stepfather. He remembered the loud crack of a leather belt and the sharp sting of its slash across his back like a whip. This one had been brought on because Bobby dared to ask his mother for some lunch money within his stepfather's hearing.

His stepfather, George, had walked up to Bobby and backhanded him across the face without a word. Bobby stumbled back, almost falling, but George grabbed him by the front of his t-shirt. He yanked the boy forward and with a low growl, said, "You greedy little bastard. I'll teach you to ask for money." Then, he unfastened his belt and wrapped part of it around his hand before using it as a whip.

Bobby had cried out for his mother, but she didn't come to help him. She never did. But that didn't stop him from crying for her. Unfortunately for Bobby, his crying only seemed to make George hit harder. George didn't just whip Bobby, he whipped him until he was bloody and nearly unconscious. Bobby's shirt was in shreds, covered in sticky blood. He'd been whipped so hard that chunks of blood and

The Wrong Stranger

skin were splattered on the walls and floor from where the belt buckle had hit his skin.

He had only been able to stand up for the first couple of blows and then had fallen to the ground. It didn't matter, though. George would show no mercy. When the beating had finally ended, Bobby was paralyzed from the pain. He tried to crawl away to his bedroom, or anywhere that was away from George. He was in a haze, barely aware of anything. His vision was blurry, all sounds were muffled; all he knew was that he had to get away. His mother came then. "Can't you try to be better for him?" she'd asked, helping him to his room and into bed, where he stayed for several days.

George had loathed Bobby for as long as Bobby could remember. Bobby's mom, Mary, had gotten pregnant with him when she was fifteen. After getting kicked out of the house, her aunt and uncle had taken her in. She met George a couple of years later. George was six years older than Mary, and at the time, she was smitten.

She had felt so lucky to have found a man to take her in, along with another man's son. "What a good man he is," she would tell herself. Her aunt and uncle liked him, too. But what Mary didn't notice was how George would pinch, push, or rough up her little toddler while she wasn't looking. There were times he might yank Bobby's hair, pinch him, or even just maliciously break one of his toys for the hell of it. Mary didn't have a clue.

George had wanted the young and pretty Mary Williams, but not her bastard brat. He decided to marry the girl and hoped that one day her little mistake would break his neck, falling down the stairs. It had started as disgust, and over the years, it grew into hatred and then loathing.

George couldn't look at Bobby without seeing his woman being with another man. It drove him crazy thinking of it.

He was a jealous man who wasn't afraid of a fight, if that's what it took to keep anyone away from his wife.

The worst part of all, after thirteen years of marriage, Mary hadn't been able to give him a child of his own.

She had borne a bastard—a fucking bastard son, for God's sake! But she couldn't even get pregnant with a *single* baby of his. It was the true reason George couldn't stand Bobby. Bobby was another man's son, not his. He looked nothing like George. Why would he look anything like him? Bobby was living proof that George had no son of his own, no child of his own. When he got drunk, he often asked himself if he was even a man, if he couldn't get his wife pregnant with his seed, and those thoughts were what sent him into a rage.

Bobby hated the beatings, but the worst part was his mother. After George would beat him, his mother would look at him in disgust and walk away. That was unless Bobby physically could not move. Then, in that case, she would help him to his room and leave him there alone. It broke Bobby's heart to see the look in his mother's eyes. He could remember a time when she would try to stop George—would at least say something in protest, but not anymore. Not for a long time. Not that it did any good anyway.

If she tried intervening, George would shove her off and might even give her a slap or punch to keep her out of the way. He never went off on her, though. His anger was only ever taken out on Bobby. Bobby didn't know what was wrong with him to make everyone, including himself, so unhappy. He would cry himself to sleep most nights, praying for God to make him a better person. Better so that he could make people happy instead of so angry.

This last time, Bobby had been afraid he was going to die. The beatings were getting worse, and one day, George wouldn't hold back. He wouldn't stop. And then that would be the end. Bobby didn't want to die. Not like that.

The Wrong Stranger

He wiped the tears from his cheeks as he sat on the curb, outside the local gas station in Eagletown, Oklahoma. Bobby stood up with finality. He had made the choice to run away to Texas and make it on his own. Unlike many other fifteen-year-olds, when Bobby made a decision, he stuck to it. He wasn't one of those 'run away to your friend's house so your mom can find you in two days' kinds of teens. He was the kind that meant what he said. If he made his mind up to run away, which he had, he was bound and determined not to just do it for some attention, but to do it for good. He would not be caught. He would not be seeing George or his mother ever again.

Bobby had been waiting at the gas station for the perfect opportunity. It had taken some time and patience, but finally, he saw the perfect person who he would approach. He decided it couldn't be anyone who looked too weird or creepy. Bobby didn't particularly care if it was a man or woman, but they had to have a look that made him feel comfortable. He didn't really want to freak anyone out, either. God help him if they called the cops before he even left town.

The person he spotted happened to be a truck driver. There were no logos on the truck or trailer, and the truck looked clean and somewhat newer, as far as Bobby could tell. When the driver got out of his truck, Bobby saw him go in to pay for gas, and he assumed, use the bathroom. The driver came back out, holding a coke bottle in his hand.

Bobby could tell he had some chew in his mouth because he kept spitting on the ground. He was whistling a catchy tune that was upbeat and made Bobby want to tap his foot. The man seemed clean enough, and although he was about George's age, which gave Bobby a moment's pause, the man seemed fit, and if it came to it, maybe he could hold his own in a fight against George. Overall, he had the look that made

Bobby confident enough to approach, and so that was what he did.

Bobby gave a friendly smile as he walked in the truck driver's direction, and once the driver noticed him, he gave a friendly smile back. "Hi there, mister."

"Hello," the driver replied with a tip of his hat.

"Do you think I could ride with you outta here? Even just for a little ways?" Bobby decided to cut straight to it, keeping his fingers crossed on his left hand, hoping the man would say yes. The driver paused for a second and looked around a little.

"Where's your parents?" he asked, smile faltering some, but still there.

"I'm running away, and nobody's gonna talk me out of it. Will you give me a ride, or should I ask someone else?" He didn't have any time to waste and needed to get the hell outta there as fast as possible.

The driver stroked his chin with his thumb and forefinger. After what felt like forever to Bobby, the man nodded his head. "Alright, you can tag along. I'm not supposed to, and I can sure get in some big trouble, but I been there before and would've given anything to have someone help me out."

Bobby gave him a smile of pure gratitude, eyes gleaming. He couldn't believe the man would really help him out; he was a complete stranger, willing to take him in. "Thank you so much, mister!" He nearly yelled because he was so excited and relieved.

The man gave a little chuckle. "You're welcome. Now you better get on up in the truck so we can head out." He opened the passenger door for Bobby and helped him up into the truck. There was a small area in back of the driver and passenger seats with a table, refrigerator, and bed. Bobby sat back there, trying to hide himself as much as possible, in case his mother or George decided to come looking.

The Wrong Stranger

A few minutes later, the driver's door opened, and the man got in to start the truck. Bobby was so relieved to have found a ride that it never occurred to him to ask where he was headed. He'd completely forgot about Texas. That he could be going anywhere in the country never crossed his mind. But did it really matter? As long as he was far away from George, he would make it just fine.

It turned out that the semi driver was headed to Seattle. Bobby never dreamed that he would visit the Pacific Northwest and felt like he was going on an adventure. He was thankful to the driver, who was helping him to start a new life. Bobby vowed that he'd never let himself be beaten and miserable again.

The driver was a kind man who empathized with Bobby. When he made his stop in Seattle, he gave Bobby some cash and some tips on the hitchhiking gig. Bobby couldn't believe when the driver tried to hook him up with a contact for potential work. He was eternally grateful, but declined the offer. Bobby wasn't sure what he was going to do with his life yet. He didn't want to take the driver up on his kind offer, only to bail out on the work that he was given and make the driver look bad. He was happy to be free but wasn't sure if this was somewhere he wanted to stay for a while or keep moving along to a different city.

25

Bobby spent a little time in Seattle, living off the cash that the truck driver had given him. It wasn't much, but enough to get him some food for several days. He didn't worry about transportation because he walked everywhere, and he didn't worry about shelter, either. He could finally live for himself and was enjoying every minute of it.

He didn't have to worry about looking the wrong way or saying the wrong thing. He didn't have to worry about the beatings anymore. And he didn't have to worry about doing anything that he didn't want to do. He felt nothing but an overwhelming sense of relief and freedom.

Instead of being afraid, Bobby was now excited to dream about the future and what he might do with his life. It was a different feeling than watching every move he made, in order to avoid getting a beating. Before, he'd been worried about surviving the next few hours without pain. No more.

Bobby was enjoying the city but thought that he might like to venture south to see some more of the beautiful state he was in. This was the first time that Bobby had ever left his home, and he didn't want to get stuck in the first place he landed. The idea of traveling sat well with Bobby, and he began to look forward to all the different places that he would be able to see.

After a few days in Seattle, Bobby started trying to hitchhike again. He found that most people were skeptical about helping a kid who was alone. The majority of the time, they would ask, "Where's your parents?" Bobby found himself lying to some and telling the truth to others, but it didn't seem to make a difference. He tried to remember the advice that the kind truck driver gave him, but after being the recipient of so many blows to the head from his stepfather, Bobby had trouble with his short-term memory.

Trying gas stations, street corners, and along the highway, Bobby couldn't get a ride anywhere he tried. He finally gave up, deciding that he would just walk until he got tired and then would continue walking when he was rested. Bobby told himself that he had all the time in the world, and if no one wanted to give him a ride right now, then that was fine. He started his journey south, trying to keep as close to the freeway as possible. Bobby reasoned that if he was close to the freeway, he would also be close to food and a potential ride while he walked.

Journeying toward Olympia, he walked south to Tacoma before continuing on. It took him four days to travel over sixty miles on foot. By the time he reached Olympia, he was exhausted. He could feel blisters forming on the backs of both of his heels. To top it off, Bobby was running low on cash. During his trek, he'd reduced his calorie intake to dollar drinks at gas stations during the day, and a dollar menu dinner at night. It had rained on and off, drenching him to the bone. He was realizing that something was going to have to change if he wanted to keep traveling, or he would not get very far.

In Olympia, Bobby was ready for a rest. He was half frozen and wet through his clothes and shoes. He decided to attempt catching a ride again while he rested his feet and tried to get warm. This time, luck was on his side.

As he was meandering along the highway, headed toward the gas station sign, he spotted a black semi parked on the outskirts of the Walmart parking lot. There were no other cars around it, and the semi driver was walking around the truck. It seemed to Bobby that he was doing some kind of inspection because he was holding a clipboard and checking things off. He wasn't sure, but the truck looked familiar. Had he seen it before? There was no way for him to know for sure; there had to be tons of black semis that passed as he'd been walking over the past few days.

Taking his time approaching, Bobby racked his brain for something to say to the driver. He rubbed his sweaty palms against his jeans to dry them off. He tried to walk noisily so that he didn't sneak up on the driver because he really didn't want to seem like a creep.

Bobby was next to the driver when he cleared his throat. "Hi there." The driver turned his head, smiling when he saw Bobby. He looked just as friendly as that first semi driver had, which comforted Bobby and boosted his courage. He asked for a ride, and the driver almost instantly agreed to help him out.

"Where you headed," the driver asked.

"South, I think."

"Alrighty, well, I'm headed to Portland."

"Sounds great. Thanks, mister!"

"What's your name, kid?"

"Bobby."

"Nice to meet you, Bobby. I'm Bill." There were no questions and no casually asking where his parents were. Was this too good to be true?

The Wrong Stranger

BILL HAD WATCHED BOBBY TRYING TO CATCH A RIDE IN Seattle. The moment he saw the kid, he knew he had to have him. The boy was gangly with sandy hair, and to Bill, he was a mirror image of Jake Carter, the little bastard who drowned Chris. He seemed to be a few years older, but it didn't matter. The kid had the exact build and appearance of Jake. Bill nearly salivated at the thought of having his way with him. He also thought that Jessica would have some particular enjoyment with this one, too.

All the women they'd picked so far remarkably resembled Joy Carter. Bill was almost certain that if he brought this Bobby boy to her, looking so much like Jake, she would be thrilled. He grinned, imagining Jessica taking her creativity to new heights. He'd kept track of the boy as he'd headed south from Seattle, making sure that he didn't lose him. It had cost him time off his schedule, driving slowly and looping around time and time again, but it would be *so* worth it.

After opening the passenger door for Bobby, Bill walked around to the driver's side. He started the truck, then looked at Bobby. "Hey, you look pretty tired and cold. If you want a rest, you're welcome to lie in back for a while. Here's a towel to dry off." Tears sprang to Bobby's eyes, but he fought them back. He was wary and exhausted down to his bones.

Bobby felt like a fool for thinking that he could just walk forever and then only making it to Olympia before he gave up. He'd been able to rest along his walk, but he'd been unable to fall into a full sleep. Now, the thought of getting a couple of hours sleep, in a bed, was like a dream come true.

"Thanks, Bill. That means a lot. I think I'll take you up on that"

"No problem! There's water in the fridge, too, if you're

thirsty." Bobby's throat was tight from fighting back the tears, so he said nothing else. He climbed through to the back sleeper where he slipped his shoes off and made himself comfortable, already feeling warmer.

Bobby wasn't really that thirsty until he thought about the water that was offered to him. He didn't want to keep taking from a kind man with nothing but his thanks to offer in return. Then, Bobby thought that taking a cold water, after it was offered, wasn't such a big deal. In fact, as he thought about it, he wondered if it might seem rude for him to not take it. Bobby stood up off the bed, opened the fridge, and downed an entire bottle. Then, he laid on the bed and let the darkness overtake him.

It was the same routine he'd gotten so used to over the years. Bill felt the familiar confidence fill him as the boy played right into his hands. This was the least amount of prep work Bill had ever done before picking up a target, which was virtually none. Even when he picked up random hitchhikers, Bill was at least prepared for them and had a place to take them. He'd always had a playroom scoped out before getting a new target. Now, though, he didn't. It was probably the most spur-of-the-moment thing he'd ever done. But after seeing this kid, there was no way he could just keep driving by. He was going to have to make some quick decisions, but Bill didn't mind. The thought of the suspense that would ensue now thrilled him.

Bill thought about the little play date that he and Jessica just had a week ago in this area. Normally, he waited much longer in between targets and never took targets in the same area twice. It wasn't just because he had to find the next one, but also because he didn't want to make any mistakes. But there was no resisting this kind of temptation. This one fell into his lap, and Bill was helpless to pass him by. The good news was they were heading out of state, and he could take the boy anywhere. After considering, Bill decided Texas would be a great place to go. The state was so big that he wouldn't have a problem finding a quick playroom.

As he drove, Bill imagined Jessica's reaction to seeing the boy. He couldn't wrap his head around the resemblance that Bobby had to Jake Carter. He looked so much like a spitting image of Jake Carter that Bill wondered if there was a dirty little Carter family secret that would explain it. He'd heard of those freak cases where random strangers looked identical but always thought they were fake or photoshopped. What were they called? Doppelgangers? After seeing Bobby, Bill was a believer.

Bill hadn't been there when Jake drowned Chris, but Bill often imagined it happening. He replayed his version of events over and over in his mind, clenching his jaw with want of payback. This was the exact opportunity they'd been waiting for, for so long. Bill just *knew* Jessica was going to relish every minute of it.

He kept Bobby sedated in the sleeper portion of his semi, as he headed toward Texas. The water bottle had enough drugs in it to keep Bobby asleep for about ten hours, then Bill let him wake up. He had to stop driving anyway because he didn't want to go over his legal driving hours.

As a semi driver, if his hours were off, it would be a headache to deal with police if he got pulled over, especially with a kid in the back of his truck. So, stopping to get some rest himself, Bill got some food for the both of them.

When Bobby woke up, he was disoriented from the drugs. "Did we make it yet?"

"Yeah, we made it. You were sleeping, and I didn't want to wake you."

Bobby blushed. "Sorry about that."

"No worries. You said you were heading south, so I thought you might want to stay with me and go a little farther than Portland." Bobby thought for a minute, not saying anything. Bill said, "If I was wrong about that, sorry, man."

"No, no. Thank you. I appreciate the ride, and your bed, and this food, too. Thanks so much, Bill." Bobby didn't want to cry, so he focused on inhaling the rest of his food. It didn't take long for the drugs to kick in again. Soon, Bobby was fast asleep again on the sleeper bed. Bill closed the privacy curtain so that Bobby would be hidden from view.

Bill climbed out of the cab and opened the doors to the attached trailer. Inside, it was full of cargo, but all the way in the far back was a false wall. The wall appeared to be the back of the trailer, but really separated a small room for Bill. It was where Bill slept when necessary. He had a camera set up to view the cab of the truck, and the sleeper area, too. With Bobby drugged, and the camera system in place, Bill felt no worries about leaving the boy in the cab alone for a while, so that he could get some shuteye.

For the rest of the trip, Bobby slept most of the time, only waking for brief intervals to use the bathroom and eat. When he was awake, Bill told Bobby that they were headed to Los Angeles. Bobby was excited about it, which meant that Bill wasn't worried about letting him wake up for small stretches.

He didn't want Bobby to stay awake for a few different reasons. Bill didn't want him to have a sense of direction or get an idea that they really weren't headed to Los Angeles. He wanted Bobby to lose his sense of time, if he had any. The disorientation that Bobby felt from both the drugs and sleeping for so long was a tool. It made Bobby more cooperative and trusting, never catching on to the fact that there was something terribly wrong.

26

Driving from Washington to Texas took three full days. Bill had been trying to time their arrival so that it would be late in the night or pre-dawn hours. Along the way, he planned with Jessica via text and phone call, agreeing on a location and time to meet. It was up to her to find a quick playroom. So far, he hadn't had to worry about information getting mixed up between Ashley and Jessica; she'd been able to keep everything straight somehow.

Because their plans were going so smoothly for every target so far, Bill was no longer worried about partnering up with her. He told himself, from day one of their partnership, if Jessica ever betrayed him, she would be the next target. He felt like his relationship with her was in a good place; Bill enjoyed the time he spent with Jessica far more than Ashley. He didn't think it would come to that, as long as Ashley didn't start getting better. Bill enjoyed the time he spent with Jessica far more than Ashley.

The arrangement that Bill and Jessica agreed on was to meet at an abandoned farmhouse that was listed for sale.

Jessica did the research for the property, and once she found it, Bill verified it would be perfect. This was the first time that neither of them actually went to the location beforehand. The farmhouse was on fifty acres in a rural area. Looking at GPS, there appeared to be no other buildings for at least a few miles.

Bill would park the truck as far behind the house as he was able, trying to keep it from front and center view. Jessica was supposed to be waiting there already. She would have an area for them set up to work. If she got there and things were not going to work out, she was supposed to tape a bright yellow piece of paper to the front door with a hazard notice on it. He would see the paper and turn around without stepping a foot out of the truck.

He realized a lot was riding on his trust in her. Bill wasn't a man who normally put his life in someone else's hands, and although he trusted her in this, the fear of something going wrong still sat with him. After she lost control and turned back into Ashley, he'd constantly had doubts about when Ashley would show back up. Apparently, Jessica wasn't in complete control like he'd originally thought. She refused to explain to him exactly *how* her personality swaps worked, but one thing was certain: Ashley could show up at any time.

Finding the agreed upon property, Bill pulled down the long driveway. There was no sign of another living soul and also no sign of a bright yellow piece of paper taped to the door. It was a cloudless night. The stars and the moon lit up the night sky so much that Bill could turn off his headlights completely and still see fine. He parked the truck, then killed the engine. Bill made sure that Bobby was still sleeping. Then, he waited. He counted to one hundred before getting out of the truck.

As soon as the driver door shut, Jessica walked out the front door. "What took you so long?"

The Wrong Stranger

He laughed, recognizing her sarcasm.

"Long time, no see." As they hugged, she grabbed his ass, and he grabbed her breasts. She ran her fingers through his dark hair, pulling him close to kiss him hard. Then, she pushed him away.

"Where is she?"

Bill had been keeping everything a surprise for her this time, including the fact that the "she" was really a "he." Jessica assumed the target was a female, because so far, Bill had only ever brought females for her to play with. For Jessica, it was all about getting revenge on Joy. But, before working with her, he'd still occasionally had male targets, especially when picking up hitchhikers. He smiled.

"Okay, what's with the look?"

"Nothing."

"Don't 'nothing' me, Bill. What the hell is it?"

Bill laughed. "Okay, I wanted to surprise you."

"Okay..."

"So, come take a look."

He walked her to the truck, opened the passenger door, and helped her up. Jessica pulled back the privacy curtain, seeing the sleeping figure on the bed. It was dark both outside and inside the truck, and she couldn't make much of anything out, except for the sleeping form. She didn't want to touch whoever it was, even though she knew Bill did a good job drugging people.

Jessica climbed back out of the truck. "It's too dark to see anything in there. What am I supposed to be surprised about?"

Bill popped his knuckles, annoyed that the surprise hadn't gone as planned. He didn't bother to ask why she didn't just turn on the cab lights or grab the flashlight from the inside of the door. Instead, he said, "Look, let's quit fucking around and get this show on the road." She'd see the boy soon enough, but right now, Bill needed to make sure this place was legit. He started for the house. Jessica caught up, and she showed him around.

"It checks out just fine." As she led him through, she pointed to a door. "The basement is there. That's where I set everything up."

Once he checked everything out and approved of the situation, Bill finally went back to the truck for Bobby. Jessica stayed in the basement while Bill pulled him from the cab. The basement was well lit with several florescent light bars hanging from the ceiling. As soon as Bill laid Bobby down, he heard Jessica's gasp. He felt a sense of satisfaction at the thought that he could surprise her, but when he looked at her pale face, he began to have some doubts. "What's wrong?" She didn't respond. She stood frozen, unmoving. All the color had drained from her. "Jessica?" She shook her head, but still didn't speak.

Bill began to worry. The last thing he needed right now was for her to lose her shit. He thought that the kid's looks would be a good thing, not bad. He'd wanted to kill the little shit as soon as he'd seen him and figured that she would feel the same way. Bill thought she would've been thrilled. She should be dancing, stripping down, and rearing to get things going. This reaction, though, was the polar opposite of what she should be doing. Maybe she just needed a second to get over the shock. She'd been expecting an adult woman, after all.

He was disappointed, to say the least, but now getting a little anxious about what she would do next. Bill tried to think of something to do or say, anything to calm her down or reassure her that everything was okay. He couldn't let her blood pressure get too high because that would probably mean a surprise appearance from Ashley.

Finally, Jessica spoke. "I'm fine. I... sorry." She looked him in the eye. "He looks like Chris."

Bill's eyes bulged. His eyebrows arched almost to the top of his forehead. "What?! No, no, no."

"Look at him, Bill!"

"No, you look again, goddammit! He looks like Jake Carter."

"Jake Car—no. What? No! How could you be so blind?"

Bill took a breath, trying to calm down. This was going to hell in a fucking hand basket really quick. He was losing control of the situation and he needed to get a reign on it. He said, "Look, please just look again." Jessica took a breath, too. She stepped closer to Bobby, turning his head so that she looked straight at him. She scanned him, taking in every detail, then stepped back again.

In a low voice that Bill had to strain to hear, she said, "It's Chris, Bill."

Now it was Bill's turn to look again. He did the same thing that Jessica had just done but still saw fucking Jake Carter. He was now grinding his teeth together in irritation. Trying not to snap at her, he said, "You know, they looked a lot alike. Same hair color, similar build..."

She thought about it, then nodded in agreement. Then, Bill asked the question that he would regret for the rest of his life. "So, what's the deal? Are we doing this or what? I mean, you can go home, if you aren't feeling this one."

Jessica looked back at Bobby, still passed out. She thought for another minute, then said, "Yeah. I'm in."

Clapping his hands, Bill cried, "Excellent!" He was done chit chatting. It was time for some action. He proceeded to tie Bobby up by all four of his limbs, then slapped the boy across the face with all his strength. Bobby's head flung back, and his lip split open. Jessica flinched at the sight. Bobby's eyes fluttered, but he still wasn't quite where Bill wanted him. Bill cried, "Come on, sugar!" Then, he slapped hard two more times, one right after the other. Bobby's nose was bleeding now, too, and the side of his face was bright red from the slaps. His eyes sprung open, now fully awake.

"That's it, baby cakes!"

Bill was excited, full of adrenaline, pumped up and ready for action. He noticed Jessica was standing by, not saying anything yet, but that was okay with him. She was leaning her back against a wall with her arms crossed across her chest. She'd been taking the lead on the last few targets, so Bill thought it was his turn anyway. He was okay with letting her stand on the sidelines for a while, especially if it calmed her down a bit. Jessica wasn't normally a big talker with their targets, so her lack of conversation at this point, wasn't very concerning for him.

Bill picked up the same pair of scissors that he'd used with Roxy and began taunting Bobby. Bobby was too young, and too out of it still, to fully understand what was happening to him, but he had a good idea that Bill and this woman were psychos. He was already on the verge of crying, both from the pain of being slapped repeatedly and also from the fear that came with being tied up in a strange place.

Now that Bill had the scissors, Bobby couldn't hold back anymore. He let go, crying, "Please, Bill! What did I do? I'm sorry, don't be mad at me! Let me go! Please don't hurt me." He wailed over and over, pleading for mercy. Bobby's entire face was beet red now. He had snot running down to his chin but couldn't wipe it away. He couldn't wipe the tears, either.

With the amount of experience he possessed, Bill was immune to the cries of a child. He was immensely skilled in his hobby, which meant that he had a significant amount of experience with all kinds of crying for mercy. He never let them get to him. In fact, it was one of the things that he loved most.

The cries made him feel powerful. Whether they were from an adult or child, it didn't matter. Bill glanced toward Jessica, smiling with pleasure. His smile slipped when he saw how pale she'd become. If he thought she looked bad before, now she was worse. *Shit.*

This was really getting to be a pain in his ass. *This kid better be worth it*, he thought. Bill left Bobby and went to Jessica. In a low voice, he asked, "Are you sure you're okay?"

She nodded without hesitating. "I'm fine. I'm just out of it, that's all." She smiled. "Keep going. It's fine, I promise."

He looked her in the eyes. "Out of it is a big deal for you." Jessica knew what he meant but didn't know how else to respond. She also wasn't sure what he would do to her if she *wasn't* okay.

"I'M FINE."

Bill nodded, going back to Bobby. "Sorry, kiddo, didn't mean to keep you waiting." He began to cut the boy's clothes.

Jessica could feel Ashley trying to get out. She was clawing her way to the surface, begging for control. It was seeing the boy that triggered it, and she didn't know how much longer she could hold on. Normally, Jessica had most of the control. Ashley was weak and pathetic.

Bill was dead wrong about the kid. Jessica wanted to laugh at his stupidity, but couldn't. He was so wrong. So, so dead fucking wrong. There was no doubt in her mind that Bobby looked just like Chris. There was no question. And Jessica knew that if that's what *she* saw, then it's also what Ashley saw. Now his stupid mistake was going to screw everything up.

As soon as Bill began to cut, Jessica was gone. It wasn't Ashley that came forward, though. It was the one who'd been hiding for years. She'd been too afraid to face life after the abuse and neglect that she'd suffered as a child. She'd hidden inside herself, protected by Ashley and then Jessica. With the sight of Bill mutilating what looked like her son, Ashley finally pushed Daisy forward.

Daisy took control, grasping it like a lifeline. The last thing that she was aware of was falling asleep in bed. She'd visited her boyfriend, Dan Sumner, and gotten home late. Now, somehow, she was standing in a basement, watching a man torture a young boy. The boy's screams were ear-splitting. Daisy wanted to cover her eyes and her ears but didn't have enough hands to cover everything. She was so afraid that she almost lost control of her bladder.

Her mind reeled. *Oh my god, oh my god, oh my god! Where am I?!* She looked around, desperate for escape. She didn't know how she could help the little boy, other than calling the police. There was no way that she could overpower this crazy man who had kidnapped them. He looked so malevolent. The look on his face had her more terrified than she'd ever been, even as a child.

Daisy saw the staircase. She couldn't believe it was wide open for her to exit. She was not tied up in any way, easily able to leave. She wondered, *what the hell is going on?* She began to sweat, thinking it could be a trap. She'd woken up in a strange situation before, but this took the cake. She began to cry, tired of the illness that plagued her. She was tired of waking up like this.

Daisy wondered if this killer knew her. Was someone else waiting for her upstairs? She felt like she could lose her mind from the fear and possibilities that presented themselves. Her head was pounding harder than ever before. She wanted to close her eyes, but even doing that was too painful.

Another guttural cry from the boy sealed the deal. Daisy knew she couldn't just stand there thinking and do nothing. She backed toward the staircase, trying to appear as casual as possible. As carefully as she could manage, she climbed the steps backwards, never looking away from the man and the boy. Sweat dripped from her brow, but she didn't wipe it. As she climbed, the pressure in her head built. Her eyes started watering from the pain, but she kept going. She thought that if she made it through this, she would never in her life forget the sound of the boy's cries.

By now, Bill was too consumed by what he was doing. He was in his own world with no one in it but himself and Bobby. Jessica would've understood well. He made sure not to touch Bobby's face anymore, after the slaps that he previously gave. Bill liked to see Jake Carter looking back; Bobby no longer existed. If he messed with his face, the image would be broken, so he left it untouched. Bill was so preoccupied that he did not see or hear Daisy moving up the staircase. He also did not hear the basement door open or her footsteps leave the house from above. As it was, Bobby's cries would have drowned out any of those sounds. Bill nearly had to put earplugs in, the boy was so loud.

As soon as Daisy made it upstairs, she looked for the front door so she could get out of the house. She was in a panic, still terrified that there could be someone else waiting to grab her.

Finally, she made it outside. There was a black semi, but no other cars. Looking around frantically, she spotted the garage. She ran to it and peered through the small, dirty window. There was a car in there. Daisy breathed a silent prayer. The garage door was unlocked. She tried the car door next. It, too, was unlocked.

The feeling of being setup for a trap grew exponentially. Daisy's head hurt her so badly that she was having a hard time thinking. She was thankful for the dark because she knew that if there were lights, she would be immobilized from the agony. Lights always made the pain worse.

She began to feel sick to her stomach and just wanted to lie down for a while. In the back of her mind, she felt a clawing sense of something dark trying to take over. The corners of her vision blurred with darkness, but she fought against it. Daisy would not black out again. Not here, not now. There was no chance that she was about to let herself do that. Inside the car, she saw a cellphone. She turned it on, then called Dan.

27

Agent Sumner was sleeping when the phone rang. He'd been going nonstop for over twenty-four hours and had been nearly dead on his feet before he made it to bed. His current case on the Hide and Seek Man was draining him both mentally and physically. Dan was close to getting the sick son of a bitch but was having a hell of a time collecting more hard evidence.

He'd tracked the Hide and Seek Man to Seattle, where he was suspected in the disappearance of a young woman. The young woman was supposed to be meeting up with friends but had disappeared. The only trace that she left behind was her wrecked car on the side of the highway.

The FBI had been called in when evidence of a semi stopping at the wreck had been found. The semi was one thing that Dan was absolutely sure tied the Hide and Seek Man's victims together. Nearly every case had a black semi-truck involved in one way or another. Dan didn't think that it was normal for a young woman to get into a horrific accident with an enormous deer, have a semi driver stop, and then not show up at any hospitals in the entire state of Washington and not call her friends or family to update them. To top it off, the buck that was found still stuck inside the car, had a slug in his head. The young woman did not own a firearm, and the trajectory of the bullet was all wrong. She was not the one to shoot the deer. So, who put the bullet in it?

Dan felt in his gut that this was the Hide and Seek Man. Some suggested that it was a coincidence, probably another sick pervert out there that nabbed the girl. But Dan knew better. There were too many similarities to other victims. There was a near obsession that ran through Dan when he thought about catching the Hide and Seek Man. He'd been warned over and over not to let the case get inside his head, not to let it overwhelm his personal life, not to let it take over, but Dan was helpless to resist. It was the first time in his career that he'd been unable to keep control.

He was thankful Daisy was so understanding about his work. She was such an amazing woman. He was crazy about her, and the fact that she was so understanding with his work life made her irresistible. Dan thought that if not for Daisy, he probably wouldn't have a personal life at all. In fact, he knew it.

He remembered what his life was like before meeting her, and it wasn't pretty. Although he'd never obsessed this much over a case before, Dan was still a true workaholic. He would rather be working on an open case than socializing or doing anything else, which was one reason he was so successful in catching the bad guys.

Meeting Daisy really helped Dan by showing him that there was more to live for than just work. Daisy opened his eyes to life with another human being, sharing interests and spending time together. He'd never lacked female attention, but she was the first female in years that he *wanted* to give him attention. He didn't need to feel guilty about being in Seattle because she encouraged him to go

The Wrong Stranger

after this case. She rooted for him and made him feel good about being so successful at catching criminals. He didn't have to feel bad for liking it or for putting in so many hours. And the thing was, with Daisy, he *wanted* to put in less hours. His internal clock automatically changed because he missed her.

Missing someone was a relatively foreign feeling for Dan. He was beginning to enjoy what missing someone meant. He was dreaming about Daisy when his phone began to ring and vibrate on the night table. In a hotel in Seattle, Dan was so tired that he slept through the ringing. His phone vibrated until it fell off the side of the table, but Dan still slept through. On the other end of the line, a panicked Daisy sobbed and cursed him for not answering. She called again and again until Dan was finally pulled out of sleep by the ringing.

His arm reached to feel for the phone. Unable to find it, he gave up, rolling back over to sleep, but the ringing started over again. In his line of work, if his phone didn't stop ringing, there was an emergency. There was no ignoring the phone. Not for Dan anyway.

He made himself wake up. Finally, he found the phone on the floor and saw all the missed calls from Daisy. Panic shot through him. He was about to call her back, but she was already calling again. "Daisy?"

"Dan! Oh, Dan!" She was crying so hard that he could barely make out what she was saying. She sounded frantic and scared.

"Take a breath. It's okay, I'm here."

"Dan! Oh my god, Dan! Save me, please God, come save me!"

"Where are you? Are you hurt?" He wanted to scream, to cry even, but he had to remain calm.

"It's some old farmhouse! I don't know where. It's so

dark. I'm in the garage, but he's going to know I'm gone. He's probably looking for me already. Oh God, what do I do?"

"Listen. You need to hide. I'll call the local police, but you have to hide, dammit! You hear me?"

"Yes. Yes, I'll hide."

"Are you hurt?"

"That poor boy. Dan, he was torturing him! Please hurry!"

"Okay, I'm going to hang up now, Daisy. Turn the phone on silent. I-I love you."

"I love you, too."

Dan hung up the phone. He had no idea where Daisy was, or what the hell was going on with her, but he'd be damned if he was about to let something happen to her. He called the necessary people to get her phone tracked, and within a few minutes, both the local police and the local FBI were dispatched to her location. Dan was booked for the next flight into Texas and would be seeing Daisy as soon as humanly possible.

He was overwhelmed with worry, but also anger. Someone was trying to kill her, that was obvious. He was thankful that she'd been able to call him, and he had faith in law enforcement to get to her location. But Dan knew well that minutes could mean life or death. After all the years he'd spent as an investigator, Dan was well versed in controlling his emotions. He couldn't let panic set it. Instead, he focused on the anger.

This was the first time they'd told each other about their feelings, and it was under terrible circumstances. Dan wondered if she only said it to him because she thought she was going to die. Or did she think that he only said it to her because he thought that? Did she really love him, or did she just say it out of fear?

What a screwed-up way for it to all go down. He was angry that he hadn't been able to tell her in a better way, or sooner. To make it romantic, like in the damned movies. Didn't women like shit like that? He wanted her to know how special she was to him, how much she meant, and the chance was taken from him. He wondered if he'd even have another chance to tell her at all.

As Dan was packing a small bag, getting ready to walk out his front door, the FBI and local police were moving in on Daisy's location. She was hiding in the garage, crouched behind some old boxes. She thought about hiding inside the car but decided against it. The fear that the psycho killer would either look there first or use it as his getaway ride overrode any notion that it might be safer, or at the very least, more comfortable. As she crouched in the dark, terror and apprehension ate away at her.

It was so quiet that the sound of her own breathing seemed deafening. Her nerves were on pins and needles. Her heart skipped a beat at the sound of a creak, and she broke out in a cold sweat. An owl hooted in the distance but was cut off. As soon as the hooting stopped, Daisy felt like her head would explode from the pain that ran through it. She started seeing black spots again, and this time couldn't keep them back. It wasn't long before she faded into the darkness.

Jessica seized control, not knowing how long it would last. She had to warn Bill before things started to get ugly. As fast as she could, she ran back across the driveway and into the house. She descended the stairs, thinking of what she would tell him. He was going to be mad as hell, but if she could give him enough warning, maybe it would make things better. She didn't know how to tell him about Daisy and didn't think there was time for that anyway. What mattered now was them both getting the hell out of dodge before the police and FBI showed up.

"Bill!" she panted, out of breath as she re-entered the basement. Jessica tried not to look at Bobby, realizing that he was a trigger. It was damned hard not to look, though, and her head was already starting to ache again. Even blocking the sight of him, there were the sounds. When Jessica called his name, it pulled Bill out of his world and back into reality.

He realized that Jessica hadn't been down there with him the whole time. "Where were you?"

"No time for that now. We've got to get out of here." She was looking the other way, trying to keep her focus on the staircase, so Bill wasn't able to look at her face. He didn't need to. Something in her voice told him there was about to be trouble. There probably wasn't time to clean up or get rid of any evidence. He thought about his options and what he would be able to do. Probably not much.

"Jessica, Look at me."

"I—come over here."

"No. Look at me. Right now, goddammit." She hesitated. Then, she looked at him. Her eyes met his. He held her gaze, then saw her eyes flick to the kid.

Jessica saw his mutilated body, surrounded by pools of blood and chunks of meat. His head was still untouched, and the look of agony that was frozen on his young, lifeless face did it. Her reaction was instant. Jessica reached a hand up to her head, as if to put counter pressure against a headache. Her eyes rolled back into her skull for a moment before her face turned into a mask of stricken horror, and she began to scream. Her cries of terror were ear piercing, making Bill wince and cover his ears.

He'd *known* Ashley would show up eventually. He'd *known* it was just a matter of time, especially with her initial reaction to the boy. He assumed that she probably called the police, which would explain why she'd left the basement in the first place. It also explained why Jessica tried to warn him and also tried to not look at the bloody mess that he'd made. She knew that it would be a trigger. He'd been so stupid to

The Wrong Stranger

give her such leeway. Bill had known there was a risk, but boy, had it bit him in the ass. He wanted to punch himself for not paying more attention to her after she'd had that initial reaction to seeing Bobby.

Bill tried to calm Ashley down, thinking that if he could get her to shut up, maybe he could knock her out and get Jessica back again. "Ashley, it's okay. Let's just take a deep breath." He reached out for her in a placating gesture, but it made her scream even louder. She wasn't climbing the stairs, trying to get away, which Bill didn't understand but was thankful for. He maneuvered himself between her and the staircase before she got the bright idea to climb them. "Ash, please stop. Let's talk about this."

Finally, she stopped screaming, and replied, but it was not at all what Bill expected. "Please let me go! You have the wrong person!"

Bill arched an eyebrow, "Look, love, I don't have time to figure out your riddles. It's time to get going now. We can have a nice little chat in the car."

"Please don't do this! Please, please! I won't tell, I swear!" Bill tried to stay calm. He tried to look like the normal Bill that she married and was used to, but it was growing harder by the minute. He was covered in the boy's blood and must look terrifying to Ashley, but there was nothing for it. He had to get them the hell out of there. Bill took a step toward her, knowing that she would back away from him. He led her this way, to Bobby, where she tripped over one of the ropes that was tied from his body to a nearby post.

She fell, twisting as she tried to stop herself from falling. It gave Bill the opportunity to grab her by the hair and slam her head into the wall. The pain was immense, and Daisy almost passed out but fought it as hard as she could. She thought if she blacked out, she would never wake up again, and no matter how bad it got, she wanted to stay alive. She wasn't ready to die. Daisy screamed as loud as she could, causing Bill to flinch. He slapped her across the face, trying to get her to shut up. He didn't want to kill her if he didn't have to. Jessica was in there somewhere, and he wanted to get her back if it was at all possible.

The slap didn't stop Daisy from screaming. She kept screaming, even though her throat was turning raw, and her head hurt the most it had ever hurt her entire existence. She screamed for her life. Bill was getting ready to bash her head into the wall again when the basement door crashed open. He didn't have to look up to know that it was over.

Police were yelling and pointing guns, spotlights blared, there were sirens going off, and someone was talking through a megaphone. Bill didn't have time to think or react. He let go of Ashley, raising his hands in the air, putting up no resistance to being arrested. He didn't understand how they'd showed up so fast. Two officers descended the basement stairs to begin with, followed by two more. Those four officers escorted Bill and Daisy to the driveway where Bill was put in a police car, and Daisy was seen by the paramedics. He didn't try to speak to her again.

As an officer was escorting Daisy away, Bill overheard part of their conversation. "Are you Ms. Daisy Taylor?"

"Yes."

"Agent Sumner wanted me to let you know that he's on a flight out as we speak. He's asked me to escort you to his hotel room if the paramedics give you the all-clear. Unless you prefer to go to the hospital to be seen?"

"Thank you." She breathed a sigh of relief. "His hotel would be amazing."

That name. Bill furrowed his brows thinking of Daisy Taylor. It rang a bell in his mind, but he had to pinpoint where. Who did he know with the surname Taylor? He flashed back to memories of Willow, all those years ago. As

The Wrong Stranger

he ducked into the backseat of the police cruiser. The door shut behind him, but Bill didn't hear it. He was too lost in thought because the pieces of a decades old puzzle were finally fitting together.

He'd been attracted to Ashley when he first met her because she looked familiar to him. He was now realizing *why*. Willow. All those years ago, she'd told him how she liked the name Daisy for her baby. Her boyfriend at the time was Joe Taylor. Bill did the math in his head. The timeline added up; she was the right age. *It couldn't be.* This woman, whom he'd married, was Willow's daughter. *His* daughter. How was this even possible?

28

From the time that Bill overheard the conversation between the officer and his wife, the gears in his head turned at a breakneck speed. He thought of nothing else, wondering if it was possible that he'd heard her name wrong. Then, Bill wondered how many personalities Ashley actually had. How in the hell did she learn about the Taylors? There was no way she was actually Daisy. He shook his head, denying the possibility. No, she'd picked another random name. It was a coincidence, that was all.

Bill kept his history at the ranch secret, not only from his wife, but from anyone he'd ever known. There was no one alive who was familiar with the history there, other than the individuals that were involved. And even those particular individuals didn't know of Bill's specific involvement, other than the fact that he was a ranch hand at the time. Bill would bet every dollar to his name that Ashley wouldn't have been able to trace him back to that ranch in Montana.

Then, he thought about the cop telling Ashley that some detective wanted her in his hotel room.

"Son of a bitch!" Bill yelled. He would've slammed his

The Wrong Stranger

hands against the back of the seat if he'd been uncuffed. There was no one else in the cruiser to witness Bill's realization that his wife was having an affair with another man. "That bitch!" he yelled again, unable to keep his anger internalized. He fumed, unable to believe she'd been able to get away with it right under his nose. How long had it been going on? Who the fuck did she think she was?

Bill's face turned red with rage. He dug his fingernails into his palms, needing an outlet. Bill squeezed his palms hard, digging his nails until he felt the wet blood on his fingertips. The pain was a comfort. He felt like he deserved it for being so blind to the situation that was right in front of him. She'd played him so well, he would almost admire it, if his pride didn't hurt so much. It didn't matter that he'd never been faithful to Ashley a day in his life. What mattered was she *belonged* to him.

Once he was booked, and alone in his cell, Bill was consumed with ideas racing through his mind. He wondered if his wife really was insane, or if she'd been playing him from the beginning. When he drifted that night, the name came back to him. Daisy Taylor. The memory of Willow with her pregnant belly surfaced. The feelings of those first nights with her flooded his vision. In his mind's eye, he saw her so clearly, as if he could reach out and touch her.

Bill felt like a ton of bricks dropped on his chest. He thought he might have a stroke or a heart attack. His pulse raced. He felt like he couldn't breathe. Bill's cell mate noticed him struggling to breathe and called for a guard. "It wasn't me," he cried. Bill closed his eyes, not believing the thing that *must* be true. The reason that he'd been so attracted to Ashley, all those years ago. The reason she'd looked so familiar the first time he saw her. The reason that her beauty had always held him captive despite his hate for her at times.

She was his *daughter*. Bill had married his own daughter.

He'd married his daughter. Ashley was really Daisy. Jessica was Daisy. The things they'd done together. They'd had a son together. His son was his *grandson*. Bill thought he really might pass out. All the color drained from his face, as the disgust he felt became overwhelming.

He was normally a man who was not easily disturbed or frightened. With his hobby, there was very little that actually bothered Bill, or made him physically ill, but this was something beyond even what he could stand.

Back when Willow was pregnant, Bill never thought that he'd come across her or the baby again. She assumed her boyfriend at the time was the baby's father. Willow was always in the back of Bill's mind, but he'd never even thought to look her up. He'd assumed that she'd be long since married with countless more children, and although he would not consider himself a kind man, he thought the best thing he could do for her was to leave her be. She was the one regret Bill had, and now it seemed it was blowing up in his face.

He'd been married to his wife for nearly ten years, believing she was Ashley. She'd hidden Daisy from him, utterly and completely. Was it possible that she *knew* he was her father and didn't care? Or knew and wanted some kind of payback? Payback for what, though? If she wanted payback, it meant that she knew what he'd done to Willow. It meant that Willow knew. Bill grimaced. No, no, it couldn't be that. There was no way she knew. *What, then?*

Bill needed to talk to her. He hadn't even thought about the legal trouble he was in. He could go to jail for the rest of his life, or get the death penalty, but somehow it didn't matter. The only thing that Bill cared about was understanding what was going on with his wife. Ironic, since for years, she'd been the last thing in the world that he'd been concerned about.

The Wrong Stranger

The police questioned Bill. They probed him, trying to get a confession that would save the taxpayer dollars and everyone's time. They tried to cut him a deal, too. If he confessed, it would mean life in prison with no parole but also no death penalty. They also wanted Bill to talk about his accomplice.

They pushed for him to give up his partner in crime, but Bill wasn't ready to spill any beans. He didn't know if he wanted life in prison or death. Maybe the death penalty would be a mercy. He also didn't know if he wanted to implicate his wife—daughter, whatever her damned name was. He couldn't think with all the fucking badgering that they were doing, so he kept his lips sealed.

Bill's lawyer was no help. "I think this is as good a deal as you're likely to get, Bill. Best thing is to tell all." Bill was paying this idiot, he wasn't even court appointed, and he couldn't believe how much he was getting ripped off.

Bill finally told him, "Look, I need fifteen minutes with Ashley. Get me that, or I'll fire your ass." His lawyer came through. The only way was to promise a confession to investigators; they were too eager to get the details.

The problem was, Bill's lawyer had a harder time getting Ashley to agree to the meeting than he did with the police. She'd been admitted to a psychiatric hospital for evaluation, after the police rescued her that night. She was associated with Agent Sumner, who claimed she'd been living as Daisy, not Ashley. Bill's attorney had to wait for her to be fully evaluated and cleared by doctors before he could set up the meeting.

29

Daisy was still freaking out when she met up with Agent Sumner in his hotel room later. She was inconsolable. Daisy told Dan how she woke up, not knowing where she was or who she was with. She thought the man had kidnapped her and the kid who he was torturing. "He seemed to know who I was," she told him, "but I had no idea who *he* was."

As soon as Dan had the facts, it took little for him to put two and two together. He realized Bill was the man he'd been searching for all this time. He was the Hide and Seek Man.

"Have you seen a black semi hanging around lately?"

She thought about it, but it was too hard to know for sure. Her memory wasn't exactly reliable, considering she couldn't remember anything between the time she ran away from home, and when their relationship started. "I'm not sure. Maybe."

He nodded. "You probably didn't because he didn't want you to. That's what he does, Daisy. He stalks women, usually in their own homes. He's called the Hide and Seek Man."

"The what?"

The Wrong Stranger

"I don't want to scare you more. Are you sure you want to hear this?"

"No! Yes. God, I don't know!" She began crying again.

"Shhh. It's okay. We won't talk about it now." Dan loved Daisy and comforted her as best he could. He believed her and vowed to see justice done. Dan was not aware of Daisy's connection to Bill, but would soon find out.

The problem for Daisy was that Dan was an FBI agent. As soon as he began doing the background research on Bill, he discovered who Bill was married to and pulled up her DMV photo. Dan's first reaction was confusion. He didn't understand why the woman who Bill was married to looked identical to Daisy, except for her eye color. Even with his years of experience, he was drawing a blank, unable to put the facts together. His next thought was that they were sisters, or at least closely related.

Dan did the research. He pulled up a whole file on Ashley, only to find that there was no other possibility. Ashley was Daisy. Daisy was Ashley. His Daisy was married. Married to a killer. *But her eyes.*

He didn't understand how she could be two different people with two different eye colors. She'd gone through the trouble to get colored contacts, but why? Dan was heartbroken and irate. His investigator instincts kicked in, telling him that she would now say anything, do anything, to get out of this situation.

The thing was, he *did* want her to talk her way out of it. He wanted her to say something that he could believe, something that would explain it all and make him forgive her. When Dan confronted Daisy, she was as shocked as he'd been. "Dan, you're scaring me," she'd said, eyes wide with disbelief.

"Oh, I'm scaring you? I'm so fucking sorry!" He couldn't help but yell at her. He was afraid, too, and felt like a fool for trusting her. Dan took her fingerprints right there and ran them through the system. There was no mistake. He showed Daisy the hard proof. "I don't even know your real name!"

"Daisy! I'm Daisy!" She couldn't believe what he was telling her. She looked away from the evidence staring at her, thinking about all the times that she'd blacked out or woken up somewhere different, not knowing how she got there. "Dan, I think I need help."

He was furious and hurt. He could barely look at her. Her tone was so believable, he wanted to punch a wall. Dan turned to look into her eyes. He could see the fear reflecting back. "Okay," he said, clenching his fists. "Let's get you some help."

Dan took Daisy to the hospital for a mental evaluation. Upon admitting herself, she stayed under the care of doctors. That was when Dan let a sliver of hope into his heart, against his better judgement. If Daisy cared enough to seek help and actually go through with it, then maybe all hope for their relationship wasn't lost.

During the months of living in a mental hospital, Daisy was under the care of Doctor Reymore. He specialized in identity disorders, which meant that Daisy was in excellent hands. He was able to break through her defenses and dig down deep into her past trauma.

Dr. Reymore helped her identify events in her past that were still causing her harm and to find coping strategies that worked. She was not cured by any means, but could now recognize her mental health state and was no longer oblivious to how she was living. He was ready to discharge her from the hospital on the condition that she continue to make weekly appointments.

The Wrong Stranger

"Doctor," Daisy asked, before being discharged, "would you speak with my boyfriend about my condition? I need to explain to him so that he'll understand, and it will help me so much if you corroborate my side."

"Of course. I don't have a problem with that at all." He smiled, reassuring her that all would be well. "I'm proud of how far you've come in these past months, Daisy."

"Thank you, Dr. Reymore. I just want to be healthy."

"I can tell. You have to be one of the most motivated patients I've worked with in a long time. Wanting to be healthy is what matters."

"Thank you for all of your help so far. Is it alright if I bring Dan to your office at my appointment next week?"

"That sounds like a splendid plan."

Daisy was relieved beyond measure. She finally understood herself and why she'd been blacking out and losing time. Daisy understood why she woke up in strange unknown places and why that psychopath thought he knew her, why he'd called her Ashley. She was his wife.

Part of Daisy couldn't believe that she had an entire other life without being conscious of it. How was she capable of marrying a man like that? She didn't understand it but was glad that at least she knew now. With continued treatment and therapy with Dr. Reymore, she was going to get this fixed. She had faith in herself, and hoped that Dan would, too, especially once he spoke with Dr. Reymore.

It wasn't hard to get Dan to go along with speaking to her doctor. He was eager to get to the bottom of Daisy's story, unable to give up the sliver of hope that he'd been hanging on to like a lifeline. The next week, at Daisy's appointment, Dr. Reymore explained everything to Dan, per Daisy's request.

"Daisy has been living with dissociative identity disorder.

You may have heard of someone having multiple personalities or split personalities," Dr. Reymore said.

Dan nodded. "I've heard of it, but I didn't think it could go this far."

"It's not normal, but as we see in Daisy's case, not impossible. Daisy has one additional personality that we're aware of, but there could be more."

This struck a nerve with Dan. "What? How can there be more? Why don't we know for sure?"

"Daisy suffered some extreme trauma as a child, which is why she developed the Ashley persona. Her brain's way of coping is to split into new personalities. The only way for us to know for certain if there's any more is to continue with the healing process. She needs to continue her therapy sessions in order for us to expose any additional personas that could be hiding."

Dan tried to wrap his brain around this new information. *She could have more personalities.* As if the extra one wasn't enough. He turned to Daisy. "Do you want to tell me about the trauma that you went through?"

Daisy glanced at Dr. Reymore. He nodded his encouragement. "I don't think I can talk about all of it yet, but I can give you the gist."

Dan nodded, waiting for her to continue.

"I was neglected by both of my parents and abused by my dad. At the time, I thought he was giving me special attention, when he was abusing me. I didn't recognize that it was abuse. I was four years old when it started."

"Jesus. Daisy, I'm so sorry." Dan held her hand, trying to give what comfort he could.

"I've had excruciating headaches as far back as I can remember. After each one, I seemed to lose time and usually wound up in strange places. I never realized what was happening to me, but apparently, my brain developed another personality to cope with the abuse. It was a way for me to escape." A tear slid down her cheek as she continued. "My mom died, and I was stuck in the house with her dead body for days because my dad was a truck driver who was never home."

"Shit, Daisy!"

"I know. After she died, I was left with him alone. He abused me for years until I ran away. By then, I was Ashley."

Dan looked back toward Dr. Reymore. "Can she still change into Ashley? And what about the eye colors?"

Dr. Reymore looked confused. "For the first question, yes, she's not fully healed yet so she can, and probably will, still switch back to Ashley when under great stress. However, now that she's aware of her mental state, we've gone over some coping strategies, and hopefully, we can minimize the frequency that this happens; she knows to watch for her triggers. Now, eye colors? What about that?"

Dan was still trying to get used to the idea of Daisy actually changing into another woman. He loved her so much, but could he live with and help her with her mental illness? It was a lot to commit to, and he wasn't sure if his love for her would be enough for their relationship. What if she didn't care for him when she was fully herself again? He would worry about it later, though.

"Her eyes are a different color from her driver's license."

Dr. Reymore asked for Daisy to look at him, so he could examine her eyes. "Hmm. Irises don't change colors, even in a situation like this. It isn't possible. Perhaps it's the lighting making her eyes look different in the picture or colored contacts."

"But they change colors back and forth."

"Yes, I can see how that would be concerning. I strongly feel that there's another explanation at play here. But the mind is also powerful beyond comprehension. It's capable of so many things that we haven't yet discovered. Really, *anything* is possible, even if we don't think it is, but that's a discussion for another day."

Dan wasn't sure what else he could say. "One more question for you, Doctor."

"Of course."

"Is her other personality, Ashley, aware of what she does while she's living as Daisy?"

Dr. Reymore had to think about it for a few minutes. "I'm not sure," he finally said. "She has no memories of her life as Ashley, so it would stand to reason that Ashley had no memories of life as Daisy, however, if Ashley's persona was more dominant, then it could have those memories and even hold more control."

"More control?" Dan really didn't like the sound of that.

"Yes. The more dominant of the personalities may be able to trigger a switch, if she wanted to be in control of the body. Research is still being done, but each patient is different, as I'm sure you understand. There are so many things we don't fully understand yet, especially in Daisy's case. Hers is one of the most extreme that I've ever seen. Just keep in mind that it *could* be a possibility."

"I thought stress was her trigger."

"Yes, it is. We know that for a certainty. However, there have been cases where the more dominant personality can still set off the trigger internally, even with no outside stressors."

Dan looked at Daisy to gauge her reaction. She'd already been aware of this when Dr. Reymore was caring for her during her hospital stay. He'd explained the mechanics of DID and what to expect, as well as what to watch for.

"Thank you. You've been a great help."

Daisy and Dan went home together. He wanted to collapse with the relief and tension he felt after speaking with Dr. Reymore. He clung to the idea that Daisy was a sick woman, rather than a cruel betrayer. She really was sick, like she had claimed, and wasn't lying about her lack of memory. She really hadn't known that she was married or any of the other things. He had a reason to trust her and to move on with their life together. But could he live with her, knowing that she could split at any moment? She could have another personality in there that they didn't know about yet. Could he be okay with that?

30

When Bill's lawyer found out that she was discharged from her voluntary stay at the hospital, he contacted Daisy to set up a meeting with Bill. Dr. Reymore gave her the go-ahead, believing that it would be beneficial to her recovery to confront her husband.

According to his attorney, Bill hadn't spoken a word to the police about anything yet. He convinced her that this was her only chance to clear the air with him before he talked to the district attorney and insinuated that it would be in her best interest to do so. Daisy had a nagging feeling that there was something else she wasn't aware of.

The deal that Bill's attorney made with the police, in exchange for his full confession, was to be completely left alone with his wife. They were to be unmonitored and unrecorded, but Bill wasn't sure how much he trusted the police. His lawyer assured him that if the police broke their word, it would be inadmissible in court. Bill didn't care. He wanted it in writing and wanted to choose his own location.

The DA refused to allow Bill to choose a different loca-

The Wrong Stranger

tion. Instead, they negotiated to have the cameras completely removed from the room. Police escorted Bill to a small, private room with two chairs and a table. There was no two-way mirror, just four plain white walls.

Daisy was afraid to meet the man who was her husband. She had no memory of him, other than that night in the old farmhouse. He'd been covered in blood at the time, and she hadn't gotten a good look at his face without gore on it. She was afraid that her fear would trigger her to switch personalities, and part of her hoped for it, but a bigger part of her didn't want it at all.

She wanted to face him. Partly from curiosity, but partly because it was what it would take for her to heal. She wanted a divorce, too, and this would be a perfect opportunity to get him to sign the paperwork.

She took a deep, steadying breath, then stepped into the room. Bill turned to her, and their eyes met. He was handcuffed to the table, unable to move. The gaze of his coal-black eyes bore into her, his expression blank. "Welcome, *wife*," he said, tone like ice.

Daisy flinched but was able to move forward to the other chair. "I have some papers I'd like you to sign," she said, pushing the divorce papers towards him.

Bill read the first few lines. He understood what she wanted from him. This was what he'd dreaded from the beginning and had fought tooth and nail to prevent. There was no stopping it now; he couldn't stay married to his daughter. "Do you have a pen?" Without a word, she put a pen into his right hand, for him to sign. "Now, we need to talk."

"There's so much I want to ask you," she said. "I don't know where to start."

Bill could tell that he wasn't speaking with Jessica. This wasn't Ashley, either. He recognized her emerald eyes. *How many are there*, he wondered. He needed to find out *exactly* what she knew about his past. What she knew about her mother. "So, I hear you have a new name."

"I've been sick. For my whole life, apparently."

Bill nodded. "I've had some idea of that recently."

She perked up, hungry for any information he could give her about herself. "Please, Bill. What can you tell me? My doctor told me I've been living as Ashley, but I have no memories."

No memories. Bill thought about that. "You were having a lot of headaches and zoning out, things like that."

Daisy frowned. She'd been hoping for something more helpful than that. "Did you know I had dissociative identity disorder?"

"Diss—what?"

She smiled. "I'll take that as a no."

"Well, I've been married to this woman for going on ten years, and it seems I didn't know her real name or actual history. Tell me about yourself, Daisy. Tell me about your parents."

Daisy blushed. This man could be charming, and his smile... Lord help her, she was beginning to understand why she'd married him. Women had to be falling at his feet. She told him about her childhood, about her mother dying and being left alone with her abusive father. She left out the details, but Bill got the picture.

When Daisy told him about the conditions that she'd lived in and how Willow was dead, Bill saw red. He wanted to find Joe Taylor and skin him alive. He'd do things to that man that he'd never done to anyone. His hands turned to fists as she told her story. When she finally finished, Bill had a hard time speaking.

"I'm sorry," was all he could manage, with a raspy voice.

"Thank you," she said, looking down.

The Wrong Stranger

"Did your parents ever talk about how they met?"

"No. At least, not that I remember. Why?"

"No reason. Just curious."

She thought it might be more than just curiosity but couldn't think why he would be interested in her parents. She let it go. "Bill?"

"Yeah?"

"Were you going to kill me that night?"

He was taken by surprise. "No. I wasn't."

"Then, why was I there?"

Bill didn't know what to say again. He didn't want to give her too much information, didn't know what she really knew, but had an idea that she really was as ignorant as she seemed. Bill realized he'd been wrong back at the old farmhouse. He thought it was Ashley that called the cops on him, but it was Daisy. Things were different. He didn't know who to be mad at anymore. She was his daughter, so technically, *still his*. He liked the sound of that. Bill didn't think he would tell her about Jessica yet. He had an idea that Jessica would make herself known when she was good and ready. "I was hoping you would take an interest in my hobby." He smiled. "I can see that I was mistaken."

Daisy was speechless. Was he serious? She couldn't tell for sure, but it seemed like he might be. Now she was the one who didn't know what to say. There was a knock on the door, and they heard, "Two minutes. Time's almost up." She looked into Bill's eyes again, wondering about all the things he could tell her. There was a lifetime of knowledge about herself that only he could tell her. She had minutes left with him and might not be able to speak with him again. Did she really want to see him again?

"What's going to happen to you?"

"I'll confess. That was the deal. Then, jail time."

"How is it possible that we've been married for nine

years, and I don't even know you? You're a complete stranger."

He laughed. "I could ask you the same thing."

"Did we—" She looked down.

"Did we what?"

"Did we love each other?"

He sighed. "No."

31

Following the meeting with Daisy, Bill gave his full confession, not only for what he'd done to the Bobby, but as the Hide and Seek Man. He wrapped up Agent Sumner and his team's case for them like a present with a pretty bow on top. They were able to successfully close the "Hide and Seek Man" case, which garnered a massive amount of publicity and boosted all of their careers.

Of course, they had no way of knowing that he was leaving out massive amounts of information, because the information that he provided checked out. Bill told no one about Jessica. He told no one about any of the other targets. What he confessed to were the cases presented to him—the ones that were suspected to be involved in the Hide and Seek Man murders.

Most of the cases were more recent, mainly when he'd been working with Jessica. Somehow, he'd let his guard down, and he was surprised at how much the police suspected. He'd thought he was getting away clean every time, but really, he'd been making minor mistakes that added up. It seemed that in working with her, he'd let down his guard a little too much. Everything that he'd originally feared had come true.

Dan and his associates were shocked at the number of victims that Bill had and was confessing to. Every file they put in front of him, he took credit for. There were no denials. He provided the details that checked out, and they had no doubt that he was the legitimate killer.

There were women across the United States who'd been abducted from their homes. There were hitchhikers that had been taken, too, some just children. Investigators knew there had to be more victims but were glad to have Bill's confession on at least these. The families of these victims would finally get closure. Bill was given multiple life sentences without parole. He was placed in a maximum-security federal penitentiary, incarcerated with some of the most dangerous felons in the country.

In the time that followed Bill's imprisonment, Daisy began a new life with Dan. He was still concerned about her mental stability but couldn't give up the woman that he loved. It wasn't her fault that she'd been traumatized as a child. He couldn't find it in his heart to hold her mental illness against her. Dan thought if he'd been raised similarly, he'd probably be a little screwed up, too. He wanted to build a life with Daisy and was willing to give it a shot if she was.

Daisy was able to control her blackouts more, but still had them occasionally. She continued to see Dr. Reymore every week for her therapy sessions. With his help, she gained a little more of herself every day. She also started to regain memories of her life, including memories of her son and what happened to him.

With the memory of her son, she struggled with falling back into depression. She began dreaming of his face and having flashbacks of his childhood. This was the time when she was the most vulnerable to switching over to an alter

The Wrong Stranger

ego, and Dr. Reymore advised both her and Dan to be extra observant in her behavior.

Because of his success with the Hide and Seek Man investigation, Dan had been assigned to another high profile case. Another serial killer. He'd become absorbed with the work again, too busy to notice Daisy's headaches coming on or her personality swaps. Because of the new case he was on, he was gone from home far more often, only showing up to shower and sleep many nights during the week. Loneliness wasn't new for Daisy. She was used to it. It was one of the contributing factors to her Ashley persona.

Despite loving his work, Dan was under serious pressure, again. Now that he and Daisy were living together, it actually made things harder for him. He acknowledged she meant well, but he was a man used to being on his own. Having her around all the time took his mind off the case and put it on her ass. He couldn't concentrate like he should, and he knew his love life was holding up the investigation. He'd rather be spending time with Daisy than doing anything else, so he avoided going home in order to get the job done. Dan was afraid if he didn't avoid her like the plague, he was going to miss something in his investigation, or worse, screw something up, or even get fired. Because Daisy never complained, he thought she didn't have a problem with his long work hours.

It was dinnertime, and Dan was gone again. Daisy was outside barbecuing when she saw the mailman walking. She checked the time on her watch. *He's really running late today,* she thought. She waved her thanks after he dropped off her mail, then headed over to see what junk there was waiting for her in the mailbox. As she flipped through the envelopes, she came across something that made her breath catch. Everything else dropped from her hands, except for the envelope that read, "Federal Penitentiary." Bill had written her a letter.

Daisy stood in her front yard, staring at the envelope in her hands, afraid to open it. She smelled her steak burning but stood frozen. One of her headaches was coming on. If she wasn't careful, she'd blackout. She closed her eyes, taking deep breaths. In, one... two... three... Out, one... two... three... Repeat. Once she thought she had herself under control, Daisy folded the envelope and put it into her pocket. She made her way to her burned meat, turning off the barbecue, then heading inside.

When Dan got home, it was early morning. As he walked up the front steps, he saw the mail laying on the front lawn. A feeling of dread shot up his spine. He opened the front door. Everything else appeared to be normal, but with the mail on the grass, he knew there was something wrong. Dan called for Daisy, but she didn't answer. There was a plate of burned steak on the kitchen table, along with an opened envelope. He flipped the envelope over, read the return address, then pulled the letter out.

Daisy,
I'll make this short and sweet. I knew your mother years ago.
I worked at the ranch that her mother (your grandmother) owned.
I'm your father.
That's right. You read correctly.
I didn't know until that night at the old farmhouse.
I thought you were Ashley.
Let Jessica out now.
I'm going to kill Joe Taylor.
-Bill

The Wrong Stranger

WITH SHAKING HANDS, DAN FOLDED THE LETTER, PUTTING IT back into the envelope. He could feel his heart wanting to beat right through his chest. *What. The. Fuck.* If this was his reaction, Daisy had to be freaking out, too. He wondered, *did she black out?* And who the hell was Jessica? His mind was racing a mile a minute.

Dan headed for the stairs. The house was dark except for the kitchen light Daisy had left on for him. He didn't want to wake her up if she was sleeping, but he needed to know if she was up. With caution, he tried, "Daisy?" There was no response. Dan flicked the switch to turn on the light at the top of the stairs, but nothing happened. He tried again, "Ashley?" Nothing. He climbed upstairs, using his phone for a light.

At the top of the landing, he turned down the hallway toward their bedroom. He placed his hand on the door handle. "Hello, Dan." He was so caught off guard, he nearly jumped out of his skin. Dan whipped around to see Daisy standing behind him.

"Daisy, God, you scared me," he panted. "I didn't hear you."

She took the steak knife from behind her back and plunged it into his heart. "I'm not Daisy," she said, twisting the handle. As the life drained out of Dan, he stared into her ice-blue eyes, thinking, *A third color?*

ACKNOWLEDGMENTS

There's an immense amount of gratitude I feel for the people who've helped and supported me during this project. My biggest supporters have been my family, especially my son. Thank you, love.

Thank you, to everyone who has read the book or a portion of it and provided me with much needed feedback. Without those beta readers, I would've had zero confidence. They helped me find the courage to move forward, and for that I'm eternally grateful.

I've been amazed in the greatest way by the wonderful writing community. I had no idea how supportive a group of people could be. It's heartwarming how amazing these people are, how encouraging, how helpful, and how much strength they provide. To each and every one of you, thank you.

ABOUT THE AUTHOR

K. Lucas is a wife and mom who resides in the Pacific Northwest. A homeschool parent and an avid reader who loves all things thrilling and chilling, she lives for the unexpected twist. Her favorite past times include reading, watching horror movies, and exploring nature.

Daisy
Willow - deceased mother
Bill - trucker
Ashley - wife
Chris - son - deceased
Ivy - neighbor - mother of Jake
Claire - real estate - killed
Jake - killed Chris
Jenny - mother of Tyler & Avery

Made in the USA
Monee, IL
26 February 2022